CRIMSON HUNTER

A Red Riding Hood Reimagining

N.D. Jones

KUUMBA PUBLISHING
CREATIVE MINDS
PASSIONATE HEARTS

Baltimore, Maryland

Published by
Kuumba Publishing
Baltimore, Maryland, USA

Publisher's Note: This is a work of fiction. Names, characters, places, and events are either products of the author's imagination or used fictitiously. Any resemblance to actual persons, living or dead, events, institutions, or locales is coincidental.

Book Layout & Design ©2017 - BookDesignTemplates.com

Editor: BFF Editing, Kathryn Schieber
Cover Design: Giusy D'Anna-Premade Book Covers Market

Crimson Hunter/N.D. Jones. -- 1st ed.
ISBN-13: 978-1732556782
ASIN: B07W3RFWHZ

Dedication

Ida B. Wells-Barnett
July 16, 1862 – March 25, 1931
Civil Rights Activist and Journalist

"The way to right wrongs is to turn the light of truth upon them."

"There must always be a remedy for wrong and injustice if we only know how to find it."

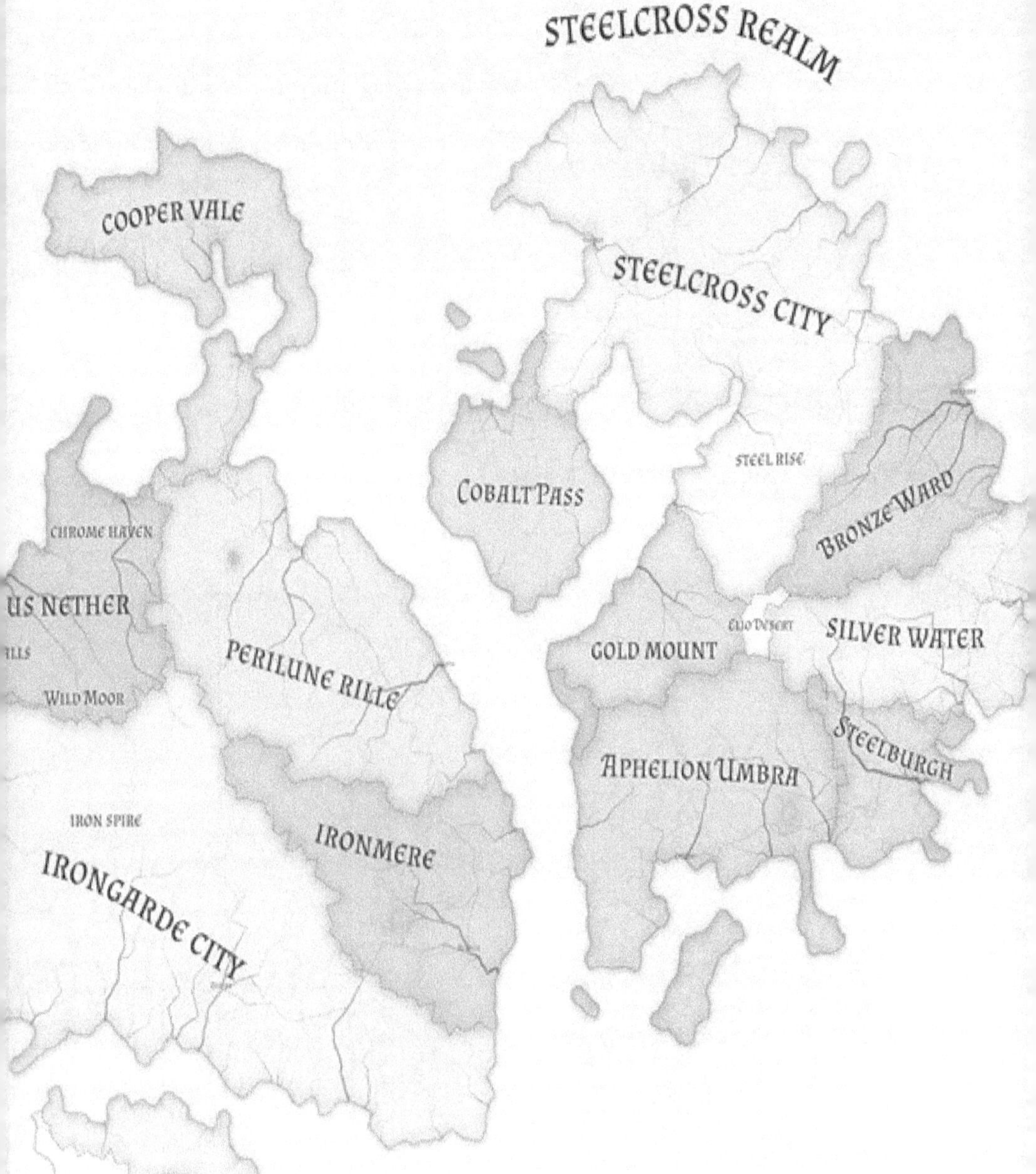

STEELCROSS REALM
COOPER VALE
STEELCROSS CITY
STEEL RISE
COBALT PASS
BRONZE WARD
CHROME HAVEN
US NETHER
SILVER WATER
CLIO DESERT
GOLD MOUNT
PERILUNE RILLE
ILLS
WILD MOOR
APHELION UMBRA
STEELBURGH
IRON SPIRE
IRONMERE
IRONGARDE CITY
IRONGARDE REALM

Glossary of Key Terms

Aku of Irongarde: Title of the consort to the Matriarch of Irongarde; Aku is a male name that means moon god

Bleddyn: One of three forms werewolves transform into; half-human, half-werewolf form; a muscular and strong body of a human male with a fine layer of black fur over thick human skin

Blood of the Sun: Name of the ruling matriarchal family of witches

Captain of the Hunter Division: Leads the Hunter Division of the Crimson Guards; responsible for the capture of muracos and threats to international security

Channon: A werewolf cub or baby

Clan of the Black Moon: The collective name of black werewolves

Crimson Guard: Collective name for Earth Rift's military and local law enforcement; responsible for protecting the citizens of Earth Rift from domestic and interplanetary threats; comprised of witches only

Crimson Hunter: Leader of the Crimson Guard; appointed by the Matriarch of Irongarde; responsible for enforcing Earth Rift's laws, particularly those that governs werewolf behavior; responsible for capturing muracos and, when ordered, executing threats to Earth Rift

Cyrus of Steelcross: Title of the consort to the Matriarch of Steelcross; Cyrus is a male name that means sun

Hunter Division: A military division of the Crimson Guard comprised of three units: Barrage, Extraction, and Guardian; responsible for the capture and/or execution of the most dangerous criminals on Earth Rift—mainly muracos

Magerun System: An aerial transportation system that connects the different regions of Earth Rift and is fueled by the sun and witch magic

Matriarch of Irongarde: Ruler of Irongarde Realm

Matriarch of Steelcross: Ruler of Steelcross Realm

Muraco: A black werewolf whose color fades to white when it becomes feral from either extreme magic lust that results in violent behavior and mental instability, or when an infected muraco's bodily fluids get into their blood

Rage Disruptor: A metal implant inserted into the brains of pubescent werewolves to monitor their rage level; it is used in conjunction with the silver snare to diminish the violent impulses of werewolves

Ravagers of the Lost Cannons: Name of Oriana's, the Crimson Hunter's, weapons, into which her arms turn from elbow to fingers; used as a method of channeling the Crimson Hunter's strong magic

Rite of Endometal Fusion: A mandatory ritual where all witches, upon turning thirteen, must submit to an injection of liquid iron or steel into their arms, legs, or both; the mixing of liquid metal into witches' blood enables them to create metal weapons through which they can channel and control their magic

Silver Snare: A spell-based collar worn by werewolves; it releases soothing magical pulses when a werewolf's anger reaches a dangerous level

Glossary of Key Locations

STEELCROSS REALM

Aphelion Umbra: Region reserved for human settlement

City of Bronze Ward: City created as a test site for werewolves and witches to live together with werewolves wearing their silver snare at night only

City of Steelburgh: Walled-off city built for muracos who've served their prison sentence but cannot be reintegrated into society

Steelcross City: Capital of Steelcross Realm; location of Steel Rise

Steel Rise: The northern skyrise residence of the Matriarch of Earth Rift; used as the residence of the Matriarch of Steelcross when there are co-rulers of Earth Rift—Matriarch of Steelcross and Matriarch of Irongarde

IRONGARDE REALM

City of Wild Moor: One of the three cities that comprise the werewolf region of Janus Nether

Irongade City: Capital of Irongarde Realm

Iron Spire: The southern skyrise residence of the Matriarch of Earth Rift; used as the residence of the Matriarch of Irongarde when there are co-rulers of Earth Rift—Matriarch of Steelcross and Matriarch of Irongarde

Janus Nether: Region reserved for the Clan of the Black Moon; comprised of three cities (Chrome Haven, Tin Falls, and Wild Moor); the only region in Earth Rift where werewolves are not mandated to wear their silver snares

Perilune Rille: Region reserved for human settlement

Blood of the Sun Decree #1
January 1, 1300

BY MATRIARCHAL DECREE, EARTH RIFT WILL BE FOREVER GOVERNED BY A WITCH FROM THE BLOOD OF THE SUN FAMILY. BE IT FURTHER DECREED THAT WITCHES ARE THE SUPREME AUTHORITY OF THE PLANET.

Alba, Matriarch of Earth Rift

1: White Moon

April 27, 2243
Irongarde Realm
City of Wild Moor

Howls sliced through the beleaguered city like deadly claws. The relentless sound shattered windows. Jagged glass shards rained down like deadly rain, cutting and adding to the pools of blood that already soaked the ground.

Oriana lifted her face to the starless night sky, sweat rolling down her brow into her dark-brown, unblinking eyes. The orders of her mother, Matriarch Kalinda, reverberated in her mind. *"Wild Moor will be our final stand. You cannot allow the beasts to claim that border city, Crimson Hunter."*

More howls cut through the darkness, followed by the tk.tk.tk.tk.tk.tk of rampaging paws. Oriana lowered her head. This was it then: the final battle of a day-long war. Countless had already died—many by her own hand in defense of her sisters—all by order of Matriarch Kalinda.

Oriana raised her arms, the liquid steel within mixed inorganic with organic—a potent witch's brew of strength and control.

"Come forth, Ravagers of the Lost." Red sun magic burst from Oriana's hands. Wild flames sparked and hissed. Channeling the flames into her arms, Oriana willed the magic to comply. From the sparks and hisses of magic, twin cannon guns formed, replacing her arms from elbows to fingers.

"Shift," Oriana ordered her Crimson Guard soldiers, trained witches under her direct command as Crimson Hunter.

Sun magic surged, turning limbs into shields and weapons.

Across the battlefield of cracked roads and burned buildings, the howling stopped. Silence descended—an emissary of violence, blood, and death.

Oriana raised her head again to the night sky and cursed the white moon glowing above. A red moon would've favored the witches. Oriana would've even been grateful for a black moon. But no, in the city she couldn't allow to fall, a white moon had risen, strengthening her enemies like nothing else in nature could, save the blood and magic of a witch.

If Oriana and her Crimson Guards didn't prevail, if she ended up food for the beasts—like the ravaged bodies of her sisters littering the landscape—her daughter would be left parentless. That, more than anything else, she could not allow to happen.

She also could not let Kalinda do the unthinkable.

Oriana focused on the enemy, their seething energy and low growls rancid in the tepid spring air. Rows of white werewolves filled the town square. As ghost white as the moon, their color differentiated them from the normal black of werewolves. Their white coats marked them as the vicious creatures they were … muraco.

Eight feet of pure muscle, the feral werewolves exuded primal might. The length of their fangs, sharp and perfect for ripping, set them apart from other beasts of prey. Their claws were deadlier still.

Magic sizzled. Perspiration drenched the red and black of Oriana's Crimson Hunter body armor, which clung to her as fiercely as her resolve. She looked around at her Crimson Guards who extended from one side of the square to the other.

The muraco horde charged.

Good. She needed the feral beasts within range of her guards' weapons.

"Barragers?" Oriana yelled.

"Ready!"

"Guardians?"

"Ready!"

"Extractors?" Oriana called out to the last group of warrior witches.

"Ready!"

"Steady," she said to her sisters. "They are almost within striking distance. Wait for my command."

The white werewolves were nearly upon them. Fangs bared, their clawed feet carved a path through the concrete. Saliva flew. Red eyes gleamed.

Despite everything, Oriana agreed with her mother. White werewolves, the muraco, were irredeemable, untamable, and feral beyond reasoning.

The werewolves lunged at them in a frenzy. Attacking claws forced the witches backward.

"Extractors, go."

A third of the wall of the Crimson Guard vanished, only to reappear behind the werewolves, shoving steel blades into thick hides. The werewolves bellowed, swinging around with lightning speed—claws curved, vulnerable throats their targets.

Slice. Slash.

Blood spurted in an unrefined arc, splashing the werewolves in their favorite liquid, their stained fur a demented painter's morbid canvas.

Oriana filled her cannons with magic, shooting over and again. The battle raged, each side losing warriors in a battle that should've never been. She ran, darted, and jumped, blasting anything with fangs and fur. Oriana fought until her body burned raw with magic, nothing to draw on but her stubbornness and will.

The werewolves fared better, the white moon strengthening them. From the way her magic tingled, the sun would rise in less than an hour. Oriana and her unit of Crimson Guard soldiers were bedraggled and outnumbered, having defended Janus Nether's three cities all day.

Wild Moor was their final stand. When the sun rose, the battle would be done, no matter how many witches were still capable of continuing the battle, no matter that the sun would recharge their magic, giving them a much-needed edge. It would be an advantage that they would be unable to capitalize upon.

"Barragers, do your worst."

Twenty-five witches converged on the werewolves, their metal blades, blasters, and phasers shoving their opponents backward. It was a magical rampage on par with the werewolves' frenzied slashes. Neither side gave an inch, a destructive storm that leveled city blocks.

Mindless, they fought. Mindless, they killed. Were her Crimson Guards any less feral than the white werewolves? No, they weren't. With this battle, they couldn't afford a sliver of mercy. So, Oriana commanded her guards to, "Push forward. Keep fighting. The sun will soon rise. Will we be here to greet it when it does?"

"No survivors," Kalinda had said. *"We need to send a message to any witch or werewolf who thinks to defy the Matriarchy."*

Bloodied and exhausted, Oriana led the charge, her cannons *booming* a welcome to the new day. When the sun crested the horizon, the werewolves didn't falter. The strength of the white moon still blazed in their veins, undimmed by the slashes of red and gold in the morning sky.

The battle was neither over nor won, but Oriana had failed. The rising sun had been her stubborn mother's deadline.

"Guardians, retrieve. Barragers, crumble. Extractors, entangle and retreat."

Crimson Guards obeyed her command. The Guardian Unit sent their magic outward. Photonic blasts of magic shriveled the bodies of their dead sisters, setting their ravaged souls free. The Barrage Unit slammed their war hammers and maces onto the ground. Shockwaves sent the white werewolves flying backward.

By the time the muracos shook off the assault and charged the witches again, the Extraction Unit had the witches tethered by a multi-looped lariat.

As if out of nowhere, a single werewolf appeared, likely from the small, dark alley to her left. He ran toward Oriana. His muzzle and claws were covered in blood. But that's not what shocked Oriana into temporary immobility.

What in the hell is a black werewolf doing here with the muracos? And without his silver snare?

He slashed at her.

She held up an arm, blocking the attack. Her belated response to his appearance was too slow. Claws sliced into her left cannon. Instinctively, she shot at him with her right. A blazing bullet of unfiltered sun magic scored his left side, knocking the black werewolf away and down.

Oriana hadn't returned the black werewolf's attack with a kill shot the way she should have. After what had happened with … *No, no, no, don't think of him now.*

She stumbled backward, eyes on the face of an enemy who shouldn't have been an enemy at all. "Get us out of here, extractors."

In a blink, they disappeared, extraction magic transporting them from Wild Moor to Irongarde City. They crashed to the ground. Oriana stayed where she was—on her back, eyes open, seeing nothing but her failure. Not the cityscape with glistening skyscrapers, the groaning witches around her, or even the sun—too new in the sky to heal her wounds.

"Are you okay?" Solange, captain of the Hunter Division and Oriana's best friend, leaned over her, dark eyes scanning her face. "Except for the arm you let that werewolf damn near take off, you look fine … Unless my tired eyes were deceiving me, that black werewolf was—"

"Your eyes are fine, and I didn't *let* him do anything. How bad is it?"

"It's bleeding, nasty-looking, and probably hurts like hell, but you won't die from it."

An accurate assessment, especially the hurting like hell part.

Solange helped Oriana to her feet. "It isn't over. Go see Matriarch Kalinda. We've lost too many sisters to the muracos. I don't want to lose any more, if they are left to storm Irongarde City."

"Neither do I, but you know what she'll do."

Solange nodded, blood and sweat matting braids to her scalp. "Our hand was forced. They left us no choice."

Two nights ago, Oriana had told herself the same when he'd come after her, snapping, threatening … and breaking her heart. *He forced my hand. He left me with no choice but to respond with violence.* The words echoed in her mind. But her heart wasn't convinced.

Oriana shook her head, adrenaline seeping from a body that wouldn't keep her upright much longer. "Why are witch lives worth more than werewolf lives?"

"Because they're our lives to protect, and we choose not to be ravaged by werewolves who sometimes wear the face of a beloved." Solange squeezed Oriana's uninjured hand, looking over her shoulder to their sisters, who were in various degrees of pain and disarray, and then back to her. "We'll get each other up and to the healers. Don't worry about us. Go see the Matriarch so we can begin to put this day, and the ugly ones that preceded it, behind us. Are you planning on telling the Matriarch about him?"

"I haven't decided."

"I always knew he was a bastard. But this …" Solange nodded to Oriana's left arm. Blood and red tendrils of magic leaked from the deep claw marks. "He's not feral. But he fought with the muracos. His silver snare didn't even activate. Is it possible he found someone to remove his rage disruptor?"

"We both know of one witch who has done it before, and she's still missing. I don't know how their paths could've crossed, though, not that it matters."

"I understand why you didn't, but you're going to regret not killing him when you had the chance."

Oriana shook her head sadly. "Like me, he's in mourning. He probably blames me for what happened. I didn't get a chance to speak to him about the night of the attack. I wanted to do it in person, to explain what happened."

"That's no excuse for siding with the muracos."

"I know." But Oriana didn't want to talk about another problem that would likely end in more violence and bloodshed.

"Take care of that arm before you see Keira, or she'll have nightmares. Hell, we'll all have nightmares after today."

Oriana hugged her friend. "You were great today. Thank you for a safe jump back here."

"It's what we extractors do. Our landing could've been better, though."

"Considering the day we've had, the landing was perfect."

They'd lost too many Crimson Guards during a single twenty-four-hour period. They would hold a mass funeral, but that would come later. Solange was right, she needed to see Kalinda—her mother would certainly never deign to leave her iron fortress to come looking for Oriana—because she'd failed her mission. Her failure would grant Kalinda the excuse to destroy Janus Nether. The region's ruin would carry a socio-political message many conservative witches, like Kalinda, supported: Witches ruled Earth Rift, not werewolves.

"You need to have that arm examined and fixed. I'll call my healer."

Oriana sat across from Kalinda in her mother's dining room, the living quarters comprising the entire top floor of Iron Spire, the Matriarch of Irongarde's fortress home. A pitcher of water and a glass had been placed in front of her and platters of food in the center of the table. She'd consumed every drop of water, but couldn't stomach the thought of eating, especially not meat, after seeing what the muracos had done to her sisters.

Within an hour of reporting the details of the battle at Wild Moor, her mother had extinguished the only shining light in Irongarde Realm. Janus Nether had been a beacon, a symbol of hope, and Oriana's dream for a better Earth Rift.

Oriana pointed to the cold, hard, metal and glass walls around them. "Tell me, Mother, what is left of us that is still human? Certainly not our hearts."

"We're witches."

Eyes that had never reminded Oriana of her own, despite what everyone said, looked at her with annoyance. Her mother understood love through a prism of power rather than self-sacrifice and vulnerability.

"What *I* did today saved us all. You were too soft-hearted to make the hard decision, so I made it for us both."

In the short time available to them before the battles, they hadn't been able to evacuate everyone from Janus Nether's three cities. How many had missed the last scheduled transport or didn't leave because they hadn't known the deadly scope of the state of emergency?

Oriana pushed the cut fruit around on her plate. Feeding her body would help expedite the healing process, but she put her fork down.

"You think me weak because I refuse to be the kind of matriarch who would unleash her ultimate power on cities of innocents."

Oriana also hadn't fought the black werewolf as hard as she should've, blocking instead of attacking. She'd omitted that detail from her report.

"You're my child, I know you aren't weak." Kalinda's eyes and lips softened, reminding Oriana of how beautiful her mother was . . . on the outside. Her oval face was a lustrous dark-brown, radiating a youthfulness that belied her sixty years. It was a shade darker than her hair, pulled taut in a bun. "You're sentimental, kind-hearted, and a dreamer. If we lived someplace else, perhaps on a planet where our magic and blood, our very essence, didn't drive our males to madness, then your idealism would benefit all and my ruthlessness wouldn't be necessary." Kalinda came and sat beside Oriana. "He would've killed you."

"I don't want to talk about that night."

"It's only been a couple of days, so that's understandable. Whether you want to hear it or not, he would have killed you."

The Matriarch's hand rose to cup her cheek. The same hand that stroked her face so tenderly had cast down Armageddon on not only the City of Wild Moor but on all of Janus Nether.

"It does you no good to dwell on the past, punishing yourself for acting from the most primal of instincts—survival. If you hadn't, you and Keira wouldn't be here. You can't possibly regret trading your daughter's life for his."

Her mother had a way of condensing emotions into binary categories—desire or disgust, hope or dread, joy or grief, love or hate.

"After this is done, I'm returning to Steelcross with Keira."

Kalinda's hand dropped to her lap, her face hardening into the emotionless mask Oriana knew well.

Standing, Oriana gripped the edge of the table to keep herself from falling face first onto the floor. When she was steady, she caught her mother's gaze. Except for the crease between Kalinda's brows, her countenance remained unchanged.

"I'll take care of the surviving muracos before Keira and I return home."

"I thought we'd gotten past our argument from the other day. Don't punish me by staying away and keeping my only grandchild from me."

At that, Kalinda's expression altered, as did her voice, breaking at the end. The hard matriarch was gone, leaving behind a mother and grandmother afraid of being alone and lonely in her iron tower of obedience and magic.

Oriana didn't know how she felt about her mother. Weariness and grief prevented her from distinguishing truth from lie. Perhaps they were all lies and only one truth—Kalinda's love for her family and Earth Rift. Or maybe Oriana only thought them lies because, sometimes, truths were harder on the digestive system than deceptions.

"I've been up all night. I'm going to bed."

Oriana exited the dining room, taking the lift to her suite one level below. Rarely at a loss for words, Kalinda had said nothing. For this Oriana was unsure if she should be relieved or concerned. Probably concerned, she concluded after showering and dressing. Wearing long sleeves so the sight of her injury wouldn't frighten Keira, she slipped into her queen-sized bed with her daughter.

Keira scooted closer, snuggling against Oriana's chest. Her warm breaths were humbling wisps of innocence she cherished more than the magic and steel that had saved their lives.

"Mommy." Her two-year-old's low, groggy voice melted her heart. Keira's eyes were closed, and she wasn't fully awake. Oriana had almost lost her daughter. Keira's physical injuries were gone, thanks to Kalinda's personal healer, but magic couldn't mend all wounds.

"I'm here. You're safe." The same words she'd spoken two nights ago in her suite in Steel Rise, an unmoving white werewolf at Oriana's feet and blood decorating the walls.

Oriana kissed Keira's forehead, feeling more like a mother and less like the Crimson Hunter and Matriarch of Steelcross. Yet, she was all three, her roles in society decreed by law.

While Oriana may find a few hours of well-earned rest, her duties as matriarch of the realm of Steelcross and co-ruler of the planet of Earth Rift, left little room for respite.

Oriana, Kalinda, and Kiera were three generations of Blood of the Sun witches, the matriarchy a family inheritance.

2: Stormbringer

April 28, 2243
Irongarde Realm
City of Wild Moor

A furious growl rolled from between his teeth. Delicious witches' scents lingered in the metallic air. Licking his claws, he tasted the residue of Oriana's magic. He still felt the burn of her counterattack to his side and shoulder. The next time he saw her, he'd make her pay.

"You're bleeding."

He growled again, a warning to Phelan to get the hell out of his face. The mood he was in, he'd rip the muraco's throat out, saving the witches the effort of killing him.

Phelan raised his face to the sunny sky, blood coating his human mouth. "Witches are at their most powerful when the sun is high. Why do you think they retreated? They lasted the night, and we were evenly matched all the way until the end." Phelan licked his teeth, clearing away blood and chewing the small piece of flesh he'd freed from between white teeth. "With the sun at their backs, they could've taken us, but they retreated."

Wounded muracos dragged themselves through the carnage, sniffing for witch remains. They wouldn't find any leftovers. Oriana had made sure of that, the murdering bitch that she was.

The witches had left Wild Moor just as the tide of battle could've turned in their own favor.

"I don't like it."

Phelan, in human form and several feet shorter than him, tapped him in the stomach to get his attention. The casual touch set off blazing heat from Oriana's attack. He growled, grabbed Phelan by the neck, and lifted his scrawny body into the air. He'd only allowed two werewolves to touch him like that. One was dead, and the other might as well be. He blamed Oriana for that too. The witch had so much coming to her.

"C-can't … breathe."

He shook Phelan, unsympathetic at the sound of snapping bones. If Phelan had stayed in his werewolf form, he would've had a better chance of surviving his anger. Stupid Phelan for shifting then deciding to touch him before he'd cooled from the battle. Phelan wouldn't die, however. Even in human form, werewolves were resilient creatures.

He dropped him to the cracked cement.

Phelan, holding his neck with one hand while pointing behind him with the other, coughed up blood onto his bare chest.

He twisted to see what had the werewolf's eyes bulging from his head. He'd lived in Janus Nether his entire life, had traveled to every part of the region. In each city—Wild Moor, Chrome Haven, and Tin Falls there were multiple starmount towers. At least two hundred feet tall and shaped like trees with a sturdy square base, the steel edifices were insulated in unbreakable glass and protected by sun magic. They were considered historic landmarks, which meant they were protected by local Crimson Guards. More, there were no records or obvious signs of their purpose. The starmount towers always reminded him too much of the buildings in Irongarde City, so he'd ignored them.

He couldn't ignore the one a block from him, though. The three crossed arms, which had always been gray like the rest of the tower, glowed a familiar shade of blood or like a red sun. The arms sparked, like Oriana's magic that still stung his side and shoulder.

"W-what in the hell is going on?" Phelan croaked from behind him.

He had no idea. The muracos had all stopped in their tracks. As if in a trance, they watched the starmount blaze to life. From the gray base, magic leapt, shooting up the tower walls like blood through veins.

He felt the tower pulse with magic, heard the crackle as it reached the glowing crossed arms, and watched as a sunbeam burst from the top of the monument just as the protective glass came tumbling down. It shattered to the ground, startling the werewolves, effectively ending whatever hold seeing the starmount come to life had on them.

He couldn't see where the beam went, but he knew what was in the direction it had gone. Two more beams shot through the sky, and he ran. He could hazard a guess where those beams were headed—the other starmount towers in Wild Moor and Janus Nether.

The muracos scattered, running in every direction. He'd left Phelan behind. He'd left them all behind. He had to get underground. Had to—

An explosion threw him to the ground. He got back up and ran faster. More explosions rocked him, sending him back to the ground. The beams were leveled at the city now instead of the sky. Howling werewolves were sliced and burned.

To his right and left, buildings burned. Unnatural flames beat against the buildings like hammerheads on fire, a magical demolition no one in the buildings would survive.

Using his claws to scramble to his feet, he ran again, dodging debris, jumping over vehicles, and staying clear of the sunburst beams.

He couldn't outrun them. The destructive blasts were too quick, too numerous, and too relentless. He thought about hiding underground, but that wasn't smart with the buildings crumbling to their foundations. He'd be buried alive.

He spun around and raced back toward the starmount tower. If only he could make it there. A speeding vehicle struck him, clipping his right leg as the human scrambled to get away. His side and shoulder throbbed even more the closer he got to the tower, witch magic calling to witch magic.

He fell onto the base, hot to the touch, with his feet cut and bleeding from the broken glass surrounding the structure. He climbed on top of the base, pressing his body against the tower wall. He heard sizzling and knew the magic was burning him wherever he touched the wall.

Other muracos fought to join him—some making it to the base, most dying a brutal death. All he could do was watch his clan lose a war he'd thought they'd won, while he took refuge at the epicenter of their pain.

He howled again, and he didn't stop until the starmount tower powered down. He staggered off the base, leaving three layers of fur and skin behind. Looking out at Wild Moor, he dropped to his knees. It was gone. Destroyed. It was a devastating strike that had only one origin.

Irongarde City.

April 30, 2243
Irongarde Realm
City of Wild Moor

Hiding in the sewers and eating rodents, he hadn't been above ground in three days. Now, he trudged through the downtown streets of Wild Moor—or what used to be the downtown area. Everything was gone—blasted to rubble and dust. Even his beloved moon had abandoned him. The grimy, black aftermath of the spell's explosive magic was too thick for the moon's glow to shine through.

In the depths of the war zone, ground zero of the goddamn matriarchs' assault, he had survived. They thought they could kill him? Fuck those bitches. He would show them. He had brought war to them once. I'll do it again.

He'd rebuild his muraco army from the ash of destruction the witches had wrought.

"Where are we going now?" asked Phelan, the first muraco to accept him as the white werewolves' leader. "Storm Irongarde City and Iron Spire?"

He coughed. The tainted air burned his lungs. The effect didn't hurt nearly as much as a werewolf, but communication was more effective in his human form.

"Not yet. We need to hunt for other muraco survivors. First in Wild Moor then in Chrome Haven and Tin Falls."

"What about the Crimson Hunter?" Adolfus, a fifty-year-old muraco with a scar that ran from chin to left eyebrow, had taken a wait-and-see approach with him when they'd been introduced. That worked for him. He hadn't been looking for friends but like-minded allies. Muracos enjoyed killing witches, and he'd needed an army for his revolution. A win-win partnership. "She'll come after us."

"It's been three days. Oriana and Kalinda think we're dead. If they didn't, Oriana would've returned by now."

The arrogant assumption that they'd succeeded in killing them all would give him and his muracos the time they needed to prepare their counterattack.

He refused to call Oriana 'Matriarch' or 'Crimson Hunter.' Those days of subservience were over. The reign of witches was coming to an end. It was time for werewolves to make a stand and reclaim Earth Rift. It was their stolen birthright. The witches had left a ready-made army for him. He wouldn't squander his good fortune.

"We first need to check Wild Moor's muraco prison for survivors. Moonblight Penitentiary is where we'll find new recruits to our cause. After that, we'll travel to Chrome Haven's Dogscar Correctional Facility. Then we'll be strong enough to take the fight to the gates of Irongarde City. We'll be unstoppable, and I'll personally devour Kalinda's heart before slitting Oriana's throat and drinking the bitch dry. Let's move out."

"How are we going to break them out?" Phelan asked.

He had no idea, but Moonblight was miles away, and the Magerun had been shut down. They'd have to hoof it, leaving him time to devise a plan.

"I'll tell you when we get there. Let's go."

He and his Clan of the White Moon shifted in the middle of the street. They were fifty strong. A small group compared to their original numbers, but their ranks would be replenished as soon as he freed the imprisoned muracos.

He took off, his clan behind him, his future in front of him.

Blood of the Sun Decree #174
August 1, 2237

BY MATRIARCHAL DECREE, THE WEARING OF SILVER SNARES IS NO LONGER MANDATED WITHIN JANUS NETHER, RESERVED TERRITORY OF THE CLAN OF THE BLACK MOON.

Kalinda, Matriarch of Irongarde
Oriana, Matriarch of Steelcross

3: Brothers

May 25, 2240
Irongarde Realm
City of Wild Moor

Zev grabbed the pitcher of frothy golden liquid the waitress delivered to their booth, drinking it down in greedy gulps.

"Come on, asshole! That's supposed to be for all of us."

He finished off the draft, one hand holding the pitcher to his mouth while using his other to flip-off his youngest brother, Marrok. He slammed the empty pitcher down. "I'm not the asshole. You are." Wiping his mouth with the back of his hand, Zev glanced around the bar, searching for the waitress. He saw a large number of people, mainly werewolves, but there were also a fair number of witches. *Slumming with the dogs.*

Zev growled, turning back to his brothers who gaped at him. "I'm not the asshole," he said again, pointing his finger at Marrok from across the table.

"Oh, I'm the asshole? You're the one who's been in a foul mood since we got here, and I told you guys the good news."

Good news, my black, hairy ass.

Marrok continued, "You don't see Alarick freaking out. He's happy for me. Aren't you?"

Zev and Marrok looked at Alarick, who hadn't said a word since Marrok dropped his bomb on the brothers.

"Just because I'm the middle brother doesn't mean I like being in the middle of the bullshit that flows between the two of you. Leave me out of it. Zev, if Marrok wants to bond himself to a witch, it's none of our business. Marrok, you know how Zev feels about the kind of witch-werewolf union you just dropped on us, so stop acting like you're surprised. All I want is a damn beer and a quiet night. It seems I can't get either because of you two assholes."

Zev punched Alarick in the shoulder, harder than he should've, but not as hard as he wanted to knock some sense into Marrok. "You always say shit like that. Stop trying to have it both ways. Either be a mediator, or don't."

He jabbed his finger at Marrok again. "Tell you what, give Alarick your balls since you won't be needing them. Or are you planning on gifting them to Oriana the night she fucks you into submission and puts a dog collar on you?"

"Too far." Alarick slipped off the booth seat, crawling under the table and coming out on the other side. He walked away, tall and broad-shouldered like all the men in his family.

"I'm going to kick your ass." Marrok stood, the tips of his fingernails lengthening, a speck of white fang peeking from under his top lip.

Zev propped his arm against the back of the booth. Since Alarick had made his usual escape, he had more leg and arm room. Now, if only that cute human would bring her ass back there and take his drink order, he could drown his worries and anger. Maybe he could convince her to come home with him or, shit, take a break and let him fuck her in a stall of the ladies' room.

"Watch what you say about Oriana."

"Why, because you looove her? Give me a break. She's just like her damn mother."

"She's nothing like Matriarch Kalinda."

"Is she going to make you wear a silver snare, whenever you want to touch her?"

"Oriana is the reason why our silver snares don't activate while we're inside Janus Nether. Unless you do something violent to cause the rage disruptor in your brain to go off, prompting the spell to form the silver snare around your neck to calm you down, you're free of the silver snare. That's Oriana's doing. Hell, she's the reason why this region belongs to black werewolves."

Yeah, they had Janus Nether, a three-city region between Irongarde to the south, Steelcross to the north, and two human regions to the east and west. Zev preferred rustic and rural life over iron and steel. But no werewolf could stand to live so far from the sweet smell and taste of witches, which meant they had to live in the metropolitan areas.

A cheer rose in the bar. Zev didn't bother to wonder what had everyone so excited. Maybe a game.

As long as they had those damn rage disruptors in their heads, triggered to magically release the silver snare whenever werewolves ventured into collar-mandated territories or became violent, he would continue to view the decree as an invisible leash, not the progressive policy it was touted as being by witches and even many werewolves … werewolves like his naïve brother.

It wasn't as if Oriana's token decree mandated humans and witches leave Janus Nether. They still resided and worked there. Although, knowledge of the new silver snare protocol in Janus Nether had resulted in many witches fleeing the territory. *Good riddance to witch rubbish.*

"It's inevitable, you know? You can't fight the urges. It's who we are."

Even if he screwed a hundred humans, none of them would satisfy the cravings of a werewolf the way his biological counterpart could. From that perspective, Zev could understand his brother's needs. But they were crea-tures of desire and lust. At some point, they'd all have to accept the true nature of werewolves.

"The cravings may be part of who we are, but we're more than that. And I'm damn sure not a monster. I'll never become that to Oriana."

Alarick returned to the table, a pitcher in each hand. Handing one to Zev, he placed the other on the table between where he'd been seated and where Marrok still stood.

"Thanks, man." Zev grabbed the pitcher, pouring himself a mug of beer instead of draining it like before. He wasn't trying to piss Marrok off this time, so he acted the role of a civilized werewolf and moved out of the booth so Alarick could slide in instead of crawling under the table again. He did take his pitcher with him, however. Zev didn't like to share, not even with his brothers. The werewolf wasn't that damn civilized.

"What did I miss?" Alarick shook his head at Marrok, who'd withdrawn his claws and eye teeth but still looked mad enough to take a swing at Zev. "Sit down and tell us about you and Oriana."

"I don't want to know about him and that …" Both brothers shot Zev a dirty look. "Fine, I won't call her an accurate but nasty name. But, mark my words, Marrok, it won't end well between the two of you."

"You don't know that." Marrok plopped back in his seat, his lean frame knocking into the table and spilling some of the beer from the overfull pitcher. "We love each other. That's all we need in order to make it work."

"So said every werewolf before his craving overtook him and his witch lover had to kill his naïve, stupid ass. We always love them. Our love for witches has never been an issue."

Alarick punched Zev in the arm as hard as Zev had hit him earlier. "You've never loved a woman, witch or human."

He shrugged, black T-shirt tight across his broad shoulders. "I never said I had. But witches are like the air we breathe, essential and all-consuming. We want them … need them … too damn much. Our lust is for more than sex, which makes us a danger not only to them but to the very fabric of our society. How can we be so perfectly matched but bring each other so much pain?"

Zev rolled his eyes when Alarick poured himself a drink and sipped it in that dainty way he'd adopted to impress females.

Alarick sat back, his expression thoughtful. "Our craving for their magic, their blood, is similar to the relationship between the sun and the moon. One cannot exist without the other, yet they can never be in the same place at the same time. Forever together, forever apart, an endless cycle."

Zev thought both of his brothers needed a serious wake-the-fuck-up call. "Well, aren't you the fucking poet of the year. Ever heard of an eclipse?"

"Say what you want, Zev. My point is sound. I don't like wearing a collar any more than you or any other werewolf." Alarick gripped his mug tighter but didn't drink. "I hated wearing that thing. But I remember when puberty hit. The bloodlust, the hunger pangs, the need to sate my lust on the first willing witch." He stared into his mug, voice lowered to a rough admission. "Even, the unwilling ones. I stalked them to their homes, to school, to the park, wherever. I couldn't stop myself. I just knew I had to be close to a witch, to taste her, to have her. So, I found one alone in the park one night." Alarick downed his beer in one long gulp. "I had her pinned to the ground, the werewolf having broken free and given chase when she ran. I overpowered her, slammed her to the ground … hard. I was out of control. She cried, and only a part of me cared. She cried, and all I wanted to do was sate my hunger."

Marrok poured Alarick another drink, no one speaking into the silence. Zev knew the blood-and-magic lust well. At some point, every werewolf did. They were animals, their human form a disguise for the beast within.

"She was a little younger than me. Eleven, twelve at the most. She hadn't gone through the change, so she had no metal to help channel her wild magic. I snarled at her, hating what the sweet smell of her sun magic had turned me into." Alarick drank his second mug of beer, nothing dainty about how he grabbed the mug, lifted it to his trembling lips, and opened his mouth, letting the golden liquid slide down his throat. "She should've fought me, but she was too scared. I imagined myself ripping into her, slashing her throat with my teeth and drinking her blood before shredding her chest in search of her heart and magic. I could see myself doing it, killing her and becoming the worst version of myself."

Marrok's arm lifted, settled across Alarick's shoulders, and pulled him in for a one-arm hug. "None of us will ever become muracos." Marrok set his own bare forearm next to Alarick's on the table. "Our skin is brown. Our fur is black. We aren't white or even gray. Our black fur will never fade because, animals we may be, but we aren't rapists and murderers. We don't hurt our witches, no matter the strength of our lust. As awful as your story is, you're still a black moon werewolf, so I know you didn't hurt that girl. Scared the shit out of her, yeah, but nothing more than that."

"Scared myself into having Dad take me to the clinic to have the rage disruptor implanted the next day, a week before my fifteenth birthday."

Zev had seen the change in his younger brother. Alarick's lust had kicked in a month early. In hindsight, he should've told their father. But he'd wanted to give the young werewolf his last taste of freedom. Werewolves weren't meant to be chained and controlled, which was what the silver snare did—a collar and leash in one ball-stealing spell. But it was the rage disruptor implant, a sophisticated witch spell, that triggered the magic that formed the silver snare. Two parts but one intricate design with a single purpose—werewolf subjugation.

Alarick's hand drifted over his face, wiping across a furrowed brow and sliding down a cheek to settle at a chin he stroked with an unspoken moroseness. "I hate the collars, but witches have a reason to fear us. They are the warm sun to our cold moon, but we can't share the same sky."

Marrok scooted away from Alarick, face drawn, jaw twitching. "You agree with Zev?"

"Most of the time, no, but about this, yes. I like Oriana. She's never been anything but kind to us. She's not her mother, but she's also only twenty-six."

"Meaning what?"

"Meaning witches and werewolves live a long time, Marrok."

"That's not what you meant."

"No, Alarick meant there's plenty of time for sweet-smelling Oriana to turn into a heartless bitch like her mother."

Alarick balled his fists, and Zev thought he would call him an asshole and punch his arm again. He didn't, but he did refill his mug and resume that damn dainty sipping. "My point is that you're both a little young and a lot naïve. You're a virgin, and I bet she is too. You have no idea how it feels to be inside a witch and to lust for more than her body, even when you're wearing the silver snare. It's not so bad, when you and a witch are scratching a mutual itch, but it's hell when you love her. The blood-magic lust is even greater."

Marrok's frown didn't surprise Zev. The young werewolf had a stubborn streak as wide as the planet, and a loving heart deeper than the biological rift between witches and werewolves. A biological rift that placed the even-tempered witches at the top of the food chain.

A goddamn matriarchy. What bullshit.

"Once I'm Oriana's consort, we're going to move to Steelcross."

"Wait, she's taking you out of Irongarde Realm? And you agreed to leave with her?" Zev ignored the pitcher of beer Alarick slid toward him. "Were-wolves don't live in Steelcross. Hell, after giving us Janus Nether, the matriarch kicked most of us out of Irongarde City."

"That was Matriarch Kalinda's decision, not Oriana's," Alarick added. "Besides, Matriarch Kalinda only booted out the werewolves who refused to wear silver snares while in Irongarde City."

"Not helping," he snarled at Alarick. "Do you hear this? Our baby brother is moving all the way to Steelcross. There's nothing but humans and witches there."

"That's only true for the realm's capital of Steelcross City."

"Which is where in the hell you'll be staying when you move into Oriana's queenly Sky Rise tower."

There's Silver Water, Cobalt Pass, and Gold Mount in Steelcross Realm too. All of these areas are inhabited by witches, werewolves, and humans, just like Irongarde Realm's Irongarde City, Ironmere, and Cooper Vale are made up of all three groups.

"I don't need a fucking geography lesson." Spittle flew, and Zev hackles rose.

"It's not Oriana's fault that when the city was founded, only witches settled in Steelcross City, and it remained that way. The same is true for Janus Nether. Werewolves informally staked claim to this region. That's why Janus Nether has the largest population of werewolves in both realms and why Oriana started her campaign to end the wearing of silver snares with us. She has a lot of great ideas. Have dinner with us tomorrow night. I'm sure, once you've heard her plans, you'll like them."

Marrok grinned at Zev, voice soft whenever he spoke of Oriana. *If I look hard enough, I bet I could see little red hearts in Marrok's eyes.*

"She's been Matriarch of Steelcross since she turned twenty-one. When there is one matriarch of Earth Rift, she splits her time between the two realms. But, when there are two matriarchs, like with Oriana and Matriarch Kalinda, they each oversee a realm. Matriarch Kalinda gave Oriana Steelcross. I'm the reason she hasn't moved there permanently. But she can't keep staying in Iron Spire with her mother. When she moves to her realm, I'm going with her."

"I don't care about her matriarchal plans or where in the hell she decides to move. I'm not stepping one foot into Steel Rise, not if it means I'll have that silver snare around my neck again. Just so I can have a meal with my brother? I won't do it, not even for you." Forgoing civility, Zev all but drowned himself in the beer, liquid running down his chin.

"I love her."

Zev burped then sneered. "So, you've said, and that will be your doom. Witches can't control their magic without a strong dampening source. If they wanted, they could level this entire city. But they won't, not because they're any more ethical than the rest of us, but because they have nothing driving them to do it, drawing out the vilest part of themselves. But werewolves …" Zev snorted. "we don't get off that lucky. If you and Oriana can beat thousands of years of genetics, well," he raised his pitcher of beer to Marrok, "cheers to unrealistic expectations. You won't be seeing me at your funeral because, well, you know, you'll be the dead fuck in the metal box."

"Asshole."

"And damn proud of it." Pushing past Alarick, Zev went in search of the cute waitress. All the talk of sex and blood had made him horny. If she wasn't available, there were other options. At least with a human female, his blood-magic lust wouldn't be an issue. With them, he could have a good time without triggering the rage disruptor, which in turn would activate the silver snare.

One day, I'll be free of the silver snare and the rule of witches.

4: Steel Dreams

May 30, 2240
Steelcross Realm
City of Bronze Ward

"What do you think?" Oriana glanced up at Marrok, twisting the edge of her blouse and biting her bottom lip. She hoped he couldn't hear the pounding of her heart.

An hour ago, they'd arrived at Oriana's home—which would be their home after their moonless sky wedding ceremony. They'd journeyed from Wild Moor to Steel Rise, which was located in Steelcross City, the capital of Steelcross Realm.

Oriana had decided to treat Marrok, who'd never been beyond Irongarde, to the beautiful landscapes between realms. So, they'd traveled via the Mage-run shuttle, a transporter tube fueled by the sun and magic. The sky transporter system connected every part of the planet, a delicate balance of metal and magic, like everything else in Earth Rift.

Oriana had then used extraction magic, the weakest of her magical abilities, to transport them to Bronze Ward, where they presently stood.

Holding her hand, Marrok continued to look around but resumed their stroll down the center of the desolate street, dilapidated brick buildings on each side. Twisted granger trees—in full bloom and with red-and-blue leaves—lined the street. They were planted equidistant in an unimaginative design typical of areas as old as this one. One tree seemed to bleed into the other, so tall and wild did they grow with nothing and no one around to stunt their expansion.

Bronze Ward was literally off the beaten path. Having gone unused for decades, it wasn't connected to the Magerun transport system.

Once they'd completed the moonless sky wedding ceremony and they were settled in Steel Rise, she'd be able to share other details of the realm with Marrok. She would begin with her decision to create Steelburgh.

"It's really rundown, Oriana. I mean, I haven't seen buildings made of brick in …" He stopped, shook his head, and smiled down at her. "I've actually never seen a brick building in person. Read about them, of course. Seen them in old vids."

They continued to walk at a leisurely pace Oriana enjoyed. Once in residence at Steel Rise as matriarch and embarking upon her ambitious plans, she would have little time for such banal pursuits. But she would, of course, do her best not to allow governance to strip her of the simple joys in life, like spending a summer's day with Marrok, dreaming of their future.

"This ward looks like it should be condemned."

"You don't like it?" She started to bite her lower lip again, but stopped. "I hoped you would. This is the place I told you about."

Marrok's frown always revealed so much. Her werewolf possessed zero ability to keep every emotion he felt from finding its way onto his handsome face.

Pushing up on tiptoe, she kissed his warm, sexy lips. "Moonvale Forest abuts Bronze Ward. Moonvale is at the base of the Blackridge Mountains. Both are protected land … perfect for werewolves."

The hand that had snaked around her waist when she'd kissed him, tugged her closer, his mouth going to her neck and nibbling. "I've never been this far north. When you mentioned giving werewolves a place of our own when you moved to Steelcross, I assumed you meant a city like Wild Moor."

Tilting her head back, she enjoyed the surge of pleasure his mouth and hands created. They stood alone in the middle of the downtown area of a ward once home to both werewolves and witches. It, like the dream that had birthed it, was abandoned—boarded-up, overgrown, and left to rot. But … just over the horizon was Moonvale Forest, verdant green as far as the eye could see. It was divided by Silentdrift Lake, the name befitting the tranquility she hoped werewolves would find there.

With two hands, Oriana took Marrok's face, holding him in place so she could look into his gorgeous eyes—light-brown with red around his irises. When in werewolf form, Marrok's entire iris was the most luscious shade of scarlet she'd ever seen. "It'll take a couple of years to turn this ward into a haven for werewolves. Once we do, though, it'll be a model."

"We?"

Sliding her lips against his, she smiled. "Yes, *we*. You agreed to be my consort, remember?"

His eyes drifted close and he murmured, "Hmm, yes. Consort ..."

Oriana hadn't asked to co-rule Earth Rift with Kalinda, but dual matriarchs weren't unprecedented. Twins Elaine and Elidi, during the eighteenth century, were the first siblings to rule together. Thea and Marisol, cousins, co-ruled for two hundred years during the early part of the twenty-first century.

But there had never been a mother-daughter rulership. The power dynamics were an issue Oriana and Kalinda were still working through. In truth, it was a constant struggle. Each gain—a dedicated werewolf region, a collar-free Janus Nether, rebuilding of Bronze Ward, and opening of Steelburgh—was a battle that left Oriana feeling as if she hadn't won, even though her mother had eventually consented.

With her hands still on his cheeks, she pulled him in for a deeper kiss. He tasted of refreshing mint and smelled of earthy wood. Marrok felt even better. His tall, muscular body wrapped around hers as he intensified the kiss. Oriana moaned into his mouth, the sun high in the sky, fueling her magic and desire.

Breathless and with great reluctance, she stepped away from him.

Marrok's heavy-lidded eyes lifted, irises redder than they'd been a minute ago. His hand rose, fingering the silver snare around his neck. Silver snares were crafted of pure silver—soft, reflective, and shiny. Bordered with reddish-brown copper, the silver snare resembled a woman's high neck collar necklace more than it did a dog's collar with buckles and straps. Silver snares weren't adorned or engraved. No werewolf tried to pretty them up or pretend they were something other than what they were—a means of control and protection. "I'm fine. I'd never hurt you."

"I know." Hands on her hips, she took in the street, trying to envision it as it had been so many years ago. "Bronze Ward was a failed experiment. Did I ever tell you that?"

"I don't believe you did." Retaking her hand, they resumed walking, her shoulder-length hair blowing in the sudden breeze.

"Matriarch Helen thought if werewolves wore the silver snares at night when they were the strongest, they and witches could live together full-time as a mated pair, like humans. Grandmother speculated that if pups from the union had the opportunity to imprint on their witch mothers, their blood-and-magic lust wouldn't be so strong. She theorized it was the absence of the maternal bond that made them so vulnerable to our magic when they reached puberty. Grandfather Tuncay—"

"Tuncay means bronze moon. That explains the name of the ward."

He led her around a corner. The condition of this street was worse than the others they'd walked down. More trees populated the area, roots having bulged up, forcing their way through the cement, reclaiming the earth the way nature was wont to do.

"Right. I like the name Tuncay. We should add the name to our list." Oriana smiled up at her future consort and father of her children.

"I bet you do like the name. Tuncay was your grandfather. By the time we have our son, our list will be as long as my arm. But I thought you wanted to have a girl first."

Oriana shrugged. "The gender doesn't matter to me but, as matriarch, it's my duty to add to the witch population, not to mention provide an heir to the matriarchy, before I birth a son of the Black Moon."

They stopped again, coincidentally, in front of a hospital.

"That's why you're trying to bring Bronze Ward back to life, isn't it?"

"Grandmother failed, as Mother has taken to reminding me. But she may have been correct about pups and imprinting. There is some evidence to support that perspective."

"What about the rest of her ideas?"

"I don't know. Mother closed Bronze Ward after my grandparents died. She refuses to discuss any of it."

Marrok stepped closer, and she thought he'd kiss her again. Hell, she wanted him to kiss her … and more. The way his eyes lowered to her lips, licking his own, his mind ran along the same lines as hers.

"Except for wearing the silver snares only part-time, your plan for Bronze Ward doesn't seem much different from Matriarch Helen's."

"That's because it isn't. Not really. Like her, I believe it's important for pups, as well as witches, to be co-parented. When we aren't, when so much of our lives are kept separate from each other, it leads to greater misunderstandings. We are as we are, Marrok. Greater minds than ours have pondered our biological compatibility yet ultimate incompatibility. Neither magic nor technology has solved the fundamental issue between us."

Placing her hand to his chest she felt his heartbeat—his werewolf strength a primal call to her witch magic.

"From my research, Grandmother, like too many matriarchs, limited werewolves to urban areas. Part of the reason our cities are so overpopulated is that two of the four realms are reserved for human residents. Mother won't agree to me building werewolf settlements in those territories, but I've been able to convince her to permit me to bring this ward into the current century and to grant those who live here access to Moonvale Forest and Blackridge Mountains."

Two years of arguing and one year of negotiating had resulted in a huge win—not for Oriana, or even for werewolves, but for all of Earth Rift. Witches and werewolves couldn't continue this way, coming together to procreate but little else for fear of hurting the other.

"You're right, I'm also doing this for both of us and our future. You hardly know your mother, and my father refuses to visit me at Iron Spire. I want us to be mother and father to all of our children."

"I want that too." Tugging her to him, he hugged her with the same fierceness she felt. "I want that more than anything. For us to be a family, the way humans are."

Oriana laughed. "You make their relationships sound idyllic. They aren't. They're complicated too."

Marrok kissed her cheek. "No relationship is more complicated than that of a witch and werewolf. So, you're giving werewolves a place to run, hunt, and play."

"Grandmother had this ward built with bricks for a reason. It's the opposite reason why we have Steelcross, Irongarde, Ironmere, and every other region with a type of metal in its name. Bricks aren't as werewolf friendly as forests and mountains, but they also aren't a constant reminder of the beast that dwells within us all."

"Witches don't have beasts inside them."

"You're wrong." Oriana lifted her hands, palms out to him. "We can wield our power like a firestorm. Witches have used the threat of werewolf attacks to stop learning and growing. We've turned over our lives to the metals we put into our bodies, using those same metals to build fortresses around our hearts, which can't cope with not having their other half. We are a doomed people, Marrok, whether we admit it or not."

"Don't say that. You sound too much like Zev."

Oriana arched an eyebrow, and he chuckled.

"Okay, you're nothing like my brother. But he used the same word—doomed—about our relationship."

She rolled her eyes. "Of course, Zev did. That explains why only Alarick had dinner with us the other night."

She hadn't been surprised. At thirty-two, Zev challenged every rule. To her knowledge, he hadn't broken any, although she wouldn't be surprised to find out he had. He was the kind of werewolf, overly aggressive and purposefully intimidating, Kalinda used to justify keeping werewolves on the proverbial short leash. Kalinda had relented some only because Oriana had asked it of her. Kalinda, despite her stubborn nature, wasn't immune to the rare moment of sentimentality. After all, she'd cared enough about Oriana's father, Bader, to give him a daughter and a son. Unfortunately, Oriana's younger brother had died at four when he'd fallen from a tall tree and broken his neck while in Bader's care. Heartbroken, Kalinda blamed Bader. Her father blamed himself more.

"Our relationship will grow on him. Zev just needs time to get used to the change. After that, he'll be fine."

Oriana doubted that, but she kept her own counsel. The last thing she wanted to do was cause any more conflict between the brothers than taking Marrok as her consort would create.

"I also don't believe you truly think we're doomed." He tapped the temple of her head. "The wheels in there are always turning. You don't want to admit you've been trying to find a solution to a problem everyone has deemed unsolvable. You're afraid."

"I'm not."

He tapped her nose. "Liar."

She waved his hand away from her face. "Fine, I am. I've scoured the matriarchal archives, going back as far as I can. But …"

"But?"

"We know there was patriarchal rule long before the brutal and life-changing war between witches and werewolves. From patriarchy and patrilineal descent to matriarchy and matrilineal descent in a single generation."

"I'm surprised any of our ancestors survived the War of Eternal Hunger. The hunger to keep power or not to be consumed by the power lust of others, I guess, is as bloody and violent as the hunger to claim it for yourself."

Very true. The War of Eternal Hunger was taught in school, although not as thoroughly as other major historical events. But few events were as significant as a war that had toppled one cultural regime only to replace it with another. Did it matter whether werewolves or witches ruled if the other wasn't elevated to equal status in society?

"There are chunks of our history that are gone. No records. Nothing. It's as if Earth Rift didn't exist until after the war."

"I know. I'm a student of history, remember?"

"Who said 'history is always written by the winners'?"

"I have no idea, but I follow your point."

Oriana didn't know if he did. For whatever reason, Matriarch Alba, the first Matriarch of Earth Rift, had all but wiped werewolves from the history of Earth Rift before her reign. Little remained to hint at what life was like for witches, werewolves, and humans before the War of Eternal Hunger. The effort to destroy over a thousand years of history would've been a massive undertaking and had to have taken years. All of which begged the question … what did Matriarch Alba want to hide from future generations of witches and werewolves? Or perhaps her motivations had less to do with hiding truths and more to do with the overwhelming desire to forget them.

" 'History is always written by the winners.' I read that line in one of Matriarch Helen's journals. Of all my ancestors, Helen was the most prolific writer. I've only read a third of what she wrote."

"Since we're in Bronze Ward, it isn't hard to figure out what part of her reign you've already studied."

"Would you like to see Silentdrift Lake?" she asked, changing the topic and, based on his response, Marrok didn't seem to mind. Although, as he'd said, he was a student of history. They would revisit this topic. Perhaps, with his help, they would solve the mystery.

"Umm, yeah, I would but, well, it's kind of far away."

"It is." Oriana crossed arms over her chest. "Your point?"

Rubbing the nape of his neck, he looked away from Oriana, kicking a piece of displaced cement before lifting his eyes again to meet hers. "Shit, you're still frowning. Your extraction magic makes me, well, umm, kind of nauseous. The jump is jarring. I don't think my stomach could take it if you had to use your magic longer to get us from here all the way to the lake."

Marrok pointed down the street, not at all in the direction of Silentdrift Lake.

With the back of her hand, she moved his arm until it pointed to the west. "That way."

"There's no need to glower, Matriarch Oriana. I still don't want you to jump us there, even if you know the direction and I don't."

"You just said I make you sick. Of course, I'm going to glower." When she went to fold her arms across her chest again, Marrok yanked her flush against him.

"Your magic, not you. Nothing about you repels me."

"First nauseous and now repels. Whoever said that werewolves weren't charming sure knew what they were talking about. You're quite handsome, though, so I think I'll keep you."

"How magnanimous of you, Matriarch."

"I am, aren't I?"

"And humble."

"Yes, let's not forget humble."

They laughed, hugging each other. Breathing in his scent, smelling the werewolf beneath the human veneer, Oriana opened herself to Marrok. Magic warmed her body, melding with the steel in her hands and arms.

"Oriana, I—"

"Trust me. I'll do better this time. I promise."

Marrok held her tighter, his head in the crook of her neck, arms around her waist.

She wound her magic around him, letting it flow from her into the midday air, a whip of magic that could, if she were in battle, be used to slice the skin and fur from a werewolf. This close, she could kill him with her magic. This close, he could sink his fangs into her, killing her before the rage disruptor registered his oxytriton spike, releasing a neurotransmitter.

When werewolves were angry, scared, or about to strike, the silver snare emitted soothing pulses sent through the werewolf's skin to his central nervous center—resulting in a calming effect. Despite witches' desire to mitigate the vicious impulses of werewolves, they had no desire to hurt them in the process. Perhaps, in the beginning when silver snares were mandated by Matriarch Alba, pain and revenge had been the goal after so many werewolves had eaten countless witches. Alba's reign had been marked by blood and broken trust.

But trust could be reformed. Time had a way of turning the inconceivable into the possible.

They held each other, Oriana trusting Marrok not to lose control, and he not moving out of her embrace, trusting himself not to hurt her and trusting her to jump them safely to Silentdrift Lake.

They disappeared into the magical ether of space. Oriana made sure to keep Marrok in the bubble of her magic, her whip around them both. She envisioned where she wanted them to land, her magic her eyes, her steel her faithful guide.

She took it slow so as not to make Marrok nauseous, his complaint valid despite Oriana's indignant protestations. She slowed her breathing, held her magic whip with one hand, and lifted Marrok's face with the other. His eyes were closed, his lips were near, and she wanted to taste him again.

She planted soft pecks to his lips, chin, and neck. Letting her lips rest against the top of his silver snare, she kissed along the rim. He sucked in a breath, so she did it again. Playing with fire, her mother would chastise, and Kalinda wouldn't be wrong.

They fell.

Splash.

Oriana spurted out water. Wet and cold, she glanced to her right and caught Marrok's equally wet face staring at her. They were sitting chest deep in Silentdrift Lake, the right bank several feet behind them, heavily blooming red mahogany trees across the lake in front of them.

She bit her bottom lip then offered what she hoped was an apologetic smile. "You're terrible at this."

"I got distracted."

"Whose fault is that?" Jeans soaked and weighing him down, Marrok pushed to his feet, his T-shirt clinging to every scrumptious, ripped muscle.

With a steady hand, he helped her to her feet. Oriana's own jeans hadn't fared any better, making slogging to the shore difficult.

Marrok's gaze slipped from her face to her chest, no doubt taking full visual advantage of a white blouse and bra that had to be damn near transparent.

When they reached dry land Oriana stopped. As if she hadn't lost control of her magic, dumping them in a lake instead of on the shore, she settled her hands on her hips, held her head high, and asked, "Do you feel nauseous?"

Marrok narrowed his gaze. "That's what you're going with?"

She shrugged. "That was your only complaint."

He threw his hands up. "Oh, I didn't know I had to ask you not to drown me. I thought not killing your future consort was a given."

"You're so dramatic. You're a werewolf, which makes you more like a floatie for your matriarch."

That earned her a snarl. "I got your floatie right here …"

Marrok lunged, and Oriana took off, running away from him as fast as her wet jeans and soggy shoes would allow. Giggling, she bolted around tall ancient trees, making sure to keep a tree between herself and the swifter Marrok.

Her strategy didn't help, especially when she tripped over her own feet, falling to the ground in a heap of wet giggling witch.

Marrok pounced, sliding into her and wrapping her in his arms, rolling them over until he lay atop her. "Got you."

"I let you catch me."

"Yeah, right. Did you say hello to the forest floor when your face met it?" Wiping leaves and dirt from her hair, Marrok smiled down at her.

Oriana's heart clenched with how much she loved this werewolf. Leaning up, she kissed the grin from his face. Kissed him until he kissed her back. Kissed him until she couldn't breathe … then she kissed him some more.

Straddling her hips, Marrok yanked off their shirts.

Reaching up, she ran her hands across his defined abs, over his hard nipples, and down his sinewy arms. Yum—dark chocolate skin and muscles had never blended together so perfectly.

"You're magnificent."

"So are you. Shit, Oriana, I want to rip that bra off you and kiss you everywhere."

She wanted the same. Oriana opened her arms to Marrok.

Without a second of hesitation, he came to her, chest to breasts, lips to lips.

They'd dated for six years. Having met their junior year of college, through a mutual acquaintance, Marrok had given Oriana his contact information. When she'd reached out to him a week later, he'd admitted, "I didn't think the matriarch's daughter would be interested in a guy she met at a werewolf-owned club."

"Are you saying you think I'm a snob?" she'd asked, trying to sound light and playful as opposed to offended and well … snobbish.

"Which answer will give me the best chance of you going out with me?"

She couldn't help herself. Oriana had laughed. "I've always been a fan of the truth."

"Then, nope. I never once thought the only child of the matriarch, reared to become the next matriarch, would be elitist. Nope, not me. I have no idea why anyone would even think that way."

She'd laughed again. The tongue-in-cheek approach had been the right move to make with a woman who, indeed, despite her true nature, was often viewed as untouchable and a snob, particularly by werewolves. In Marrok's unique way, he'd charmed her, leaving her wanting to know more about him.

Marrok now worked his way down her chest—licking and kissing. It wasn't enough. She burned for him, her skin no longer wet from the lake. Oriana wanted Marrok to remove her bra. She craved the feel of his mouth on her aching breasts. More, on her throbbing sex.

Experience, however, told her Marrok wouldn't take the initiative. Oriana cupped him on the outside of his drenched jeans. Squeezed. Rubbed. She smiled when he moaned, eyes closing and hips pushing into her hand.

Acting quickly, before he regained his senses, she unbuttoned and un-zipped his pants. Slipping her hand into his jeans, Oriana followed the path of dark, curly stomach hair into his boxers, and around an erection harder than her Ravagers of the Lost cannons. She stroked him in earnest, pleased with his guttural moans and hungry kisses.

Oriana contemplated rolling him over, straddling his knees, and taking him into her mouth. She'd never pleasured him that way. Every time she'd tried, Marrok had stopped her. Not because he hadn't wanted her mouth on him as much as she desired the taste of him on her tongue, but because he viewed oral sex as a slippery slope. For Oriana, oral sex was meant to be slippery, no slope necessary.

She gripped him harder, increased her pace, and wedged her other hand between their bodies, working at her own zipper. All the while she hoped Marrok would, for once, accept the path she was leading them down. They were alone, engaged, and ready.

Damn, if Oriana were any more ready to become Marrok's lover, she would combust from the heat of the long wait. From his heavy breathing and fast rutting into her hand, Marrok's own explosion was a few strokes away.

"O-Oriana. Shit. That … that's soooo good." Marrok bit her neck, his penis growing and pulsing in her hand. "I'm going to …"

Come, yes, on her stomach. She milked him until his penis stopped twitching and his breath came in slow gulps.

"Y-you're not supposed to do stuff like that."

If Marrok meant his words to be a scold, he should've communicated the same to his still-hard penis. *Bless werewolf stamina.*

Marrok rolled off her, grabbed his shirt, and used it to wipe Oriana's stomach and hand clean. Kneeling beside her, his eyes traveled from her face to her breasts and then to her undone pants. Marrok exemplified the word wolfish. They were in a forest, he was a werewolf, and she was reclined before him, weak from her arousal and the leftover enjoyment of watching him orgasm. Would Marrok continue what Oriana had started, or leave her horny, hot, and unfulfilled?

"The ceremony is in a month. But it feels like another six years."

"We don't have to wait. We could," Oriana's gaze fell to Marrok's lap, his erection tenting his boxers, "play around." Lifting her eyes, she found his glued to her face. "Just a little playing, if you want."

"You know I want. You're counting on me wanting to do more than play around."

Of course, Oriana was, but she wouldn't press the issue or complain if Marrok decided they'd played enough for one day. Protocol dictated that matriarchs maintain their virginity until they took a consort. One of the many reasons she loved Marrok was his decision to abstain from sex along with Oriana. She hadn't asked or expected it of him, especially when they'd begun dating.

"I can smell your desire for me."

"Not very romantic, my love."

"Maybe not, but neither was shoving your hand down my pants and jerking me off."

"I heard many sounds coming from you, but not one of them was a protest."

Marrok reclined beside Oriana, his nearness a tangible temptation. "My father didn't raise a fool." He kissed her, his tongue slipping inside her mouth and his fingers into her panties—exploring. "Or a selfish werewolf. I won't make love to you before our wedding, but I'll repay the pleasure you gave me. I'm still seeing stars." Nose lowered to her neck, sniffing her. "I like this scent on you. I want more of it."

She shivered, wanting more of Marrok but accepting the boundary he'd drawn.

Oriana's legs parted, relaxing as Marrok's thick digit penetrated her—not deep, but inside her enough to offer her more than teasing thrusts. Two fingers stretched her. Slick from her desire, his thumb rubbed her clit, drawing it to a hard, pulsating erection.

She gripped his shoulders, pulled him to her, and claimed his mouth again. The closer the night of the ceremony drew, the more impatient Oriana became to consummate their relationship physically. They had to be the only twenty-six-year-old virgins on Earth Rift. Delayed gratification wasn't a virtue she valued, certainly not with Marrok's tongue and fingers simulating a joining of bodies and hearts.

Her stomach tightened. So close. Yes, so close. "Marrok, please. Please." Nails dug into his bare back, and his hips lifted, needing him deeper. "Marrok. Please. I need. I need …"

"I know, baby, I know. But I can't cross that threshold inside of you. That's for our wedding night. I'll give you all of me then."

"But I want … I need you now." His fingers weren't enough, not after so long.

But then he rubbed her in *just* the right spot, and she moaned loud and long. Yes, Marrok had found Oriana's need, the place inside her that had her biting his neck and squirting her release.

Ironically, or perhaps typically—she lacked the experience to know—falling apart in his arms made her want him even more. Marrok didn't help the situation when he sucked on the fingers that had been inside her; their gazes locked. Damn, she could come again from the sheer pleasure of watching him enjoy the taste of her.

How they'd abstained for so long, she didn't know.

"That is so hot."

"You taste good. You'll taste even better when my lips are on you and my tongue is in you. I can't wait."

Neither could Oriana. Her sex quivered at the thought, Marrok's husky voice a carnal promise she couldn't wait to indulge.

Knowing they'd gone as far as they dared, Oriana and Marrok dressed, her clothes even more uncomfortable over sensitive post-orgasm skin.

They got to their feet.

"This place smells nothing like the cities."

Marrok's contented awe reaffirmed her commitment to breathing life back into Bronze Ward.

"No metal. No towers or skyrises. No witch magic. Nothing but fresh, clean air. You should shift. I know you want to."

"But …"

Oriana could sense his desire to run wild and free in his natural form.

"I shouldn't. I couldn't."

"You should. You can. This is what I want to give to the werewolves in my part of the realm. To all of Earth Rift, but that's a long-term goal that may never happen if Mother fights me on it. But this" —she playfully smacked his chest — "I can give to you now. Go, run, be happy. I'll return in a couple of hours."

"You don't have to leave. I said I wouldn't hurt you."

"As I've told you many times, I'm not afraid of you in werewolf form. But I want you to experience the lake and forest without worrying about what you think I'm thinking and feeling. With a matriarchal override command, I can force the recall of the silver snare, if you like."

He appeared scared to death at that prospect, so Oriana let that offer go unanswered.

On another note, Oriana looked down at her disheveled clothing. She may have landed them in Silentdrift Lake, but she was fairly certain, without Marrok as a distraction, she could magic jump into her bedroom without anyone seeing her.

Her hair must look terrible. She pushed the wet strands behind her ears. "Have fun. Don't get into trouble while I'm gone."

"How can I? There's no one else out here." Marrok popped the button on his jeans, his arched eyebrow and grin a challenge.

She gulped, called her magic, and jumped to Steel Rise. The wedding ceremony could not come soon enough for Oriana.

June 8, 2240
Steelcross Realm
City of Steelburgh
Crimson Guard Headquarters

"They're a bunch of animals." Forehead pressed to a window, Abelone despised the sight below. *Muracos: filthy, untrustworthy, barbaric.* Not just the creatures walking up and down the steel-smoothed street, but the entire worthless city.

"Every time you come here, you stare out that window. You just passed them on your way in. No need to torture yourself by watching them go about their business."

"They have no business to go about." Opening the window, Abelone leaned out and spat. Not waiting to see which werewolf it landed on, she slammed and locked the window. Turning, she shrugged at Bharavi's crinkled nose and shaking head. "What?"

"That was nasty, even for you."

"Don't make it sound as if you care any more about them than I do."

Her long blonde bangs covered one eye. Abelone had considered cutting her asymmetrical bangs to match the rest of her hairstyle. She preferred short and simple to long and annoying. But Bharavi enjoyed running her fingers through the sun-kissed locks, so the too-long bangs with otherwise cropped hair was Abelone's concession to a witch whose shiny midnight hair fell to her waist. It was too much for Abelone's taste, but it was silky-soft, like Bharavi, so she didn't complain. Much.

"Come. Sit. And stop glowering."

"I don't take orders from you." Abelone stalked away from the window to sit in the chair on the other side of Bharavi's desk. Crossing her legs, she let her foot swing forward and back, lightly kicking the desk with each frontward motion. "We shouldn't be here." Cocking her head in the direction of the window, but meaning all Steelburgh, she amended, "*They* shouldn't be here."

Dressed in her knee-length white coat, name badge hanging from the breast pocket, Bharavi inclined her head. Dark eyes shimmered with the same disappointment Abelone had seen in the gaze of every Crimson Guard assigned to police Steelburgh, the city Matriarch Oriana had created to house the muracos who had served their prison sentences but who could not be released back into society.

"At least you don't have to examine them. They like it too much. The touching, the closeness, the small examination room filled with my scent. I can hear them breathing me in—sharp, greedy inhalations."

Forearms that had been leaning on the desk crossed over chest, a self-defense posture Abelone knew well.

"I replace their rage disruptors when they arrive. But we both know if they worked properly on them, they wouldn't be here. Muracos serve no purpose, have no greater goal than to see us dead. Matriarch Kalinda should've never agreed to Matriarch Oriana's whims."

Bharavi, a forty-eight-year-old physician, liked Matriarch Oriana—her wit, sensitivity, and intelligence. The girl possessed a kind nature her mother lacked, as well as magical abilities beyond her years. Underneath her kindness, however, was a bullheadedness all too common in young witches. Girls Matriarch Oriana's age thought they knew more than they did, including how the world worked and what needed doing to keep it from disintegrating into chaos.

"I was thinking." Bharavi pushed a button on her desk, darkening the window to prevent Abelone from looking out. Not that she could see anything from her seated position other than buildings across the street and the graying sky. "We could request transfers. I'm sure Matriarch Oriana would grant them. She's reasonable and would likely approve our requests if we explained why we want to change our assignments."

"Matriarch Oriana is more spoiled than reasonable."

Bharavi's eyes darted in the direction of the door. "You need to watch what you say about the matriarch, and where."

Abelone rolled her eyes. "It's just Misae in the front office. Your assistant can be trusted. Don't break out in a sweat. I'll close the door, if it'll set your mind at ease."

"I'm closer to the door than you are." Bhavari scooted her wheeled chair to the door. Just as she'd been when Abelone had entered Bhavari's office, Misae sat at her desk, viewing something, probably medical files, on a computer screen. Bhavari pushed the door closed.

"You look like a kid—rolling your chair back and forth. Get yourself situated and finish what you were saying."

"Fine." Bhavari readjusted her desk chair, the rolling having triggered the height feature. "Matriarch Oriana isn't a spoiled brat. She's just young. I remember when we were her age."

Uncrossing her legs, Abelone sat up straighter, wishing she could squelch her worries as easily as she'd adjusted her position. "We were in our twenties once, true, but we never made decisions that risked our hard-won place in society. Matriarch Oriana thinks she can tame werewolves. She can't. She thinks our laws are too rigid and unfair to them. They aren't. She thinks her kindness will be appreciated and returned. She's wrong."

"What if she's right, Abelone? I mean, it would be nice if werewolves and witches could get along better than we do now or have in the past. Would that be so bad?"

Sweet, conflicted Bharavi. Abelone loved the healer, but her vacillations had the unpleasant effect of a low-grade headache.

"No, not bad, but highly unlikely. You're the healer. You've treated them, researched them. They are as they are. If they weren't so unstable, our lives would be different. I told you what my father did to my mother."

"I know, but—"

"She begged him to stop. But he wouldn't. I hid under my bed, listening to her plead with him. By the time law enforcement arrived, Mom was dead, and Dad was gone. Since Dad had turned into a muraco, Crimson Hunter Shams was called in to track him down. When she found him, he attacked her, leaving her little choice but to use deadly force."

Local law enforcement didn't hunt, fight, or even guard imprisoned muracos. Those dangerous duties fell to the Hunter Division of the Crimson Guard, led by the Crimson Hunter and her second-in-command, the captain of the Hunter Division.

"I'm sorry."

"Mom didn't even fight back. She let him take her away from me without casting a single spell. I hated her for a long time, even while I mourned and missed her."

"Ah, sweetie. She loved you." Bharavi moved from the chair behind her desk to the chair beside Abelone, a surgeon's hands taking hold of a soldier's. "She loved him too. Your mother didn't want to die. Most people don't. Could you use an offensive spell against me?"

"That's not the same."

"It's the same. You love me, so you wouldn't want to hurt me, even if I were trying to harm you. Your mother loved her mate. She tried to reach the heart and mind that loved her in return.

"She was sentimental and stupid, and it got her killed."

She'd known, when her mother had ceased crying and screaming, that she wouldn't be coming for her. Abelone had cried—more terrified of being left alone than of being her father's next victim. She'd had to be coaxed, by an officer with kind eyes and a gentle voice, to come from under her bed. That night, when she'd been carried down the stairs, blood on the walls and floors, she'd promised never to be a werewolf's victim. As soon as she was old enough, Abelone joined the Crimson Guard. She wouldn't permit anyone, not even a matriarch, to threaten the stability of a system intended to protect witches like her mother and little girls like Abelone had once been. It wasn't perfect, but the system gave more than it took.

Bharavi pressed a kiss to lips that felt too cold, her hands clutching Abelone's. "It's all right."

"It's not. What Matriarch Oriana has done is dangerous. I know her decisions originated from a good place. She wants to do right by witches and werewolves. But werewolves will interpret her actions as naivete at best, a weakness worth exploiting at worst."

"You're plotting."

"I'm not."

"You are. What you haven't done is acted on what I see percolating in your eyes."

Dropping her hands, Bharavi shifted to kneel in front of Abelone. So beautiful. She'd been attracted to her from the start, not because she was the prettiest girl she'd ever seen, but because Abelone's introverted nature called to her own. They were a good match, their marriage still strong after fifteen years. Abelone's father may have loved her mother, but his love hadn't prevented him from clawing her chest open and devouring her heart.

"I showed you the announcement. Matriarch Oriana will take Marrok of Wild Moor as her consort next month."

"They're a cute couple. I'm happy for her."

"Why?"

"Because we all want to be loved and give love in return, sweetie. She's trying to be a good leader."

"She's misguided."

"Yes, she is. But we'll survive her youthfulness."

"What if we don't? What if she keeps giving werewolves more and more rights? What role will her consort play in the government?"

"None. Why should he?"

He shouldn't, but werewolves in Janus Nether no longer wore silver snares and muracos who served their prison sentences now had Steelburgh instead of living the rest of their wretched lives in a maximum security prison. Neither should've occurred, but both had, thanks to the young matriarch.

Abelone had already spoken to a few Steelburgh guards, though she hadn't told her wife. That argument would come later. The other guards agreed with Abelone. If Matriarch Oriana wouldn't see what she was doing to Earth Rift and the impossible situations she was creating for her sisters in magic, they might have to take drastic measures to get Matriarch Kalinda's attention.

If provided with the right motivation, Matriarch Kalinda would step in, ending the werewolf threat. Sacrifices would have to be made. Abelone was prepared to suffer the consequences for her actions. Something else she hadn't shared with Bharavi.

Abelone encouraged Bharavi to rise from her knees with a gentle tug to her hands. She got the message and retook her seat beside Abelone. "Hold off on the transfer requests."

"Why? You hate it here, and I go where you go."

She should take her wife away from Steelburgh. Hell, out of Steelcross and away from Matriarch Oriana's bleeding-heart policies. But they couldn't run from this. If left unchallenged, Matriarch Oriana would continue nipping away at the fabric of their matrilineal system, one ill-advised decree at a time.

Perhaps, with a consort in residence, she'd come to see the true nature of werewolves. Abelone's loyalty to the realm superseded her allegiance to a young matriarch who spat on the legacy of her foremothers.

"I do hate this city. But at least here I can help guarantee the animals stay in their cage, a threat to no one."

"No one but us, you mean."

"I'd kill them all before I'd let them hurt those of us who work here."

"You're still plotting."

Bhavari's comment hadn't sounded as disapproving as it had earlier. Good.

"If I am, can I count on you?"

Bharavi kissed her again—longer and sweeter than the last time. "As I said, where you go, I go."

Abelone didn't want to die, and she sure as hell wouldn't wish that fate on her wife. But the future of the realm was more important than their lives.

She did have a plan—one that could end in their own deaths but the continued life of witches.

A fair exchange.

Misae pretended not to notice when Dr. Bhavari closed her office door. She'd kept her eyes focused on her computer, as if she hadn't heard Abelone refer to the young matriarch as "spoiled."

Closing the electronic file, Misae contemplated her next steps. She hadn't heard much, except for Abelone's normal grumblings. The witch complained about everything from rainy days to shift hours. The guard could be blowing off steam, fussing for the sake of complaining, and nothing more. Yet, Abelone's seriously angry tone had Misae rethinking her interpretation.

What if Abelone and Dr. Bhavari were planning on doing something they shouldn't? Then again, what if the privacy they sought had nothing to do with Matriarch Oriana but everything to do with the convenience of spouses working in the same building?

No good ever came from jumping to conclusions. Misae tapped the screen, opening another medical file. Until she knew differently, she'd give Abelone and Dr. Bhavari the benefit of the doubt. She liked Abelone well enough, and respected Dr. Bhavari, although the healer had a few quirks she found strange.

Still, Misae had been assigned to Steelburgh for a reason, and it wasn't only because she had experience working with incarcerated muracos.

She'd keep her eye on the couple. A very close eye.

5: Moonless Sky

July 3, 2240
Steelcross Realm
Moonvale Forest

"How long are we going to have to wait?" Zev complained, his deep voice loud against the quiet of the dark night.

Marrok was about to tell his oldest brother to go screw himself, but Alarick stepped in. "Stop being an asshole." Alarick shoved Zev, who leaned against one of the towering red mahogany trees. "This night isn't about you. It's about Marrok. So, shut the hell up and relax."

"I'm just saying. Why in the hell do witches have to take so damn long to do everything?"

"I beg your pardon?"

Marrok and his brothers snapped around. Zev really was an asshole. Had the jerk forgotten who'd transported them to the forest? The clearing was the same location Oriana had jumped them to in May, near Silentdrift Lake. He'd relished every minute of the two hours as a werewolf Oriana had given him. The time had passed too quickly, Marrok hadn't been ready to leave when Oriana had returned for him. She'd promised he'd see the river and forest again soon. Back then, he'd had no idea she'd meant the location to be the spot for their moonless sky wedding ceremony.

"Present witch excluded, of course," Zev said with a politeness Marrok knew to be false.

Their beautiful mother, Lita—five-six, slim, with almond-shaped eyes—ran her hand through dark, curly hair they'd inherited. Unlike Marrok and his brothers, who kept their hair cut short, Lita's grew long and thick, an attractive halo of coils as lovely as the fifty-five-year-old.

"Sorry, Mom," Marrok said, offering Lita a sincere apology. He walked away from his brothers to his mother. "Thank you for being a part of this."

"No one says no to a matriarch."

Eyes dropped. "Oh, I see."

He felt the touch of a warm, soft hand to his cheek. "No, you don't see, and I should've stated that differently. Yes, Matriarch Oriana asked for my presence, but she didn't make it an order, not even one couched to sound like a request or invitation. She didn't arrive on my doorstep as Matriarch of Steelcross but as the witch who loves my youngest son."

Lifting his eyes, he asked, "If I had invited you, would you have accepted?"

"Yes, of course, I would've." The hand on his cheek slid to his silver snare. "I've always loved you boys. I know I haven't told you and that I haven't been a proper mother to you."

"You, umm, you love us?"

As if his unsteady voice and doubting tone broke Lita's heart, tears filled her eyes. Her hand fell away from his collar, fisting the side of her ceremonial robe. "Staying away from you boys was the hardest decision I've ever made."

"Self-preservation makes people do things they may not have done otherwise. Living in a house with four werewolves wasn't an option, not if you valued your life." He smiled, making light of his pain over her abandonment and hoping she'd stop weeping. He never could stomach the sight of a crying female.

She shook her head, tears falling from eyes nearly the same shade of brown as his. "Ask any werewolf why the mother of his children leaves him and their pups, and you'll receive the same wrong answer." Lita shifted slightly toward the coastline behind her, taking in his kneeling father who stared out at the lake. "I'm sure Io has told you boys that witches leave because we're afraid of our werewolf lovers and sons." She turned back to Marrok, wistfulness having replaced tears. "While true for some witches, it isn't for most, and rarely for mothers." Lifting her hand to the silver snare again, she thumbed the collar. "We keep our distance for protection."

"I know. You need to protect yourselves from us."

"No, to protect you all from us. If we maintain our distance, we aren't a temptation. It's a fight you cannot win, Marrok. Werewolves have no control over their blood-and-magic lust. That's not their fault."

"It's our curse."

"It's a condition of life we've made the best of." Lita's hand rose to his cheek again. "I walked away because of love, not fear. At some point, every witch lover and mother will make that heart-shattering choice."

With a jerk of his head, Marrok stepped away from Lita. "No. Oriana won't leave me. She loves me."

"She does. And I love Io." Lita glanced back to his father, as enraptured by the peacefulness of their surroundings as Marrok had been the first time he'd seen Silentdrift Lake.

Love? Not past tense. Surprising. Does Dad know? Probably not. Then again, maybe he feels the same way, which would explain why they cannot bear to be in the same room with each other for long. I thought it was hate. Perhaps it's been repressed love all along.

"As matriarch, Oriana will deliver a girl first," Lita said, her focus still on Io. "It is then you'll understand why Io never wanted a daughter. I grew to despise the fear I saw in my own father's eyes when he looked at me, fear that the scent and sight of me would drive him mad enough to attack me."

This was the last conversation he needed to have before starting a life with Oriana. He wanted to stop the words flooding the air between them. But Marrok couldn't deny how much he feared harming Oriana. He'd never experienced the kind of craving Alarick had described, and he hoped he never would.

Lita grasped his hand, twining her fingers with his. "I'm telling you something today I should've told you years ago. I know now is not the ideal time for this kind of mother-son conversation. Then again, perhaps it's the perfect time. No doubt, Matriarch Kalinda would've shared the same with her daughter. Considering Matriarch Oriana hasn't changed her mind about taking you as her consort, she listens to her heart. Know this, Marrok: witches always protect those we love, even when it seems our actions are anything but loving."

"Are you saying Oriana will hurt me if she thinks I'm a threat to our daughter?"

"I'm saying Oriana will do most anything to spare you the pain of living with the guilt of hurting your child." For a third time, Lita looked to Io. "That's the reason why your father never wanted a daughter. Losing a mate is far less painful than the anguish that accompanies the death of your offspring at your own hands. So, we had three sons. In the end, Io had you boys, and I was left with nothing but regrets." She squeezed his hand. "Love fully yet fairly, Marrok. Cherish the time you'll have with Oriana."

Marrok looked away from his unhappy mother to his frowning brothers, to his brooding father, and back to Lita. Why in the hell had any of them come, if they felt so strongly against the union? He didn't need their presence if it didn't also come with genuine happiness and emotional support. Marrok wasn't naïve, and neither was Oriana. They'd calculated the risks against the love they had for each other. It wouldn't be easy, but they'd find a way to make it work.

He stepped away from his mother, releasing her hand.

"Marrok, no, no, I'm sorry."

"For telling me Oriana will, at some point, either leave me to spare me the temptation of wanting to consume her, or kill me to protect our daughter from me, or kill me to protect me from the guilt of having murdered my own child? Even if any of those awful things come true, tonight sure as hell wasn't the time to bring them up. Thanks for that, Mom. You sure know how to make a werewolf feel good about himself and his future."

Marrok stalked away from Lita, trying not to care he'd made her cry or that her warning, brutal as it was to hear, had come from a place of love and concern. He and Oriana should've kept their families far away from their special event. That opinion solidified in his mind when a stony-faced Matriarch Kalinda and a glowering Bader arrived with Oriana, a perfect landing that couldn't have been his witch's doing.

Solange stood beside Oriana, the only smiling guest, which said a lot, considering the witch was hardcore law enforcement. Then again, so was Oriana.

She hadn't stepped down from the post of Crimson Hunter since becoming a matriarch. Marrok supposed she eventually would turn over the high-ranking position to Solange. None of that mattered now, though, not with the way Oriana was beaming at him, her smile bright enough to vanquish the ugly conversation he'd had with his mother.

Needing to cleanse his emotional pallet, he strolled up to Oriana, lifted her off her feet, and swung her around. He breathed in her lemon scent, wishing they were alone and that he didn't have to place her back on her feet and deal with their pessimistic families.

"What's wrong?" she whispered against his ear.

Marrok wouldn't give voice to the fears Lita had brought to the surface. "Nothing. I'm fine. I just missed you. Two weeks without seeing each other, you know?"

He had missed her, that Oriana would believe. The rest of it she wouldn't. He'd tell her the truth later. She would know that too, without him having to assure her that his prevarication wasn't intended as a true deception.

She kissed the spot he loved just behind his ear. "I can have Solange take them home. Her extraction magic is advanced enough where she can perform double jumps with a single spell. She can have them back home in less than two minutes."

Marrok set Oriana on her feet, already feeling better. "You'd do it, wouldn't you?"

"I won't have you upset the night of our union. Out of respect for our families, I invited them, but what you think and how you feel are more important than their offense." She glanced around Marrok. "Zev looks like he couldn't care less. Say the word, Marrok, and this night will be just for us."

Strange as it may seem to others, Marrok often forgot Oriana was a matriarch. To him, she was simply Oriana of Irongarde, the woman he adored, the woman he would do anything to make happy. Yet, there were times when the softness he'd come to know and love was replaced by a will of iron and a spine of steel.

Her arms hadn't transformed into her Ravagers of the Lost cannons. She also didn't wear her Crimson Hunter's body armor or hold the Blood of the Sun wand of Steelcross, symbols of her dual roles. Yet, there was no denying Oriana's readiness to go into battle for him, if only against their disapproving families.

A lesser werewolf would've hidden behind the might of his witch, but what kind of consort would Marrok be if he began their union as a sniveling coward?

He kissed her, on her lips, with tongue, and uncaring what anyone else thought. Except for, well, Oriana's father, Bader, who growled at Marrok.

"You aren't her consort yet. Kindly remove your hands from my daughter."

Oriana giggled into his chest and, just like that, the twenty-six-year-old woman was back, the monarch gone. "Father—"

"There is a protocol, Oriana, and this isn't it," said Bader, consort to Matriarch Kalinda, his title of Aku of Irongarde decades old. "Come, you are Matriarch Oriana of Steelcross. This will be a proper moonless sky wedding ceremony."

Her father, with shoulder-length dreadlocks with streaks of red in the front—just as in Oriana's hair—stepped forward and waited, his hand outstretched. Oriana nodded to Bader, accepting his proffered hand.

Bader's smile was one Marrok had never seen the man offer anyone before. It revealed a depth of emotion Marrok feared, based on Lita's words, he would come to comprehend all too well. Unlike Io, Marrok couldn't talk Oriana into giving them only sons. He observed Bader, regal in his Aku of Irongarde ritual robe—black with red trim, matching red buttons on sleeves and front. However, what most caught Marrok's attention was an image displayed on the robe over his heart but which he'd also seen on the werewolf's chest —the Aku Moon of Irongarde—a bluish-white new moon under a blue, white, and green Earth.

Matriarch Kalinda wore a black, hooded pullover robe with wide, hanging sleeves and a black center inset with red ribbon lacing. His mother wore the same style of robe as did Solange and Oriana. Yet, Oriana's robe came with a red center inset with black ribbon lacing. Her hood and sleeves were two-sided with red-and-black double-knitting. Black hair piled atop her head, her red streaks left out—an accent that contoured a cheek, drawing the eye downward to her cleavage, the perfect location for his gift.

As if pulled by the moon the darkness hid, they walked to the edge of the coastline, joining Io. Marrok, his father, and brothers all wore forest-green ceremonial robes made of soft suede. Taffeta trim in the same forest-green color accented the mandarin collar, sides of the open front, and the shoulders to the hem of the wide sleeves. The belt was made entirely of taffeta, lending a shiny appeal to the family robe.

His family stood in a line behind him—Io to the far right, Lita to the far left, and his brothers in between. Several feet in front of him stood his smiling witch. Oriana's parents flanked her, with Solange behind and to the right of the matriarchal family.

They all stared at each other, no one speaking for an awkward three minutes. Behind him, he heard the first of what would be many bones cracking then reforming. Io, his father, had begun the ritual, although tradition dictated the witch's father should've been the first in werewolf form.

Marrok's gaze shifted to Bader to see if Io had offended the man by taking the lead. More snaps sounded behind him, and Marrok wanted to curse and snarl at his brothers. But the Aku of Irongarde appeared unfazed by Marrok's family's lack of etiquette. He turned to see three fully shifted black werewolves behind him, standing upright on their hind legs, discarded robes at their clawed feet. Marrok allowed himself to observe his mother who, to his surprise, didn't look afraid. Then again, perhaps it was not surprising, based on their conversation. Lita did, however, shake her head, face awash with embarrassment.

Yeah, Marrok could relate.

"Do you wish to shift?" Matriarch Kalinda asked Bader. "I'll hold your robe, if you do."

The older man seemed to consider his estranged mate's offer, his face suddenly impassive. Marrok wondered what emotion Bader didn't want to be revealed to the matriarch. Maybe the same one Lita had kept from Io all these years. No way this side of the moon did Marrok want his and Oriana's union to end up like either of their parents'.

Bader raised Oriana's hand to his mouth and kissed the back, a smile accompanying the loving display. "I think not. If I do, I won't be able to touch our daughter like this." Bader's attention shifted to Marrok. "What about you? When will you shift?"

Bader still gripped Oriana's hand. Marrok wondered whether the werewolf would willingly release her into his care when the time came.

"Not yet. I have a present that requires a gentle, human touch."

At the mention of a gift, Oriana's smile widened. "I don't see a pocket in your robe. Where on your body have you hidden my present?" Her tone had taken on the low, seductive voice that always had the effect of tempting his restraint. "Will you permit me to search you to find out?"

"Oriana," her parents half groaned, half scolded.

"Daughter, at least maintain the illusion of decorum until after the ritual … *and* until you and Marrok are alone." Matriarch Kalinda reached behind Oriana, pulling her hood over her head. She did the same with her own hood, as did Solange.

Marrok didn't have to look behind him to know Lita had followed suit, but he did. Lita smiled at Marrok the way she had when he was a boy and she tucked him in at night. She would kiss his cheek and say, "Good night my bright moon." His mother loved him. Hearing her say the words healed a fissure in his heart he'd pretended hadn't existed. Marrok loved Lita too, and wished, for the millionth time, that the rift that kept werewolves and witches apart could be mended. He would help Oriana with her research. Hopefully, somewhere in the matriarchal archives, they would find a solution.

Lita moved to stand directly behind Marrok, followed by Io, Zev, and then Alarick, a matrilineal descent hierarchy.

Across from Marrok, Bader kissed Oriana's hand again before standing behind her, with Solange claiming the location behind him. Only Marrok, Oriana, and Matriarch Kalinda remained where they were. Mother and daughter were equals in their society, and Marrok's rank would soon match that of Bader's, making him the second most powerful werewolf in the realms.

Marrok couldn't care less about prestige or power. The only privilege he coveted was that of loving and being loved by Oriana.

"On this moonless night," Matriarch Kalinda began, the opening lines to the ritual, "we've come together to witness the commitment of the sun to her moon."

Oriana took one step forward.

"Together they are magic, mysticism, and might. They are born as stars, a fusion of heat, light, and life."

Another step.

"Together they are strength of heart and sincerity of soul. She is every sunrise and sunset."

Bader's baritone voice followed Kalinda's soft, assured tone. "On this moonless night, we've come together to witness the bonding of the moon to his sun. Together they rule the sky, a merging of opposites. Unity, cooperation … his moon and her sun are better together." Bader's eyes, which had moved from one person to the next, making sure to include them all in his message, shifted to Marrok and stayed. "We are every moonrise and moonset. Every phase of the moon runs through our veins and is felt in our hearts and minds. Do you feel them, Son of Lita of Ironmere City?"

"Yes."

"Do you know them, Son of Io of Chrome Haven?"

"Yes."

"Then convince me you deserve the heart and hand of the Matriarch of Steelcross."

Marrok knew the words that came next in the ceremony. They were simple enough to recite. But Marrok had interpreted correctly the Aku of Irongarde's unspoken challenge. He wanted a guarantee no werewolf, including Bader himself, could offer a father-in-law, much less the witch he loved.

Marrok had told Oriana, dozens of times, that he'd never hurt her. He'd meant those words with every fiber of his being. He simply didn't think himself capable of harming her. Realistically though, was that a promise he could keep, regardless of his intentions? The sad, disturbing truth was that he could not. Even as Marrok watched Oriana watch him, her smile dimmer for the gauntlet her father had tossed down, his mind revolted against the possibility of him giving her a reason to walk away from their union.

If Alarick were in human form, he'd likely whisper to Marrok that Bader was an asshole. As convenient as it would be to cast that judgment at the older werewolf, Bader wasn't an asshole but a father who wanted more for his daughter than what he'd been able to provide for her mother.

Marrok reached behind him, unclasping the necklace hidden under his silver snare. "New Moon. Waxing Crescent." One step put him closer to Oriana. "First Quarter. Waxing Gibbous." A second step. "Full Moon. Waning Gibbous." Silver necklace in hand, he leaned down and placed his gift around Oriana's neck, a silver crescent moon with a dangling nebula pendant in the center, a swirl of yellow, pink, purple, blue, and red—the colors of witch magic. "Last Quarter. Waning Crescent." He kissed her cheek. "Eight phases of the moon, and of my beating werewolf heart. Every phase belongs to you, Oriana. You're my sol, and I'll forever be your" —he winked at her— "heavenly body."

She grinned up at him, suppressing the laughter he saw in her wide, bright eyes. Because Oriana was an unrepentant flirt, she licked her lips, a sensual glide from one corner to the other, her eyes never leaving his.

Her parents couldn't see her, but his mother damn sure could. Lita's whisper: "By this time next year, I'll have a granddaughter to spoil," was a reminder of how the ceremony would end.

The palm of Lita's hand settled against the center of his back, her low voice reaching him again. "Well done, son. It's time for you to shift. She's ready to take you as her consort, but as the werewolf you are and will forever be."

He nodded, acknowledging Lita's words, as well as Oriana's smirk and raised eyebrow. The woman could be a menace. Marrok wasn't shy about his body, no werewolf was, but the way Oriana watched him disrobe, through lust-filled eyes, he feared he would embarrass himself. While Matriarch Kalinda and Bader couldn't see how their daughter looked at him, with open desire, they most certainly could see his reaction to her.

Oriana's royal blue eyes dropped, not to his lips, as they normally did when she wanted a kiss, nor to his chest, which she loved to snuggle against, but to his dick. She licked her lips again, and his dick twitched. She grinned, winked, and opened her mouth to say something inappropriate, no doubt, but closed it when her mother sighed, "Whatever you're doing to make Marrok cringe with embarrassment, please stop. No one here, especially Lita or I, want to see …" She gestured in the general direction of his groin.

He swore his brothers laughed at him, as much as they could in werewolf form.

"Marrok, please proceed, so we can complete this ritual. It's clear to all present that my daughter is incapable of acting the role of a proper matriarch."

"Trust me, Mother, I've been nothing but a proper matriarch, all these years, thanks to Marrok."

"That's good to hear," Bader said, "but more than I wanted to know. I agree with Kalinda. Let's proceed."

Lita backed up, giving Marrok space to shift, not that he needed much.

He lifted his face to the sky, to his beloved moon. Willing his body to obey, he began to shift. Bones cracked, beginning at his feet and moving up his body. Falling to his hands and knees, back and hip muscles pushed out, lengthening, contorting, strengthening. Claws formed, knuckles bulged, jaw broke, and the silver snare adjusted to accommodate his thick neck.

All the while, Oriana watched him in silence. He'd never shifted in front of her before. A part of him felt self-conscious, insecure even. Irrational, considering witches were werewolves' natural mates. Except for the blood-and-magic lust, nothing about werewolves turned witches off.

Oriana had always claimed he didn't scare her, even when he towered over her, like he did as a werewolf.

She closed the short distance between them, pressed her hand to his chest, over his heart, and he waited for what would come next. Oriana had never used her magic on him, but she would have to claim him as her consort, the same way Matriarch Kalinda had claimed Bader decades earlier. Yet, he sensed no magic emanating from Oriana.

"You're magnificent, Marrok. Please kneel."

Without haste, he complied. Dropping to his knees, he was nearly eye level with his witch. To Marrok's delight, Oriana pressed her body to his, wrapping her arms around him and hugging him to her.

She felt amazing—soft, warm, curvy.

He returned her embrace, careful to keep his claws away from any part of her.

Oriana kept them there, her small hands stroking his back, his neck, his face. She even kissed his cold nose, sending shivers of need and want through him. "I'll always take care of you," Oriana promised. "Your heart. Your mind. Your soul. Our offspring. Every part of you is mine to love and to protect."

A witch's pledge to her werewolf mate. More, a matriarch's oath to her consort.

Her hand found the spot over his heart again. He still didn't feel her magic. Nipping his ear, she spoke words so low they had to have been meant for him alone. "I will not brand you with the mark of the Aku of Steelcross. I will not burn my symbol into your skin, although you are burned into my heart. You are my moon, as I am your sun. But our life together will be an endless total eclipse, a rare phenomenon we'll embrace with both hands, fighting to be the exception to the Earth Rift rule."

She nipped his other ear, and a moan slipped from him. He held her tighter, wanting everything she offered.

"I love you, Marrok." Removing her warmth, she stepped back, every bit a matriarch when she said, "Stand Marrok of Wild Moor."

He did.

"From this day forward, you will carry the title of Marrok, Cyrus of Steelcross, Consort to Oriana, Matriarch of Steelcross."

As he looked around at the gathered guests, their faces registered the same shock which washed over him.

His witch had given him, a werewolf of the Black Moon Clan, a title that literally translated as *sun*. Only witches were named after the magic-giving star. He had no idea what it meant or even what he wanted it to mean.

Oriana had a way of knocking him on his ass without lifting a pretty, manicured finger. There were no words … not that he could speak as a werewolf.

Marrok shifted, quicker than ever. Then he was pulling her to him, kissing her laughing, smiling face. "You don't need magic to stun everyone around you. I love you, my wicked, little, red witch."

Oriana smacked his naked ass and jumped them away from Silentdrift Lake, his stomach plummeting to his feet.

Blood of the Sun Decree #3
April 1, 1309

BY MATRIARCHAL DECREE, WITCHES AGE THIRTEEN AND OLDER MUST COMPLETE THE RITE OF ENDOMETAL FUSION. FAILURE TO COMPLY WILL RESULT IN THE MATRIARCHIAL FAMILY HEAD'S LOSS OF STATUS UNTIL WHICH TIME THE OBLIGATION IS FULFILLED.

Alba, Matriarch of Earth Rift

6: Young Love

July 3, 2240
Steelcross Realm
Steel Rise

They materialized in a dark room, crashing to the floor with a hard thud. Marrok swore, and Oriana could relate. Damn, who knew landing with a six foot, two-hundred-pound, muscular male atop her would hurt so much?

Marrok glared down at her. "I guess you're going to blame *this* messed up landing on having gotten distracted as well."

Oriana's hands landed on Marrok's ass with a loud *smack*. "Yes, it's your own fault for having such a sexy body. A body, by the way, you've refused to let me sample properly."

"Yeah, right. You aren't capable of limiting yourself to a sample."

Marrok settled more comfortably atop her, pushing her ceremonial dress up her thighs and wedging himself between Oriana's legs. "Your so-called sample sex would've had us going all the way."

"You would've enjoyed it, if we had."

A big hand pushed her dress farther north, holding it in place while lowering his face to her neck. "Hell yes, I would've enjoyed it. Right before your parents found out and had me castrated. Matriarchs are supposed to be untouched until they take a consort."

"I thought you were going to say innocent."

He kissed her neck. Sucked. Bit. Licked. "There's not an innocent thing about you except for this." Marrok's erection rubbed against her panty-covered sex, setting off sparks of heat and desire.

They moaned, him against her pulsing neck, and her against his broad shoulder.

Marrok did it over and again, rocking into her with his long, hard penis. *Yesss.* Oriana loved and appreciated how much Marrok respected her, including his insistence on upholding an outdated custom no one, except for heirs to the matriarchy, was expected to adhere to. That didn't, however, mean she had appreciated the creative ways he'd taken to rejecting her advances. Pride should've had Oriana ceasing her flirtations, but stubbornness had proven a greater motivator.

"Are we in Iron Spire or Steel Rise?"

"Steel Rise." She bit his shoulder, tasting his salty, woodsy flesh. Delicious. "My extraction magic may not be as good as Solange's, but I am capable of not overshooting my destination by an entire realm."

"So you say. At least no one saw us, and we made it to your suite without me throwing up all over you."

Oriana glanced around the room, which was difficult when pinned to the floor. But she could see enough to know whose suite she'd jumped them into, and it wasn't hers. Umm, she'd just keep that fact to herself. No need to worry her consort with inconsequential details that would have him stopping what he was doing with his mouth and hips.

She'd waited years to get him exactly where he was—between her legs and at the hot core of her desire. Oriana had no plans of moving from this room until she was breathless and boneless.

"Rip them."

The hand that had been exploring the edge of her panties stilled. Yet, she felt a suddenly pointy fingernail and observed Marrok's irises shift to pink.

"I can see you want to, so do it."

"I shouldn't. It's your first time. I'm supposed to be soft and gentle with you. A werewolf can't have everything he wants."

"You can if your witch also wants it. It's also your first time, but I have no intention of being soft and gentle with you." Widening her legs, she pushed up, grazing herself against his erection. Then she was kissing Marrok—deep and hard.

Her panties fell away, a single flick of Marrok's elongated nail having sliced through the silk garment.

"Yes," she hissed against his ear. "Rip everything off."

This time, he didn't argue, not even a silent rebuttal in the eyes that watched her for a consent she'd granted years earlier.

His grin was masculine satisfaction personified. "Hell no, not innocent at all."

Careful slice after careful slice had Oriana's ceremonial dress cut to shreds, with pieces of fabric scattered around her on the floor. If someone came upon them, Marrok's big body over hers, his hands holding her wrists over her head, Oriana's dress torn, and she splayed like a starfish, they'd either draw an absolutely correct conclusion or a horribly inaccurate one.

"We should at least move to the bed. A gentleman doesn't deflower his bride on a cold, hard floor."

"You're a werewolf."

"Which doesn't make me a rutting animal who's so full of lust I'd take you on the floor, no matter how much you tempt me. Up, Oriana."

He jumped to his feet, scooping her up afterward and depositing her on the big, fluffy bed she'd been on many times. Not in this context, though. The room hadn't been used in over a year, she rationalized. Changing the linens wouldn't be enough but she'd have time to set right what they were about to do there.

Oriana was happy to accept Marrok's weight atop her again. They kissed—unrushed, long, and deep.

"I've dreamt of this." Warm breath caressed a nipple before Marrok's wet mouth claimed it. "… of tasting all of you …" Tongue rimmed, and lips sucked. "… of having free rein to touch you as much as I like." A hand played with her other breast, fingers twisting her nipple, pinching with a firm softness. "Your legs around my waist. Your pussy squeezing my dick. Your mouth anywhere you want to put it as long as it's on me."

Damn, where had this Marrok been hiding? If he kept talking like this, she'd come from the images alone. Hmm, his voice, deeper than normal, prompted so many sensual ideas.

"What else?"

"So much."

"Tell me." Oriana had never ached this much for him or been this aroused. Her magic sizzled underneath her skin. Electric charges detonated every place they touched, shocking her senses and feeding her arousal.

"Telling is good." Marrok shifted down her body, leaving a trail of wet kisses as he went. "But I'd rather show you."

Red irises looked up at Oriana from a head between her thighs. Shit. Could Marrok feel the pattern of shockwaves running up and down her legs?

He sniffed her. Marrok ran his nose along her sex, inhaling her the way he would if he were in werewolf form. There went the electric shocks again, supercharging her center and curling her hair.

"You have no idea how good you smell to me. Or how hard I get from your scent, knowing I'm the only werewolf who's ever made you perfume like this."

"Marrok." His name came out as a low moan. Her legs trembled, and her sex wept for him.

He nuzzled her again. His nose rubbed up and down, getting coated in her moisture. "So sweet, baby. You smell so sweet to me." Instinctively, her hips rose. "That's right, mark me with your scent."

Werewolf sex play, while still in human form.

"S-stop teasing," Oriana panted.

"Not teasing. Taking my time."

She wanted to tell him to go faster, to dive in with his lips and tongue before she embarrassed herself by coming from the friction of his nose against her clit. But she didn't have to because Marrok covered her mound with his mouth and, *yes, yes, yes*, it felt so damn good to be claimed this way.

Marrok didn't suck her so much as slurp her into his mouth, all thick, full lips and long, wily tongue. Yanking her forward, big hands on her thighs, Marrok pulled her even more onto his tongue, keeping her pressed to his mouth as he feasted.

Oriana couldn't look away from what he was doing to her. Her eyes were blown wide. Her mouth was wide as well and couldn't keep from moaning loudly. Her hand settled atop his head, fingers gripped his scalp, and she gave a little push downward.

Marrok growled animalistically, making her stomach flutter as he devoured her in the one way witches did not mind being dominated and feasted upon by their werewolf lovers.

A long, wide tongue penetrated her—deep.

Oriana cried out, her hands fisting the bedsheets. Marrok fucked her with his tongue, a tongue that was more werewolf than human. She couldn't keep her eyes open a second longer. They slammed shut.

Marrok wasn't in his bleddyn form—half-human, half-werewolf. They couldn't have unprotected sex that way as it would result in a male fetus. She had to first give birth to a female, the next Blood of the Sun matriarch. But he could shift individual parts of himself, and Oriana couldn't help how her magic and blood flooded the area where his bleddyn tongue plundered her depths.

Furry hands held her open wide, Marrok's tongue a relentless piston moving in and out of her. Over and over he licked her, his nose a constant, hard press against her clit. Oriana screamed and came.

And came.

And came.

He sucked her clit, a luscious pull, and she came a fourth time.

Marrok moved up and loomed over Oriana, arms on either side of her, caging her in the most mouthwatering way. "Are you okay?"

For all that he'd turned into a werewolf oral sex god, Marrok was still the same sweet, considerate male who protected her honor when she'd been ready to throw it away for a stolen moment of fleeting carnality.

Oriana sucked in a breath, letting it out slowly. She smiled, and the lines between Marrok's forehead receded. "I'm fine. Better than fine. I had no idea you could be so inventive."

"Neither did I." Leaning down, he pressed a shy kiss to her lips. "You inspire me."

"Hmm, I like the sound of that. What else do I inspire in you?"

"Show not tell." Gentle hands twined in her hair, fingers massaged her scalp, and hips surged forward, joining them in a breath-stealing entry.

She gasped.

He stilled.

Oriana thought he'd ask about her well-being again. Instead, Marrok moved experimentally, and they moaned through their smiles. She'd had him in her hands before, knew he was big. But having Marrok inside her put his size in a different perspective.

Her eyes rolled back, her mouth fell open, and she met his thrusts with her own.

The first time was hard and quick. The second time playful and slow. The third time had them drenched in sweat, Oriana astride Marrok, hands gripping the headboard, their rhythm desperate, cries thunderous.

"O-Oriana. Oriana."

She loved the sound of her name, groaned as it was, on Marrok's sensual lips. He came, hands holding her waist as he surged upward, pressing all of himself into her.

Leaning down, she kissed her consort. "I've wanted this for a long time."

Marrok gathered her in his arms, her head on his shoulder, sheets everywhere except on the bed. "Sex with me?"

"Well, yes, of course. But I meant us. As much as I hope our union won't end like everyone else's, I know for that to happen we must figure out the secrets of self."

"You mean figure out why werewolves lust for witch blood and magic?"

"Also, why witch magic is so hard to control without the aid of a channeling device." Sitting up, she held both arms in front of her, showing them to Marrok. "I've never told you this story, but on my thirteenth birthday, I went through the rite of endometal fusion. It was a grand event at Iron Spire. Food, music, decorations, and presents. Did you know no werewolf is allowed at the ceremony, not even a witch's father?"

Oriana lowered her arms. She'd begged Kalinda to invite Bader. *"The rite of endometal fusion is a sacred ceremony for witches only,"* her mother had told her. *"They have their rites, and we have ours. You'll see your father soon, Oriana. Stop crying, and go get dressed. Your guests will arrive soon."*

They hadn't been her guests but Kalinda's. That day had been the beginning of the distance her father had placed between them.

"Yeah, Dad told me what he knew."

She nodded, lost in thought. "I knew I would all but lose my father when I turned thirteen and my magic and scent increased beyond my control. I knew it, but the knowledge did nothing to lessen the pain of it actually happening."

From their many conversations over the years, Oriana also knew Marrok had lost his mother at an even younger age. Most witch mothers stayed with their pup until a year or two before they began puberty and had the rage disruptor injected. With Zev being six years older than Marrok, Lita would've separated herself from the boys when Marrok was eight to Zev's prepubescent fourteen.

Nothing about their familial relations brought them more pain than the separation of parent from child. Oriana hated it. They all did, so why did everyone accept the misery as inevitable?

"I've heard it doesn't hurt when a werewolf receives the rage disruptor injection. Is that true?"

"For the most part." Marrok patted his chest. "Come back down here."

A tempting offer she would soon take advantage of, but not before she told him everything she'd been holding inside. Oriana couldn't share such thoughts with Kalinda and while she could confide in Solange, she wouldn't put her friend in an unfair position to keep a secret that challenged one of the most important Blood of the Sun decrees.

"I was placed on an altar. Correction, I was strapped to an altar."

"You were what?" He sat up, angry about a pain that was thirteen years old.

"The straps didn't hurt."

"You say that as if it excuses the act of grown witches strapping a kid down against her will."

"Not against my will, Marrok. It's the law. Even my mother is beholden to laws that came before her reign."

She wouldn't reveal how her mother had come to a sobbing Oriana later that night in her bedroom, comforting her with kisses and apologies.

"I was injected with liquid steel." If she concentrated, Oriana could still feel the metal burning its way through her arms, her body fighting against the invasion before succumbing—an unnatural fusion of organic with inorganic. "I screamed until I passed out. I have no idea what happened after that. When I came to, I was in my bedroom, magic-laced gauze on my arms from elbow to wrist. The healing itched and burned, and my arms were so heavy."

"Come here." Holding her close, he hugged her to him and kissed her forehead. "Rage disruptors, silver snares, rites of endometal fusion, they're all bullshit. None of them is a normal practice. How in the hell can it be normal for us to live like this? And we do it to ourselves. It's a vicious cycle."

"I know. I want it all to stop."

"So do I. But the decrees, as awful as they are, exist for a good reason. Witches and werewolves love each other, but we can't truly live in peace, not as long as werewolves are threats to witches. I don't know what in the hell to do about that."

Separating herself from Marrok enough to meet his eyes, she voiced the unthinkable. "I won't submit our daughter to that kind of pain."

"What are you saying?"

"No rite of endometal fusion. I won't do that to our child, not when she's too young to understand or to fully consent. I won't do that to her."

"If you don't, you'll lose your position in society."

"I don't care."

"Yes, you do, Oriana." Marrok took her face in his big hands. "Yes, you do. You were raised to be a matriarch, to rule with intelligence, kindness, and empathy. As Crimson Hunter, you help keep our planet safe, not only from feral werewolves, but from magic-abusing witches and criminal-minded humans. You love those roles, and you're good at both."

"I love you and our future children more. I won't have our offspring subjected to liquid steel or silver snares. Both are barbaric, and I'd overturn both decrees today, if I had a better way of bridging the rift between witches and werewolves."

With a gentle tug, Marrok coaxed Oriana down onto the bed and his chest. "The pattern of your thoughts is so much worse than your extraction magic. If we take this leap—"

"*I'll* take the leap, you don't have—"

"Unless you were lying about me being your Cyrus of Steelcross, whatever in the hell that actually means, then what we do we do together." He touched her flat stomach, his palm warm. "In my human form, I can give you a witch. We may have even created one tonight. The thought thrills and frightens me but not as much as losing you and her. Once you give birth, we'll have twelve years to figure something out."

"That's not a lot of time."

"It isn't, but you're the one who wants to rip apart the system your ancestors built."

"I don't wish to rip anything apart. It's already torn, Marrok. I want to mend, to build … to start over if that's what it requires. I want us to live without fear. Something tells me we never truly have, even before the War of Eternal Hunger. Because happy witches would never have battled their mates, fathers, brothers, and sons to the death."

"By our own government standard, what you're saying would be deemed treason."

"I know." Propping on an elbow, she grinned down at him. "Cyrus of Steelcross is a title with no ascribed meaning, Marrok. I won't dictate what kind of consort you'll be. You won't command me, and I don't expect you to be commanded by me because I'm Matriarch of Steelcross. That's why I'll never physically mark you. Human couples wear wedding rings as symbols of their union. I don't wish to imitate them. We require no symbols, but if you need one, you have the new title. Define it as you will."

"You sound very much like a matriarch, but your words are nothing any matriarch would ever say. Be careful, Oriana. You need to go slow to go fast."

She kissed his chest. "Change is normal, even inevitable, but the unknown scares the shit out of most people." She settled against his side.

"An endless solar eclipse, huh?"

"Not a perfect analogy, but yes."

"You're a madwoman."

"You married me. What does that make you?"

Marrok's rumble had her smiling. "A lovestruck werewolf who'd do anything for his outrageous witch."

"Blasphemy." Oriana pulled Marrok on top of her, opening her legs and body to him again. "Mmmm, yes, no more talking."

He made love to her again, one leg propped on his shoulder, the other hitched around his hip. *So good.*

Lights turned on.

A female screamed.

Oriana swore.

And Marrok bolted off her, a string of curses following his retreat.

"*Oriana,*" her mother and consort yelled at the same time.

Cringing, she reached for her extraction magic, looped it around Marrok's waist, and jumped them out of Kalinda's bedroom. First thing tomorrow, she'd buy her mother a new bed.

July 15, 2240
Irongarde Realm
City of Wild Moor

"I can't believe he married her and moved to Steelcross."

Alarick downed the rest of his beer. "Shut up about it already. I'm tired of hearing you whine about Marrok and Oriana. It's done. He's happy, and so are Dad and Mom."

Snatching up his own mug of beer, Zev coated his mouth with the bitter taste, swishing it around before swallowing. "Lita isn't our mother. She's the incubator who gave us birth."

"Watch your mouth, or so help me, I'm going to hurt you."

"What? Since when have you taken her side over mine?"

"You've always talked a lot of shit, especially about witches. I don't know what your deal is, and I've never cared enough to think too hard on it. But I won't sit here and stay quiet while you talk shit about Mom. If Dad were here, he'd knock your teeth down your throat."

"Because he's as witch-whipped as Marrok is—and you too, from the way you're acting. Calm down and order another drink."

"No, I'm done."

"Come on. What's your deal?" Zev raised his fist to punch his brother in the arm, but Alarick slapped his hand away with such force Zev's instinct was to strike back.

He felt it, the silver snare materializing around his neck, followed by a hiss of magic from his reformed silver snare, dulling his anger, his urge to lash out in violence. Unballing his fist, Zev tried to fight against the magic seeping into his body, but it was a battle he couldn't win easily—not as long as the damn rage disruptor functioned.

When a black werewolf did manage to hold on to their rage or hunger long enough to resist and act on their violent urges, they turned into a muraco.

"You can't even control your anger enough to avoid setting off the silver snare. It might not last, but Marrok has the right idea. At least he's living his life, which is more than I can say for the two of us. We work all day then come to this bar and get drunk. I'm twenty-nine and haven't let myself fall in love with a witch since I broke up with Noor."

"She dumped you. If you're going to tell the story, don't lie about how it ended."

"You're an asshole."

"And proud of it." Zev gestured with his hand around the busy bar. "Take your pick."

"I don't want—"

"A human female? Yeah, that's your problem. Witches will be the downfall of every werewolf. Dad still pines for Lita, although she left his ass the same way Noor dumped you. Give it a few years and Marrok will be back in this booth with us, tail between his legs, because Oriana kicked his dumbass out of Steel Rise after she used him to get the next heir to Earth Rift. That's all we're good for, Alarick, in case you're too stupid to figure it out. If the witches could get pregnant any other way, they wouldn't need us at all. They tried, you know, but conception can only happen the old-fashioned way. Which means they need us, at least for that."

Zev snapped his fingers, but the redheaded waitress ignored him, her rolled eyes and nasty attitude ensuring she'd never get another tip from him.

"Something is seriously wrong with you."

"You're just mad because you can't deal with the truth. Unlike you, I won't lie to myself. Witches and werewolves can't ever be anything more than lovers by necessity and enemies at heart. Two alphas can't coexist without going for each other's throats. We once had the witches by the throat, now they have us by our balls. One of these days, the pendulum will swing back to werewolves. With a little push, we can see it happen in our lifetime."

Glancing around the bar again, this time making sure no one was listening, Zev slid closer to Alarick, who watched him as if he were a giant arachnid about to strike. Not a chance, since he'd triggered the silver snare. It wouldn't disappear until he was "symptom-free" for twenty-four hours. *One way or another, I'll free myself.*

"Listen, there's this group I've heard about."

Alarick's eyes narrowed. "What kind of group?"

"The kind that has connections with a special doctor."

Zev slid so close to Alarick he could smell, under the scents of mint toothpaste and beer, the witch he'd obviously been with before meeting him at the bar. *Interesting. Who's the witch, Alarick, and why haven't you told me about her? I'll get the truth out of you later.*

Zev pointed to his head. "… a doctor who removes rage disruptors."

Alarick's eyes snapped to the crowd of people in the bar then back to Zev. "Are you trying to get our asses thrown in jail?"

"It's fine, no one is paying any attention. But yeah, we should take this convo to a more private place. Your apartment is closest. We can go there."

"Hell no. Whatever shit you're thinking about getting into, don't. Leave that underground dirt alone. That's white werewolf shit that'll get your ass killed or imprisoned."

"Marrok is Cyrus of Steelcross. He'll have my back, if something happens."

Alarick ran a hand over his face, shaking his head like an agitated Io. Out of the three brothers, Alarick was most like their father in temperament and mannerisms.

"No matter what fancy title Oriana gave Marrok, she's still Crimson Hunter. If you're caught without your rage disruptor and hanging out with muracos, there's nothing Marrok will be able to do to save your werewolf hide. It isn't even fair of you to expect him to bail you out of that kind of insane situation."

"We're brothers. We're supposed to have each other's back."

"I do have your back, which is why I'm telling you to stay the hell away from the muraco underground. Once you take that step, Zev, there's no coming back. Our disruptors are tracked. As soon as they go offline, Oriana will know. It's her job to know, to hunt down rogue werewolves."

"To kill them for seeking their freedom, you mean."

Alarick did that face wipe and head shake thing again. "Have you ever truly listened to anyone other than yourself? If you had, you'd know Oriana uses lethal force as a final resort. She and the Hunter Division of Crimson Guards aren't executioners and not every rogue werewolf is muraco. But yeah, Oriana is Crimson Hunter for a reason, and it's not because her mother is matriarch."

"Only thing you've said is that our baby brother married a witch willing and capable of killing a werewolf because she's killed them before."

"You really hear only what you want to." Digging into his pants pocket, Alarick pulled out a few bills and slapped them on the table. "You're my brother, and I love you. So, hear me when I say, stay away from that doctor and the underground werewolves. Stop looking for trouble before someone comes looking for you." Alarick slipped from the booth, shoving hands in the front pockets of his black jeans. "I'm serious. For once in your life, don't be selfish. If you don't care what happens to you, think about your family. Think how Marrok will feel if his mate has to hunt down his rogue brother."

"What about our freedom? Does that mean nothing to you?"

"We aren't slaves to witches, Zev. That's the part you keep forgetting. If we're slaves to anything, it's to our blood-and-magic lust. If you want to fight something begin with that and stop blaming witches for our shortcomings as werewolves."

"You're delusional."

"I'm tired is what I am, and I have work in the morning. So do you. Take your ass home, and forget we had this conversation. I'll do the same. See you next Saturday at Moonvale Forest for our run. Marrok said Oriana will send someone to pick us up."

From the way Alarick said that, his brother had a specific witch in mind he hoped Oriana would send. Maybe it was the same witch he'd gone down on before Zev had interrupted his evening by inviting him for a quick drink at their favorite bar.

First Marrok and now Alarick. I'm losing my brothers to witches. Something must give, and it won't be my relationship with my brothers.

Zev relaxed against the booth, as if he hadn't a care in the world. "Yeah, you're right. I'm going to have another drink then I'll be off too. Forget I said anything."

"It's already forgotten. Goodnight, bro."

Before Alarick reached the double doors that would take him into the hot summer night, he had his phone out and pressed to his ear.

Zev growled low in his throat, yanked out his own phone and checked his savings account balance. *Shit. Not enough.* The rage disruptor removal procedure was expensive, borderline robbery, but it would be worth it to have his freedom.

He slid from the booth, mentally calculating how many overtime hours he'd have to work and how long it would take him to raise the money he needed. *Too many and too long.*

But Zev left the bar, committed to a plan that would be well worth the wait.

7: The Future

December 31, 2240
Steelcross Realm
Steel Rise

With a swipe to the left, Marrok turned the page on his handheld mage tablet, continuing to read Matriarch Helen's diary entries. Not even Oriana had read these historic documents, although only she and Kalinda were privy to the matriarchal archives.

It's taken years to build Bronze Ward, but Tuncay and I have worked hard to turn our dream into a reality. Few thought we could do it. Even fewer believe it will be a success. But Bronze Ward is just brick and mortar. Its physical construction is only the first step in our much bigger dream. The opening of Bronze Ward tomorrow will be an important first step along what will be a lengthy journey.

I must admit, I'm frightened of what will come next. While I am responsible for every life on this planet, I feel a greater responsibility to the new residents of Bronze Ward. Friends have taken to calling the project a "grand experiment." I dislike the skepticism in the name, but my feelings don't make the not-so-subtle judgment any less true. Bronze Ward is an experiment. There's nothing inherently wrong with experiments. Except this one involves people's lives. If I'm wrong, witches and werewolves could die.

I don't share my fears with Tuncay. As matriarch I must have the right answers, even when I'm uncertain. Rulership is a weighty burden. Too heavy, some days. I'm grateful for Tuncay, but even he cannot help me carry the load of being a matriarch. He battles his own demons. Our individual burdens are why we've decided to postpone parenthood. For now, Bronze Ward is the newborn we must raise and nurture into a well-adjusted, fully functioning adult. For that to happen, we need to survive its infancy and toddler years.

Fireworks blasted. Marrok smiled, looking up from the tablet to the windows across from their bed. A rainbow of color lit up the night sky and their bedroom. Sparkling lights and loud revelers on the street below heralded the new year.

"So loud," Oriana complained from beside him, covering her sleepy head with a pillow. "Why must they be so loud? Until werewolves migrated here, Steelcross was a quiet city."

"Steelcross hasn't been a quiet city since you became its matriarch."

Oriana grumbled something he couldn't hear, likely a curse.

He slid down the bed, curling himself around his grumpy witch. "How are you feeling?"

"Tired. A little nauseous."

"So basically, the same as when you crashed, face-down, two hours ago."

"It's your fault."

"I know. My fault." Marrok snatched the pillow off Oriana's head. This time, there was no doubt his witch cursed him—in two languages, no less.

"You and your determined sperm."

"The morning sickness will pass. You could always take something or use magic to alleviate your discomfort."

"No magic. Blunt force weapons. That's all witches are."

Marrok wouldn't argue with her. He never did when she got like this. Until living with Oriana, he'd never known how much witches struggled with controlling their powers even after going through the rite of endometal fusion.

Daily, he witnessed the physical and emotional toll on his mate. Carrying their child added to the demand for self-control.

"What can I do to help?"

Shifting in his embrace, she faced him. The red streaks in her hair seemed even brighter every time a firework crackled outside their bedroom windows.

"Have you learned anything new from the archives?"

"Not much. There's a lot to go through."

"I know. We need to devise a plan of attack. Twelve years, remember?"

"I know I'm the one who mentioned twelve years to find a solution, starting once you gave birth to our daughter, but we shouldn't put a ticking time bomb on our child."

"I don't mean to, but that's how I feel."

"If you think like that, it's going to take all the joy out of becoming and being a mother."

Burrowing against his bare chest, she didn't speak, so he didn't either. His father hadn't prepared him for this kind of life, for living with a witch who, most days, glowed like the sun but other days was quiet and pensive. He was learning about her, as much as she was learning how to live with him.

Marrok inhaled her scent. Always lemon, even after she showered.

"When are you leaving?" Oriana asked, her lips grazing his chest.

"I'll return to Dad's house in two days."

Blindly, she reached for his silver snare, finding it easily. "I hate that you feel a need to put distance between us."

"So do I. You know I don't want to leave, especially when you're expecting. But we agreed. Short breaks from each other, the way Matriarch Helen suggested."

"Screw my grandparents and their short breaks. That's not a viable long-term solution."

"It's all we have. You smell too good, Oriana. I'm drawn to you more every day."

"It's the sex."

He swatted her ass, and she smiled up at him. "I won't lie, sex is part of it. Alarick warned me."

He'd told her his brother's story, which she waved away with, "He was a boy just coming into his full werewolf powers. Between a fifteen-year-old Alarick and the eleven-year-old girl, she was the more dangerous of the two. We aren't prey but predators. He's lucky she didn't kill him."

Oriana's way of viewing werewolves and witches never ceased to amaze and confuse Marrok.

"The temptation *is* greatest when we make love. There's more than sexual hunger inside me."

"Does your hunger make you want to kill me?"

"How can you say that without fear? You act as if my confession isn't like that ticking time bomb we just talked about."

Rising onto her knees, she shoved his right shoulder. Obligingly, he moved onto his back, watching as she straddled his waist, as naked as he was. For a minute, he only noticed the gorgeous breasts before letting his gaze drift down to the small baby bump. Despite his own worries, he couldn't wait to become a father.

Lita had told him to love "fully yet fairly." It hadn't been fair of Io only to give Lita werewolves. Until their talk, Marrok hadn't considered how selfish his father had been. He'd viewed Lita's leaving their family from a narrow perspective, one born of limited knowledge and unconscious bias.

"Now that I'm pregnant, you can have sex with me in your bleddyn form, if you want."

His witch had a frightening knack for seeing into his mind. Not that he'd been expressly thinking about them having sex in his in-between form, but that his parents had either only had sex while Io was in his bleddyn form or his father had made certain he and Lita used a contraceptive when they had sex while he was in his human form.

"We've never done it like that before. It's a new year. I think we should." She sat more firmly on him. "At least one part of you is interested, so stop looking at me as if I suggested we have public sex. Sometimes, I think you're a prude."

"You say shit like that to get under my skin. You know I'm not a prude, and you damn well know you would never have sex in public. I don't know why we're having this conversation when we're supposed to be outside celebrating the new year with residents of Steel Rise, which you seemed to have forgotten. You must've also forgotten that you're the one who organized the party you've complained is too loud."

"Yes, I did, so we could have a party for two in here. No one wants anything from their matriarch when music, food, and alcohol are free and plentiful. Besides," she licked her lips, "I want to see your bleddyn."

"See or feel?"

"Both."

He laughed at the lust in her eyes, moaning as she stroked him. Marrok could shift right there in their marital bed, giving them both what they wanted. But the energy Oriana displayed came from her exhausted reserve not from hours of rejuvenated rest.

"Another time."

"Are you sure?"

The fact that she wasn't persisting, using flirtations or jokes to get her way, was proof enough he'd made the right decision. Bleddyns were demanding lovers. It would be much more rigorous than having sex in human form, although far less than mating with a fully shifted werewolf, which no sane female willingly did. Witches weren't animals. Their bodies *were* structured, however, to be able to mate with the half-human, half-wolf bleddyn form.

The first trimester of his mate's pregnancy, however, wasn't an ideal time to have that kind of sex. Bleddyns didn't make love, they fucked—hard and with the intent of getting his mate with a channon, a werewolf baby.

Sitting up, he adjusted her on his lap, giving her a taste of what she wanted.

Eyes closed, her forehead fell against his as she languidly rode him.

"As a bleddyn, I'm bigger." He pushed into her. "Longer." Another deep thrust. "Thicker."

Oriana's eyes popped open, and he thrust into her again.

"No matter my form, I can make you scream and come for me. But yeah, my bleddyn will more than feed your witch hunger."

Oriana's magic sparked to life, strong sizzles from her hands onto the shoulders she gripped.

He winced in pain, the shock a burn to his senses and skin.

She stopped. "I didn't mean to hurt you. I'm sorry."

"I'm fine. It's nothing."

"It's not nothing. I burned you again."

"It was a mistake, and I'll heal. Ignore it, Oriana, and make love to me."

"I can't ignore—"

Marrok kissed her, silencing her fears and building tension. He kept kissing her, unwilling to release his witch until she understood he'd take a hundred magic burns from her, if she found pleasure in his arms.

He had a theory, though, because he didn't think her burns were simply a byproduct of her strong sun magic. He kept hoping to find evidence to support his theory in the matriarchal archives. To date, he hadn't.

Marrok wanted to try something with Oriana but now wasn't the time for experiments, not when she was pregnant, tired, and emotional. Not that Oriana would agree anyway to a half-baked scheme that could leave him hurt or dead.

More fireworks exploded, and so did Marrok.

"Happy New Year, Oriana. I love you."

Blood of the Sun Decree #2
March 1, 1309

BY MATRIARCHAL DECREE, THE REGIONS OF PERILUNE RILLE IN IRONGARDE REALM AND APHELION UMBRA IN STEELCROSS REALM ARE RESERVED TERRITORIES FOR HUMANS.

Alba, Matriarch of Earth Rift

8: Ticking Time Bomb

February 29, 2241
Steelcross Realm
Copper Vale City

Abelone sipped from her glass of red wine. The bottle had been an early anniversary gift from Bhavari who sat opposite her at their small dining room table. Beginning tomorrow they'd have two weeks leave to look forward to, so tonight was a perfect time to sit back, relax, and enjoy the light-bodied flavor of her drink. She closed her eyes, savoring the taste of cherry on her tongue.

"Someone's ready for vacation," Bhavari said.

"How right you are."

Abelone peeked at her wife through a barely opened eye slit. As always, Bhavari was lovely—her black hair glossy and straight, her dress form-fitting and sexy. Bhavari liked to dress up, no special occasion required. Abelone knew she hadn't seen Bhavari in the emerald green dress before, a cool color that complemented her fair skin and dark hair. Like the red wine, the new dress was an early anniversary gift.

"We should talk about last week's meeting."

"Don't ruin my good mood with talk of work. For once, let's have one meal without Steelburgh creeping into the conversation." When Bhavari didn't reply, Abelone sighed, opened her eyes, and sat up straight, her wine glass joining her dinner plate on the table. "Okay, I'm listening."

"It's been a week."

"I know. You just reminded me." Not that Abelone needed the reminder. They'd taken the most dangerous step in their plan. They couldn't act alone. "I've already heard from a few of them, if that's what you want to know."

Bhavari poked at the remnants of food on her dinner plate. She'd eaten most of the green goddess cobb salad with chicken Abelone had prepared, attacking her dinner the way she did when she skipped lunch. Forgetting meals was a bad habit Bhavari had adopted long before she and Abelone met. Neither their marriage nor Abelone's admonishments had altered Bhavari's behavior. The best Abelone could do was cook, keep to a regular dinner hour, and make sure she kept the fridge stocked with Bhavari's favorite foods.

"What about Misae?"

"Your little assistant confirmed."

"Good. It would've been awkward working with her if she hadn't."

Bhavari stopped toying with her salad, exchanging her fork for her glass of water. She might have fine taste in wine, but two years of dating a college student who was a high-functioning alcoholic had left the proverbial bad taste in her mouth.

"What about the data technicians?"

"Not yet."

"We need them onboard. We can't do anything without the techs."

"I know. Calm down."

"I am calm." Bhavari reached for Abelone's wine glass, lifted it to her mouth, then visibly shuddered at what she'd been about to do. She handed the glass to Abelone, shaky hands making for a delicate transfer. "Okay, I'm not calm."

"I can see that. It'll be fine." Abelone drained the last of the wine, in case Bhavari had another moment of weakness.

Bhavari hesitated then said quickly, "It's not too late for us to back out of this. We haven't done anything wrong. Not really. Talking about a crime isn't the same as actually committing a crime, is it?"

"We can alter our course, if that's what you really want."

Eyes that had been staring at the wall across from the dinner table turned to Abelone. "She'll have the baby soon."

"I know."

"Her consort is everywhere. In everything."

"I know that too."

"I thought when she became pregnant so soon after marrying it meant she finally understood the role of a matriarch. But, from what I hear, she involves him in most of her government affairs. Where she goes, so does he. She even gave him a sun title."

Abelone was tempted to repeat the same two words. She knew everything Bhavari had mentioned. The entire planet knew because Cyrus of Steelcross was more than soundbite news. The populous seemed to be split over how they felt about Matriarch Oriana's relationship with her consort. Or rather, Matriarch Oriana's unspoken insistence on upgrading her consort's status in the government above that of any werewolf, including her father, the Aku of Irongarde.

"She doesn't understand what she's doing."

Abelone reached for Bhavari's trembling hand, pleased when her touch seemed to have the desired effect of calming her. "Matriarch Oriana is blinded by sex, love, and her own naivete. It could take her years to finally see the true werewolf she married. By then, it may be too late for Earth Rift. We need to rip the blinders off for her."

"Are you sure we're on the right path?"

Abelone was positive of two facts. One, Matriarch Oriana, if left to her own devices, would destroy everything witches had built since the time of Matriarch Alba. Two, anyone involved in the plot would die. She hadn't been that explicit during last week's meeting, but she could see the understanding in everyone's eyes. Well, everyone except for Bhavari, who foolishly clung to the belief that they could go against the matriarchy and survive.

If Abelone were more concerned with growing old with Bhavari than protecting the witch way of life, she would tell her wife the truth and retreat from her decision. But she could do neither. Someone had to show the young matriarch the error in her thinking. She despised the stench of betrayal that clung to her, but she loved witches and Earth Rift more.

"I'm positive we're doing the right thing."

Bhavari smiled, relieved, and Abelone felt the smallest pang of guilt.

The doorbell rang, a perfect distractor from the unwanted emotion. They weren't expecting a visitor, and Abelone jumped, literally, at the interruption.

"I'll get the door," she said, already out of her seat and moving away from the table. Abelone wasn't surprised Bhavari followed her to the front door, but her mouth fell open when she saw the person outside. If she stumbled backward, gasping, and stammering out, "G-good evening," well, no one could blame her.

March 27, 2241
Irongarde Realm
Iron Spire

"You can't hide in here forever. Trust me, I know."

Marrok recognized Bader's voice but didn't lift his head or acknowledge the other werewolf's presence in the library beyond a nod.

"Kalinda won't leave Oriana's side, and you're afraid to stay there. As I said, I know that kind of fear." The couch cushion beside him dipped. "You're a father now, Marrok. There's no greater responsibility … or greater fear known to a werewolf than being a father to a witch. Daughters can gut us unlike anything else in nature. Here I am, back in Iron Spire, a place I swore never to step foot in again. But I couldn't stay away, couldn't miss the occasion of my daughter giving birth to her daughter."

Shoulders hunched, T-shirt clinging, and mouth dry, Marrok stood on unsteady legs. For a second he swayed, a memory of a fiercely focused Oriana bearing down, pushing their daughter into the beautiful yet harsh world, seized him. Stumbling forward like a drunkard turned away from a bar after last call, Marrok grasped the corner of a desk.

"Slow, deep breaths, Marrok. Slow, deep breaths. The last thing Oriana needs is her consort passing out, hitting his head on his way to the floor, and ruining a priceless rug with his blood."

Marrok had never known the Aku of Irongarde to laugh or make a joke. He had seen him smile but only in Oriana's presence.

"Was that meant to be a joke?"

"If you found it funny, then yes. If not, then no. Oriana is the humorous one in the family, not me and certainly not Kalinda. If I hadn't been there at Oriana's conception and birth, I would swear Kalinda and I played no role in making her."

Still holding on to the desk's edge, Marrok turned to face his father-in-law. As always, Bader dressed to impress—shined shoes, creased dress pants, and a crisp white shirt with diamond cufflinks. All that was missing were the suit jacket and tie he'd arrived in. He'd removed them nine hours ago before drinking the first of several cups of steaming coffee. The aku didn't appear as if he'd spent those hours pacing, awaiting the delivery of his first grandchild.

"Oriana looks like you."

"She resembles her mother more. Even the shade of their blue eyes are the same. Oriana is the only bright spot left between Kalinda and me." Leaning against the cushions, legs crossed, arm stretched out along the back of the couch, Bader appeared like a werewolf of leisure, not a male baring his heart. His scent, if not his eyes, gave away his pain.

"I guess Oriana does look more like her mother, but she doesn't have Kalinda's rough edges."

"When Kalinda and I first married, neither did she. Ruling a planet has a way of turning leveled glass into jagged shards."

"Is that a warning?"

"No. And I wasn't only speaking about my mate. I'm not the same werewolf she took as a consort. I've disappointed her, as much as she's disillusioned me."

Bader bit his lower lip the same way Oriana did when she was deep in thought or nervous.

Marrok wanted to ask him a personal question. With the sentimental mood Bader seemed to be in, now might be his only chance.

"Have you ever been tempted?"

The way Bader's dark eyes hardened like twin pieces of marble, he thought the werewolf would tell him to go screw himself. But he didn't. Instead, Bader lowered his arm and leg, eyes softening with the movements.

"To hurt my mate or daughter, you mean?"

Marrok nodded, shifting to rest one hip on the edge of the desk, tension radiating from shoulders to toes.

"Not tempted to hurt, that's not the correct word to describe the feeling." Bader's hand rose to his stomach. "It's more like an extreme sensation of starvation, of a hunger so deep and consuming I could feel it at the cellular level. My stomach rumbled, growled from the pain of needing to be fed."

The hand on Bader's stomach clutched at his shirt, as if he could feel his hunger pains from the mere telling of his truth. His jaw set and brows pinched.

The memory haunts him. I wonder when he last felt that way.

"I'm sorry. I shouldn't have asked."

"My son is gone, and with him my heart and marriage. I can't have either back. Witches are even less willing to forgive than werewolves. But I'll tell you what I would've told him. Love with all your heart. Hold nothing back. Treasure the small things—your daughter's laughter, your mate's hand in yours, how your heart skips a beat when you see them, knowing they love you as much as you adore them. When you feel yourself starving for the taste of their magic, step back, breathe, but never, ever walk away from them. We all think that's the answer, the only way to survive each other, but we're wrong."

Marrok planted both feet on the floor, leaning against the desk instead of sitting on it. "Wrong?"

"One hundred percent wrong." Bader slid to the edge of the couch, the palms of his hands on his knees. "You're old enough to feel the hunger, even if you haven't yet had the gnawing pangs of starvation."

Yeah, he'd felt the hunger for magic, especially since sharing a bed with Oriana. Their short breaks helped. When he returned, he felt better, more in control.

"It's always there. Once we reach puberty, the hunger stays with us, even when we aren't in the presence of a witch. I can't remember what it feels like to be full, to have my body satisfied on a bone-deep, primal level. The contentment of being full, of not wanting anything else because you're stuffed, isn't an experience known to any mature werewolf."

Io had shared a similar perspective with Marrok, but the conversation had ended with, "And that's why we'll always lose our witches, why they'll never completely trust us not to hurt them." But Bader disagreed?

"I don't understand."

"Witches grow up thinking they can't rely on their fathers, while werewolves are raised believing their mothers will grow to fear them."

"Isn't that what happens? After puberty, witches can't depend on their fathers because they're no longer in the home. The same is true for werewolves. Their mothers leave, afraid of what will happen if they stay."

Bader's headshake had the hair jewelry dangling from his dreadlocks rubbing against each other, producing a soft wind chime sound.

"Self-fulfilling prophecy. We believe it, so we make it true. I left my family because my father left his, as my grandfather did, and his father, and every other male in my family who had a daughter. I was told that's what real werewolves did, if they loved their mate and daughter. 'You never want to hurt them,' my father told me. 'A werewolf must protect his witches, even from himself.' "

"How can we do both? Protect them and stay with them?"

Twelve years. That's all the time he and Oriana had to figure out what they could do differently to save their marriage and their family. Marrok didn't doubt Oriana would reject the rite of endometal fusion when the time came. She wouldn't permit anyone, including Kalinda, to bully her into subjecting their daughter to what she viewed as a barbaric practice. But the personal cost would be high, greater than he thought Oriana could fully grasp. In essence, she would be shunned.

Unless Kalinda and Bader wanted to suffer the same fate, Oriana would lose them too. Worse, how would Oriana feel if her parents chose her over everything else in their lives, leaving the realms without a legitimate line of matrilineal matriarch and a long-standing aku? What would happen to Earth Rift without the traditional succession plan? Would war erupt, as witches and werewolves fought themselves and each other to claim what the Blood of the Sun family left? None of the possibilities would bode well for Earth Rift.

Oriana couldn't abdicate the matriarchy. Not for him. Not even for their children. Where did that leave them?

With a ticking time bomb.

"I've been reading Matriarch Helen's private journals."

Sliding back against the cushions, Bader re-crossed his legs and arched an eyebrow. "Why?"

Marrok didn't know how much Oriana had confided in her father beyond her plans for restoring Bronze Ward. He shoved his hands into his pants pockets, wishing he could fake cool calm as well as the aku.

"Haven't you ever wondered how Helen and Tuncay did it for so long?"

"They took breaks from one another. It's not a mystery, Marrok. We've all tried that strategy. A week or two at first. Then a month. Then three. Before you know it, a year has passed, and you begin to feel like a guest in your own home. So you leave again, staying away even longer because you think it's better that way, that you're a burden and your family is happier without you. Distance has a way of adding to our delusions. We tell ourselves we're doing it for their safety when, in truth, we stay away because it's easier than staying and fighting the perpetual hunger. Naturally, the bond that brought the witch and werewolf together strains, frays, and eventually breaks."

Once again, despite his relaxed posture and matter-of-fact way of sharing the pitfalls of his marriage to Kalinda, Bader's scent betrayed his regret and loneliness. Combined, they smelled like lemongrass to Marrok. His whole life he'd been familiar with the smell, beginning with his father. Most mature werewolves reeked of it. He'd learned to ignore the smell, to interpret it as a natural and immutable part of life.

As a new father and a consort with only a year of marriage behind him, Marrok dreaded the day he too would stink of lemongrass. That innocuous smell would represent all he had lost and everything he had failed to protect.

His mate.

His daughter.

His heart.

"Helen and Tuncay's love story was tragic. Kalinda never talks about her parents. If I were you, I wouldn't mention that Oriana gave you access to Helen's records."

Bader glanced at the wall clock above the library door. Marrok realized he'd been gone too long. It didn't take two hours to wash a newborn, move Oriana from the birthing room to her bedroom, and for Oriana to nurse their daughter. He needed to get his butt back to his family.

"Oriana is the only person who has managed to get around Kalinda's rough edges, as you called them. Bronze Ward is a perfect example of what I mean. For a while, Helen and Tuncay did something right, something other than taking breaks from each other. I don't know what new idea they'd devised, probably another experiment like Bronze Ward."

Marrok thought he knew what the deceased couple had done, and it had been a risky experiment. A risky, *failed* experiment, because everyone knew how Helen and Tuncay's love story had ended. Happily-ever-afters did not exist for witches and werewolves.

Marrok pushed to his feet, sure-footed and ready to see his girls. Running away resolved nothing. He agreed with Bader on that point.

"Feel better?"

How could he? Between Lita's and Bader's advice, he had no clear path to guarantee he wouldn't lose his family in the end. He felt like he was wading in waist-deep quicksand, nowhere to go but down.

"I'm going to go see my mate and daughter. Coming?"

"No."

"Suit yourself. Do you want me to tell Kalinda where to find you?"

He doubted Bader's right eyebrow could reach any further northward.

"Okay, I guess you don't." Marrok strolled to the closed library door, opened it, but didn't exit. "Is it true that Matriarch Helen died performing an advanced-level spell that resulted in malfunctioning weapons she couldn't control? And that the weapons, somehow, severed her arms and legs?"

Bader's sigh was heavy. "I don't know. I don't think Kalinda does either. What I do know is that Helen locked herself in her bedroom with her trusted Crimson Hunter. Helen's magic was unmatched, wilder than anything I've ever seen. Only Kalinda could bypass her mother's barrier spell to get us inside her room. But it was too late. Flames were everywhere, but that didn't stop Tuncay from charging in there. Kalinda would've followed him, but …"

Marrok turned back to Bader. The werewolf hadn't moved, but his tone and face were no longer cool and calm. For once, the emotions on his face matched his scent—horror and sadness.

"I stopped my mate from going in. It took all my werewolf strength to do it, too. We fought, right there in front of her parent's burning suite. We fought, and I was never more afraid in my life."

"That Kalinda would hurt you?"

"No, that I wouldn't be strong enough to stop her from killing herself. When Tuncay ran in there, in his human form, he had to have known he wouldn't survive the wild sun magic in that room. But he went in anyway, choosing to die with his witch rather than living without her."

Marrok stared at Bader, mouth clamped tight. What the hell could he say? The tragic tale explained so much about his mother-in-law. Her rough edges were born in witch fire.

"I lost Kalinda that day. Long before our son was born and died, I lost my mate. Oriana's rite of endometal fusion ceremony was a convenient excuse for us to put a halt to the pretense. I traded my daughter for the relief I felt at no longer living with a woman who hated me for loving her."

"She would've died with her parents, if not for you."

"A part of Kalinda did die with Helen and Tuncay. What remained was a witch whose final memories of her parents were their cries as they burned. She wouldn't have been able to save them, whether I'd stood in her way or not." Bader's hand lifted to his chest, right above his Aku of Irongarde symbol—Kalinda's mate mark. "Since then, she's never been able to separate the worst day of her life from the werewolf who forced her to live in a world without her parents. After that … we eventually were able to do our duty for the realm, giving them their next Matriarch of Earth Rift."

In an atypically ungraceful move, Bader flopped onto the couch, his hair jewelry producing a discordant bell sound fabled to ward-off evil spirits.

Marrok didn't believe in evil spirits but something terrible had laid claim to Earth Rift.

"Whatever you and Oriana are doing with Helen's journals, you need to stop. She and Tuncay plotted and planned and got in way over their heads. Their schemes killed them and Helen's Crimson Hunter, Farkas. It took four witches to extinguish Helen's flames, that's how potent her magic was without the steel buffers in her arms and legs."

For all that Kalinda had followed Matriarch Alba's decree and had Oriana injected with liquid steel, she'd limited it to her arms. From that precedent— and perhaps small act of defiance—other mothers followed her lead. The more he learned, the more he realized how little the people of Earth Rift understood their matriarchs—current and past.

"I see so much of Kalinda in Oriana. But my daughter is more like her grandmother than I realized. You've studied Helen. Do you disagree?"

Marrok shook his head, wishing he hadn't seen the same drive in Oriana that he had read in Helen's journals. Their passion to end the divide between witches and werewolves were undeniable, admirable, but also too terrifying for Marrok to stand by and let Oriana go it alone.

"With or without me, Oriana won't stop until she has her answers. I'll keep her safe, make sure she doesn't go too far."

"I'm sure Tuncay thought he could do the same for his mate. In the end, Helen trusted Farkas more than she did Tuncay. Why do you think that was?"

Again, Marrok stared at Bader. The day of his daughter's birth shouldn't be accompanied by this kind of brutal conversation. Yet, like Lita on his wedding day, Bader had decided to add a gray cloud of truth to his sunny day.

"From what I've learned of Tuncay from Helen's journals, he loved her, which means he would've tried to stop her. Tuncay wouldn't have wanted

Helen to risk her life on an experiment that could kill her. Like you with Kalinda, he would rather be hated than watch her die, knowing he could've saved her. As Crimson Hunter, it was Farkas's duty to do the will of her matriarch, even if she disagreed."

"I can't lose my daughter, Marrok. Do you understand?"

"I won't fail Oriana."

"That's just it, Tuncay didn't fail Helen. Yet she still died. Do you know why Oriana is so bad at magical jumps?"

"Because she doesn't practice and knows Solange will bail her butt out of any situation?"

Bader laughed and, yeah, so did Marrok because it was the truth, and they needed the emotional release.

"Well, yes, but that's only partially true. When I said Oriana was like Helen, I wasn't only talking about their passion and purpose but also their powerset. Extraction magic, as difficult a spell as it is, is the only spell Oriana doesn't practice because that's her small way of reminding herself to take care with her high magic level and position as matriarch. When you're born to rule and everyone on a planet of billions, except for your mother, is expected to bend to your will, that depth of power can be both intoxicating and corrupting. Like Helen, Oriana's magic literally runs hot, even with the liquid steel in her arms."

His healed burns were proof of how hot Oriana ran when in the throes of passion, her mind not focused on controlling her wild sun magic but on giving and receiving pleasure.

"She needs you, more than you realize. And Kalinda needed me more than I realized."

"What about the hunger?"

"You won't die from it. Some days you'll wish you could, though. Other days you will think you'll do anything to make the pain go away. But you won't. You must trust, no matter how bad it gets, how starved you feel, that you'll never hurt your mate and daughter. I didn't have enough faith in myself. But Tuncay did. If one werewolf could survive the hunger, we all can."

Bader rose and, to Marrok's surprise, the older werewolf hugged him. Not one of those one-armed "manly" hugs either, but the both-arms-around-his-neck kind of hug a father bestowed on his son.

He returned Bader's hug. Marrok was raised in a house of males, and Io was an affectionate father, as quick to display his love for his sons as he was to get in their faces when they did something wrong.

"She's not afraid of you."

"That's what she says."

"Believe her." Bader stepped back from Marrok. "Until that day we fought, I never believed Kalinda. But she truly wasn't afraid of me. I also knew, no matter how hard she fought, she wouldn't do anything to truly hurt me. I used her love against her that day. We both knew it, and she despised me for it. She still does."

"Time has a way of healing old wounds, at least that's what my father says. I don't think Kalinda hates you."

"You're twenty-seven. Talk to me when your marriage is older than my cufflinks."

"Was that another joke?"

"It depends. Was it funny?"

"A little."

Bader smacked Marrok on his shoulder. "Then it was a joke. You better go see Oriana. I've grown fond of you, so I'd hate to have her magically jump you to the top of Mage Peak before you've had a chance to give Keira a brother and me a grandson." Bader pushed him out the door. "Go, and … don't tell my mate where to find me."

When Marrok entered Oriana's bedroom he took in the scene before him. Oriana slept in their bed with Kalinda seated in a chair beside her. Keira was nestled in a bassinet in front of Kalinda.

Marrok smiled at his mother-in-law … and lied. "Bader wants you to know he's in the library if you want to talk before he leaves for the night."

Yeah, Marrok may have been only twenty-seven to Bader's sixty-four, but he intuitively knew that Bader wouldn't have mentioned not telling Kalinda where he was if he didn't think she would seek him out. More, if he didn't want to be sought out by his mate. Sometimes, all the encouragement a were-wolf needed was for a witch to make the first move.

"Thank you, Marrok," Kalinda whispered, her eyes on her sleeping daughter. "It was a hard labor, but she did great."

"No magic. No medicine. The story of Oriana's pregnancy."

"You forgot stubborn."

Marrok walked Kalinda to the suite door. "She was stubborn before her pregnancy. Don't forget about Bader."

When she paused, hand on the doorknob, Marrok wondered if he'd over-played his hand with the reminder. But she just shook her head, as if tossing out whatever notion had occurred to her.

"Goodnight, and congratulations on the birth of a healthy baby girl."

"Thank you."

Stripping down to his boxers and tossing his clothes onto the bedroom's settee, he went over to his daughter. "Hey, cutie," he cooed, noticing his daughter's big, royal blue eyes were open. "Look at you. What a beauty." Careful to hold her securely, he lifted Keira into his arms, the newborn tiny, yet solid.

Sitting on the edge of the bed opposite where his mate slept, Marrok held his daughter. "It was love at first sight." He snuggled her soft cheek with his nose. "Don't tell your mother—she'd be jealous—but you're my best girl, my absolute favorite little witch."

She smelled faintly of lemons, but also a floral scent uniquely her own. As Keira grew, her baby scent would yield to the scent of her magic—were-wolves' olfactory temptation. Kissing her delicate forehead, Marrok breathed her in and vowed to embrace the advice he'd given Oriana months ago. He would enjoy parenthood, and he would try not to think of the next twelve years as a ticking time bomb.

Having rocked her to sleep, he returned Keira to her bassinet. Dimming the light, Marrok joined Oriana in bed, spooning closely, arm around her waist, head on the same double pillow.

Closing his eyes, he began to drift off to sleep. But a low, soft voice murmured, "Best girl, huh? Favorite witch?" A sharp elbow to the gut had him coughing and laughing.

"You're number two, if that makes you feel better. If we have another daughter, however, you'll drop to number three. But hey, third place? That's not bad."

Oriana laughed.

Marrok grinned. He didn't see the pillow before it smacked him in the face.

9: Accountable

January 10, 2243
Steelcross Realm
Steel Rise

Oriana read the report in her hand—twice—before handing it to Marrok. "Are you sure?"

Solange, who sat at the opposite side of the conference table from Oriana and Marrok, frowned and nodded.

Marrok balled the paper, tossing it into the wastebasket at the end of the table. Oriana wished she could dismiss the details of the report as easily as Marrok had made the shot.

Solange's gaze slid to Marrok. After nearly three years of marriage, Oriana still needed to remind witches, including her best friend, that Marrok was entitled to access the same intelligence as Oriana.

"Let's not travel this road again, Solange." Without looking, she placed her right hand atop Marrok's left. "Go on."

"Of course. A recent audit of our rage disruptor tracking system revealed data gaps."

"I read that in the report. Is the count accurate?"

She had to ask, although Solange wouldn't have requested a formal meeting if she hadn't tripled checked the auditor's findings.

"Thirteen hundred, give or take a hundred."

Marrok turned his hand over, pressing his palm against hers and lacing their fingers when she would've slammed her hand onto the table in anger.

"How in the hell did we lose track of thirteen hundred werewolves?"

"No answer I can give you will satisfy. Outdated program? Lazy technicians? Skipped maintenance checks?"

"Lazy technicians, maybe. We can check the dates of maintenance reviews. But an outdated program, doubtful. Unless werewolf DNA can change, and our magic expires like meat or medicine, the program works as it should. The auditor concluded the same. Why then, in your report, did you suggest a system glitch as the cause?"

"I have no idea why the system isn't able to track their silver snares. But a glitch makes the most sense."

"Not the silver snares," Marrok said. "The system tracks rage disruptors, not silver snares."

"Technically, you're both correct. One device, two parts, and three spells to make the mechanism work seamlessly. It's perfect symmetry. Foolproof. Failproof. So why don't we have tracking data on over a thousand werewolves?"

"I don't know. I only learned of the glitch two days ago and haven't completed my investigation yet."

"Until we have evidence to support your contention, I'm not going to assume what happened was a system failure or glitch. What's the demographic breakdown of the missing werewolves? That wasn't in your report."

Oriana and Solange had been friends since childhood. Solange's mother had served as Oriana's tutor. Professor Soleil oversaw her magic training when it became obvious to Kalinda that an impatient mother training her stubborn daughter led to nothing but frustration and tears. Solange and Professor Soleil had moved into Iron Spire. With another child in residence, the spire no longer felt as lonely, and Oriana's days weren't filled with boredom.

They'd turned the spire into their personal playground and, for the first time, Oriana had a friend. Solange had viewed her as more than a matriarch-in-training. Cheeky as hell, badass to the bone, Solange's loyalty to Oriana was known throughout the realms, as was her dedication to the Crimson Guard.

Oriana had never known her friend to lie to her, not even about dating Alarick, although neither Solange nor Alarick would describe their secret relationship as dating. Maybe it was just "screwing" as Solange had told Oriana, with more vehemence than the conversation had warranted.

What had always been true was that Solange placed kinship above everything else. Her integrity and loyalty served her well as captain of the Hunter Division. With those traits, however, came blinders, invisible to all except those who knew Solange well.

"Tell me what you don't want to say. You know I'll drag it out of you. You're better than the report you gave us. Tell us everything you know. Leave it to me to decide what's important."

For a beat, Solange appeared as if she would argue, eyes intent, lips parted, shoulders stiff. Then she scooted closer to the table, fingers locked in front of her, and made a short nod of acknowledgment. "They're all muraco."

Oriana opened and closed her mouth three times before she could wrap her mind around Solange's simple but devastating sentence. "Are you saying we can't track thirteen hundred muracos or that we don't know where they are?"

"Umm … both."

Maybe she should smash her head instead of her hand against the table. This couldn't be happening. But it explained Solange's hesitance.

As Oriana had suspected, not a glitch, although she preferred Solange's assumption to the conclusion she had drawn.

"Wait, wait." Marrok sounded as dazed as she felt. "I thought we were talking about missing werewolves in the non-literal sense. But that's not what you just said. You mean there are muracos who are physically gone not missing in the sense of us being unable to track them by their rage disruptor?"

"Yes, gone in every sense of the word, except for dead, which I'd take over them being free and on the run."

"If the escaped muracos have infected black werewolves with their saliva or blood, we have no way of knowing how many muracos are actually on the loose." Marrok kissed her hand before releasing it. "This is bad."

"The understatement of the year, my love. Only a skilled witch with the right training and medical tool can remove a rage disruptor from a werewolf's brain. If not done correctly, brain damage or death will result."

It went without saying that no werewolf was officially trained in the technique. Even the number of witch healers licensed to insert rage disruptors was few, all vetted through a rigorous process. Unlike the number of missing muracos, the list of licensed healers capable of removing rage disruptors was short.

There were also only a few locations where large populations of muraco resided. If Solange knew muracos were missing, it would follow that she knew from where. Considering how hesitant her friend had been to share all she'd discovered, and that she still hadn't uttered the word hanging between them like rotten fruit on a dead tree, Oriana knew where the muracos were missing from.

"We have a serious national security issue on our hands." She'd have to meet with Kalinda, who would have more questions for her than she had posed to Solange. Oriana wasn't looking forward to that discussion. When it came to certain topics, Kalinda had a one-track mind. She viewed all muraco as irredeemable werewolves deserving of death. Their laws, however, prevented Kalinda from executing muracos without first attempting imprisonment.

Werewolves, even muracos, weren't without their civil rights, even under a matriarchy. Black werewolves may have had no more use for muracos than Kalinda did, but the matriarchy would have a full-scale riot on their hands if the white werewolves were denied basic civil rights. Kalinda was too wise to risk an avoidable war.

Still, they had to be captured and returned to custody. Oriana would attempt to bring them in alive, but if Kalinda ordered the Crimson Hunter to execute them, Oriana would have little choice but to obey. She both gave orders and took them. Being matriarch didn't shield her from the latter. Only Kalinda had the power to compel Oriana to do something she didn't wish to do. Killing over a thousand werewolves, even muraco, would have her stomach and mind revolting the entire time.

Solange pushed another report across to Oriana, which she promptly slid to Marrok to read. "That's a list of the highest crime areas in Janus Nether."

Marrok read the report, frowning the entire time. "A werewolf knows another werewolf, even when in human form." Marrok tapped the side of his nose. "No way could a muraco hide among black werewolves, and us not know. They carry a scent unique to only them." He touched his nose again. "While I don't have personal experience with muracos, Dad swears, when in werewolf form, muracos smell like an overcooked rock doe. So, no, they couldn't hide in Janus Nether. But they could hide among humans. Aphelion Umbra and Perilune Rille—I suggest looking there first. The Magerun would allow them to slip into Steelcross or Irongarde, kill a witch here and there, without local enforcement realizing the murders were anything other than the normal crimes committed by witches and humans. It isn't as if only muracos kill. As long as they don't kill while in werewolf form, law enforcement wouldn't have a reason to focus their investigation on werewolf citizens."

Solange pointed in the direction of the wastebasket. "Did you happen to read the date when the muracos went missing before you crumpled the paper?"

"Yeah."

"Notice anything, *Cyrus of Steelcross*?"

"Captain." Oriana let Solange's title be warning enough. "Make your point without the sarcasm."

"My point is that the muracos went offline three years after the signing of the Blood of the Sun decree that made it legal for werewolves to go without their silver snares while in Janus Nether."

Per the new decree, the rage disruptor tracking system had been adjusted. Serial numbers of rage disruptors for all werewolf residents of Janus Nether had been moved to its own file. The system was reconfigured to release silver snares both when werewolves reached a certain oxytriton level and when rage disruptor trackers registered travel beyond Janus Nether's borders.

Solange inclined her head to Oriana before shifting her attention to Marrok. "Maybe the muracos did go to one or both of the human regions. If they did, I don't think they intended to hide there indefinitely."

"I wasn't implying they were, only that it would've been impossible for them to conceal their true identities for long or without questions being raised if they were in Janus Nether. One, they would've had to keep their shifts limited to their homes, erasing a major plus of living in Janus Nether. It being a witch-free zone means we don't have to worry about spending lots of time as werewolves. It's freeing in a way I can't begin to explain."

Marrok brightened, as he spoke of Janus Nether. Watching him, silver snare around his neck, she realized, for the first time, how much she'd given him with one hand but had taken with the other. She'd worked hard to convince her mother to make Janus Nether a collar-free territory. Then she'd married Marrok, taking him away from the first place he'd experienced a semblance of the freedom witches and humans took for granted. Even as Cyrus of Steelcross, she couldn't grant Marrok the same freedom he'd known in Janus Nether, making him no different from any other werewolf in Steelcross or Irongarde.

"Two, after a while, someone would've noticed the muracos' lack of a silver snare. We all trigger our rage disruptor at some point. It's impossible not to. We aren't robots, Solange. We get angry, just like everyone else. We fight, can even throw a few punches before the magic from the silver snare kicks in and calms us down."

Marrok refilled first Oriana's glass with water then his own. He held out the water pitcher to Solange, offering to fill her glass, too, but she demurred. "For obvious reasons, muracos aren't wanted anywhere. They have no community, no family or friends who still claim them. They want to live without constraints, to have something of their own. But they can't because they only know how to take and destroy."

Her gaze on Marrok, Solange considered his words, tapping her fingers on the table. "You're talking about a rebellion."

"It's what Oriana meant when she mentioned a national security issue." Marrok looked to Oriana for confirmation, and she nodded. "Yeah, they're biding their time, living among humans until they have what they think is a solid plan to challenge the matriarchs. When they do, they'll move to Janus Nether, infecting as many black werewolves as they can with their tainted fluids. Exposure to their saliva or blood is all it will take to turn a black werewolf into a muraco. The region is close to Irongarde City but have few witches living there to oppose them. They can attack black werewolves and, because of the silver snares, the black werewolves won't be able to successfully defend themselves."

Yet another way the matriarchy had diminished their males. They couldn't even protect themselves because witches had built a system around their own defense.

"What makes you think they aren't already in Janus Nether?" Solange asked.

"I can't know for sure, of course."

Oriana nodded, acknowledging Marrok's words. "It'll be several investigative teams' tedious assignment, but I need all Magerun footage examined since the muracos went offline. We have their names, though they're unlikely to still be using them. We also have their DNA on file and images. Between the two, the teams should be able to determine if, when, and where they used the transporter system. If they have moved to Janus Nether, I doubt they did it in large numbers. That would've been too obvious, but a few here and there and sprinkled between all three cities, is more likely. I also need to speak with everyone with access to the tracking system."

Marrok tucked a strand of hair behind her ear, sending inconvenient frissons of awareness through her. "You can use the word interrogation in front of me. I know what you do as Crimson Hunter."

No, he didn't. At least not all of it. This meeting wasn't the time to disabuse him of his assumption. That would come later … but far too soon for Oriana's liking.

"We have a lot to do." Solange grinned from Oriana to Marrok, her shit-starter friend shining through. "So, Cyrus of Steelcross, while Oriana is organizing every detail of our investigation, you will have plenty of time to have a Crimson Guard jump you to Iron Spire and provide Matriarch Kalinda with an intelligence report. I'm sure you know she prefers her updates to be made in person."

"Sure, I'll go, if you're the one, Captain of the Hunter Division, to jump me there, staying in the room with me until the meeting is over." Marrok returned Solange's smile, plenty of playful sarcasm about a task neither of them would happily volunteer to complete.

"Cut it out, you two, or I'll take both of you with me."

"No thanks, Matriarch." Solange stood, slim and fit in her black captain's uniform and boots, her rank insignia—a circular red brush stroke design—on her left shoulder.

"Oh, we're back to Matriarch. A minute earlier, I was Oriana. Where's your spine, Captain?"

"Right where it belongs. In my body. I'll need it when we go hunting and for, well, walking and living."

"Coward."

"A coward with an intact body." Granting Oriana a smile, Solange stepped away from the conference table. "Seriously, Oriana, if you want us to go with you, you know we will. Your mother is going to go ballistic, and I can't blame her. We dropped a huge ball. She made you Crimson Hunter, gave you Steelcross, promoted me as your captain, and accepted Marrok as your consort. I know none of us takes any of that lightly."

"We don't. Mother will be angry and disappointed. Just as we all are. But she's made plenty of mistakes during her time as matriarch."

Marrok cough-laughed. "That's what you're going with? Really, Oriana? Kalinda will eat you alive, and you'll be the one returning home with parts of your body missing, not just the spine she'll rip out of you."

"Okay, Consort, what strategy would you use?"

"Consort, huh? You're going with that play. Fine, add all of Kalinda's poor decisions and mistakes together, add about twenty more for good measure, and tell me what you come up with that rivals us losing track of thirteen hundred muracos."

"Point taken. Just so we're clear, you two are blameless." They began to protest, but she raised her hand, and they quieted. "It doesn't matter that you're my captain or that you're my consort. I'm Matriarch of Steelcross. I'm accountable for everything that happens in this realm, just as protection of Earth Rift's populous falls to me."

Oriana didn't know if she would, in time, become the leader Earth Rift needed and deserved. What she did know, however, was that she needed to ascertain the muraco threat level … then neutralize it.

The muracos had escaped from a location directly within her realm of control, and she hadn't known. Worse, they were aided by women she thought of as allies. The thought of their duplicity hurt worse than being injected with liquid steel.

Solange moved toward the conference room door. "I'll leave you two alone to talk. Call me after you return from Iron Spire. We have a lot to do. The more I think about it, Marrok's probably right about the human regions. I'll pull together three investigative teams for the footage analysis. When they finish, we'll have data upon which we can make strong decisions." Solange smiled her shit-eating grin again. "Try not to jump into a locked closet."

"Once. I did that once when we were ten, you mage cow."

"Once is all it takes. You were in there for three hours because you made a mistake and cast a looping spell."

Oriana slapped her hand over Marrok's mouth. "She's not funny. Stop laughing."

"After a housekeeper found her, she told everyone we were playing hide-and-seek and she had won."

Solange tossed some braids over her shoulder with a smirk, stuck out her tongue at Oriana, the way she did when they were girls, and left.

"Yuck! You got saliva on my hand."

"I was laughing. That's what you get for covering my mouth." Marrok wiped away laugh tears—his grin big, beautiful, and very sexy.

Oriana kissed him.

Winding his arms around her waist, he slid her from her chair and onto his lap. "Kiss me with your magic."

"You know that doesn't work."

"It does, just not as much as we want it to. But it does work, just as Matriarch Helen wrote."

"We aren't having that conversation now." She tried moving back to her chair, but strong arms kept her put. "Marrok, no."

"Why not? The little magic you feed me through our kisses helps with the hunger pains."

Opening the first four buttons of his shirt, Oriana's fingers hovered over the red rash that began at his nipples and ended at his belly button.

"It's nothing."

"It's not nothing. When I burn you when we make love, at least you heal soon afterward. But these kind of burns stays with you for days. You're allergic to my magic."

"That's not what your grandmother wrote."

"I know what she wrote." Oriana tried pushing from him again, but his arms tightened around her. "Dammit, Marrok, I don't like hurting you, even if the magic kisses give you enough control where you don't feel a need to take short breaks from me."

"I'm not allergic to your magic. I'm allergic to the steel in your body. It comes out in any magic you use on a werewolf. That's what Matriarch Helen wrote. We both read it."

"True, which reminds me of another thought I had. I'm positive Mother never read Grandmother's journals. If she had, she would never have given them to me."

"You're probably right about Kalinda. The most important point isn't Kalinda's perspective but our actions. You aren't your grandmother, and I'm not your grandfather. We don't have to go to the lengths they did. I can take the rashes, if it means I get to stay with you and Keira." Warm lips nuzzled her neck. "Rashes heal, but our hearts won't if we're forced to stay apart."

"We still don't have a solution to our ticking time bomb issue. Mmm, yes, that's good. The things you can do with your lips and tongue."

"Don't tempt me. I'll have you on this table and—"

Oriana kissed him again, pushing wisps of magic from her mouth into his. Careful, she emitted a measured dose. Too much, and he'd be in bed with a fever, painful rashes covering his body.

Through trial and error, they'd learned how much of Oriana's steel-tainted magic Marrok could "safely" consume, just as Helen and Tuncay had done. Helen had recorded every experiment in her journals, noting the amount of magic used each time and details of Tuncay's reaction. Helen had theorized that the amount of magic a witch could "safely" use on a werewolf depended on the strength of the witch's magic, the werewolf's age and overall health, and how strong his cravings were for witch blood and magic. Helen's formula for her consort was more of a guide than an exact recipe.

The way Marrok gripped her waist, claimed her mouth, swallowed down her magic, fierce and desperate, she knew he wanted more. Not sex, although he'd take the offer. He always did. But more of her magic. His need pulsed in the air around them, could be tasted on the tongue plundering her mouth.

She pulled her lips away from his.

"Don't stop." The words were spoken around elongated eyeteeth.

Oriana touched a fang.

Marrok pulled away from her touch. "Don't do that. I don't know what would happen if you cut your finger and I smelled and tasted your blood."

Fangs retracted as quickly as they'd appeared.

Oriana trusted Marrok not to hurt her, but she wouldn't tempt fate. Marrok finally let her go, and she returned to her chair.

"Thank you."

"You won't be thanking me when you break out in another rash. This isn't our answer."

"And you doing what Helen attempted is?"

"I won't ever do that. I promised you I wouldn't." Oriana didn't have a death wish, so keeping her promise would be easy.

"We'll work something out before Keira turns twelve."

"I hope so."

"We will. As soon as we deal with the muraco situation, we can turn our attention back to our research. Are you positive we have all of Matriarch Helen's personal records?" Marrok asked.

"I assume you don't think we do, if you're asking."

"I'm unsure. Some entries are daily then the next is weeks or months later."

"She was busy. Most days, I'm lucky to get home before you put Keira to bed."

"That's only because you're also Crimson Hunter. But, yeah, I know matriarch's schedules are tight."

"But you still think journal entries are missing?"

"Not just single entries. More like entire journals. They're all dated, so it's easy to follow. Haven't you noticed how one journal will end on a topic, but the next will pick up with a different one?"

"Yes, but, as I said, I took that to mean Grandmother was too busy to fill in what happened in the interim. It's not as if she wrote her journals for anyone other than herself. She was her only audience, so it makes sense that she wouldn't write every detail of her life in her journals."

"I know, I know."

"You're frustrated." Touching the side of his face, she smiled when he turned to kiss her palm. "I'll ask Mother if there are more journals. Based on what we've read, I think it's safe to conclude that Grandmother figured out why Alba destroyed so many historical records."

"You think that because of Helen's final experiment?"

"Yes." Oriana lowered her hand to her lap. "Maybe you're right about missing journals because I've read nothing to explain why she thought it a good idea to cut into her arms and legs. We've read her archives, so we know she wasn't insane, but she wound up killing herself and others in a dangerous experiment. I have no clue what she hoped to achieve."

"I'll reread her journals while you're away hunting muracos. Maybe we missed something. Or I could go with you. Come on, don't shake your head."

"I won't risk you getting bit by a muraco. You know what'll happen if you do."

"Madness or death," he droned, his voice lacking the seriousness the awful possibilities warranted.

"The saliva of a muraco is more poisonous to black werewolves than metal. With my magic kiss, you'll only get a rash and fever, but contact with the blood or saliva of a white werewolf will change you in ways I don't want to think about."

The prospect of her sweet Marrok turning feral—not because his bloodlust had been so great he'd pushed past the magic in his silver snare to attack a witch and drink her blood, but because a crazed muraco took away his free will—brought out every protective instinct inside her.

"I'll be careful. I could help you."

"No!" Shit, she hadn't meant the word to come out as a command, but Marrok's flared nostrils confirmed he'd heard the unintended order. "I didn't mean—"

He shoved his chair back, putting more than physical distance between them. "I get it."

"You don't, and I don't have time to argue."

"We aren't arguing. I said I get it."

One of these days Marrok would learn how to align his facial expressions with his lies.

"I'm sorry for hurting you. I want our marriage to be one of equals. I'm trying my best, but it's not easy. The kind of marriage I want us to have goes against everything I've seen and been raised to believe. You're free to make your own decisions, Marrok, regardless of whether they conflict with my opinion and desires. At the same time, you need to know I'll never shirk my duty."

"As matriarch and Crimson Hunter?"

"No, as your mate."

Pulling her chair farther from the conference table, Marrok knelt in front of her. Hands grasping hers, he brought them to his mouth and kissed. "You can't stand between me and everything. That's not how life works."

"I refuse to accept what you're saying." She knew Marrok was talking about more than just himself. "Keira is our daughter. I won't let her be hurt. Ever. And I won't have our son injected with a damn rage disruptor. I hate you being in that silver snare."

Oriana refused to cry, but she couldn't help the high pitch her voice had taken or the tremors running though her body. She wanted to sink into the strong arms Marrok wrapped around her, to give in to the unacceptable because battling a tidal wave wasn't a war any mortal could win.

Her life would be easier if she accepted the way things were, the way society had been for over a millennium. Except … Oriana's life wouldn't be easier because she wouldn't have Marrok … and she wouldn't have herself.

"You're stubborn as hell."

"I know." A tear escaped. Two. Three. More. "I couldn't bear it if something happened to you. I would kill every muraco if it meant keeping you safe."

"That declaration is scarier than your stubbornness. I think I know how Tuncay felt and why he ran into Helen's burning room."

"Because he loved Grandmother."

Leaning back from Oriana, Marrok used the sleeve of his shirt to clean her face. "Yeah, that. But also because she'd spent years working her ass off to give him the same freedoms she'd had her entire life. I'm not blind, Oriana. I see the way your eyes fall to my silver snare when you think I'm not paying attention. You're guilty of nothing. You haven't wronged me."

She glanced down at his open shirt, rash redder after their magic kiss. "It's not about personal wrongs but group oppression. We're products of this society. But where it's granted me power and privilege, it's given you limitations and self-doubt. I may not have created this lopsided system, but I've benefitted from it more than most. If those in power aren't willing to make personal sacrifices, to stop being so damn entitled and scared, then what hope is there for us?"

"Go slow to go fast."

"You keep telling me that. But when is slow too slow?"

"I don't know."

"You do. It's now. It's the reason why we have thirteen hundred unaccounted-for muracos. I wish I could convince myself Mother won't sanction their deaths, but I know she will. I also wish they only had their rage disruptors removed because they want to live in peace and not hurt anyone. But I know, *we know*, oppression breeds hatred, even in the most unlikely of places. We're way past the point of going slow to go fast."

"Where does that leave us then?"

"With me tracking down as many muracos as I can find, and with you re-searching anything that could help us. If Grandmother found something, maybe you can find it too."

Oriana allowed herself to be pulled to her feet when Marrok stood. She thought he would say something about that being the same plan they'd had since the day they married. Or that it had taken Helen decades to unearth whatever it was she'd figured out and that they had far less time than that.

Marrok didn't. He only smiled down at her, his hands still holding hers. There it was. Bold and bright and unapologetic.

His love.

His faith.

She cherished one but felt the undeserved weight of the other.

"Be safe, Oriana. How can we make that son you keep talking about if you let those muracos eat you?" Gathering her close, Marrok whispered into her ear. "I'm the only werewolf allowed to eat you. Remember that."

January 11, 2243
Irongarde Realm
Iron Spire

"Just because it's midday in Steelcross doesn't mean it's the same time here. You also don't jump into your mother's bedroom without warning."

Oriana sat at the foot of Kalinda's bed, smiling as her mother grumbled her way to full wakefulness. Considering what she had to tell Kalinda, Oriana should've been on her best behavior when approaching her mother at two in the morning. But the imp that still lived inside Oriana reared her head and couldn't resist irritating Kalinda. A short-sighted decision since she was there for a serious matter that wouldn't leave either of them smiling.

Kalinda pushed up in bed, propping herself against her vintage, bamboo headboard. The nightstands flanking her bed matched the headboard. For all that Kalinda surrounded herself with steel and iron, not a single piece of furniture in her suite was crafted from metal.

Until her marriage to Marrok, Oriana hadn't understood her mother's outward love of metals but personal preference for natural composite materials like bamboo and other true woods. Oriana surveyed the large bedroom. Nothing had changed since she'd last been there. But the absence of metal reinforced what she'd come to understand about her mother.

"Why are you smiling at me?" Kalinda's hand rose to her head, pushing back stray hairs that had come free of her loose ponytail. "I must look a fright."

"No, you're beautiful."

Whatever self-consciousness that had momentarily gripped Kalinda seeped away with the narrowing of her eyes.

"Why are you here in the middle of the night? Since you're still wearing a silly grin, I assume Keira is well."

"She is. You should visit more often."

"Or you could've brought my granddaughter with you." Kalinda's eyes swept over her king-sized bed. "There's plenty of room. Bring Keira to me tomorrow. She can stay until one of us tires of the other."

Oriana grinned, but wanted to roll her eyes. "You're warm-hearted beyond words, Mother."

"Indeed. Now, tell me what you've done or failed to do."

Kicking off her high-heeled shoes, Oriana drew her legs onto the bed, sitting cross-legged and facing her mother's outstretched legs. "When Marrok moved to Steel Rise, I had my suite redecorated."

"I am aware. I've been in your suite of rooms. Why are you telling me what I already know?"

It was a pointless stalling tactic, but one Oriana found amusing.

"Wood furniture. No metal."

"Again, I know."

Oriana pointed to the open bedroom door that led to the sitting area then to the bathroom to her left. "Your suite is also metal-free. You even have bamboo floors throughout."

"Yes, I'm well acquainted with my living space. Are you planning on stepping down from the Matriarchy and taking up the glamorous career of interior design?"

Despite Kalinda's haughty tone, Oriana heard the smile in her voice, although she wore a too-familiar scowl.

"I changed the furniture in my suite for Marrok's comfort. Why did you change yours?"

Kalinda's right eyebrow rose, lips thinned, and hands twisted in the duvet across her lap.

"Better question, why did you keep the bamboo and wood furniture after Father left?" Oriana snapped her fingers. "Oh, I have an even better question than that one. Has Father been back in this room since the two of you separ—"

"Oriana!"

Kalinda's embarrassed snap shut her up.

"You're an awful brat when you've done something terrible you don't want to confess. One would think you'd be a model child on those occasions, but you're the queen of emotional distractions. Stop wasting time and tell me what's happened."

When Kalinda crossed her arms over her chest, not a sliver of softness coming from her, Oriana stretched out on the bed, resigned to her fate. She shared every ugly detail. Oriana may have taken a playful detour when she'd arrived, but once she began speaking of the offline rage disruptors and missing muraco, she delivered the news with the gravity the situation deserved.

When Oriana was a girl, skipping from one topic to the next, Kalinda never treated her youthful musings as unimportant. She listened with patience, if not feigned interest. Kalinda had a way of making Oriana feel as if her opinions mattered. She still treated her that way, maintaining eye contact and not interrupting until Oriana had exhausted herself.

When she finished, an apology spilled from her.

Kalinda said nothing, but magic sparked from hands curled into fists. She didn't even look at Oriana. Her eyes were closed, head and shoulders pressed against the headboard, as if forcing herself not to lunge at Oriana, shaking her shoulders while yelling, "I told you we weren't ready, but you wouldn't listen. You had to have things your way. It will be your fault if anyone is injured or killed as a result of your idealism."

"I'm sorry, Mother."

"Stop saying that," she barked, eyes now wide-open and glowering. Rubbing the bridge of her nose, Kalinda appeared outraged enough to break the metal wall around Steelburgh with her bare hands. "I don't want to hear another apology. They're meaningless. Being sorry solves *nothing*. You've already determined the culprits. The reason behind their traitorous actions is simple. It's the same objection I had when you started your damn crusade."

Force of habit had Oriana opening her mouth to contest her mother's reductionist way of viewing her efforts to bridge the divide between witches and werewolves, but a scalding look from Kalinda had her swallowing her pride and closing her mouth.

"Be that as it may, we can't excuse what they've done. You know the penalty for such an act, and so do they. They knew they would be caught. It was inevitable, and so is what you must do."

She'd overhead people refer to Kalinda as "heartless" and "cold." Oriana couldn't fault their assessment, not that she agreed. But Kalinda's steely calm was legendary, even among her family and friends.

Kalinda had indeed warned Oriana. Her mother's wisdom hadn't been lost on her. She had known Kalinda had a point, but she'd thought her perspective the more valid of the two. She still didn't think herself wrong, at least not in the grander scheme of where she believed Earth Rift needed to go as the planet and its people moved forward.

"No one is a villain here, Oriana. And when this is over, you won't feel like a hero. There are no winners. In this, we're all losers."

When Oriana was twelve, she'd been thrown from a horse. No broken bones, but she'd run into her mother's office with plenty of cuts and scrapes, her face streaked with dirt and tears. Kalinda took one look at Oriana and asked, "Did you get back on your stallion?"

She'd wept out, "No. He's too big for me."

Kalinda had stood from her desk, walked to a bleeding, shivering Oriana, placed her hands on her shoulders, and turned her back toward the office door. "If you're going to cry, at least do it atop your mount."

Ashamed and angry, Oriana had stormed from her mother's office, crying for a different reason. Two days later, she was back in the stables, staring down the horse that had thrown her. The animal wasn't her enemy. He was just doing what came naturally to him when she tried to make him submit to her will. Eventually, she did ride the stallion. Kalinda didn't praise Oriana or even comment on her success. A week later, however, she found a new saddle on her saddle stand with a brass plate that read: Oriana-MoS.

Of course, at twelve, she hadn't been Matriarch of Steelcross, but Kalinda's vision for Oriana was clear. Oriana's vision for Earth Rift was equally as clear, but not everyone shared her outlook for the future.

"Do your duty, Crimson Hunter."

Oriana felt twelve again, sensing her mother's hands on her shoulders while she pushed her toward the door. As a child, she'd misinterpreted Kalinda's response, and she had good reason to think the Matriarch of Irongarde heartless and cold. Yet, whenever Oriana fell or failed, Kalinda was there, stern and unyielding, telling her in a dozen different ways to cry all she wanted as long as she did it from atop a fear she'd conquered.

Rolling off the bed, she found her shoes and put them back on. "I'll take care of it."

"I know you will. Afterward, return here at a decent hour, and bring my granddaughter. We'll speak then about how we'll handle the muraco situation." Sliding down the bed, Kalinda snapped her fingers, and the light Oriana had turned on when she'd arrived winked out. "Go home, daughter, and rid your realm of our betrayers. Treason deserves only one response."

Oriana stood there beside Kalinda's bed. The stallion had truly been too big and wild for Oriana to handle with ease, but Kalinda had gifted it to her anyway. She had to have known Oriana would fail. What twelve-year-old wouldn't have?

Yes, she'd failed, but she'd also learned the power of perseverance at an age when falling had far fewer consequences. No, Kalinda wasn't heartless or cold but she was one hard-as-steel mother and teacher.

"Did you give me all of Grandmother's journals?"

"Why would you think I haven't?"

"There are time gaps, which makes me think I don't have them all."

"At this point, don't you think you have more important issues to contend with than my mother's old journals?"

"Yes, but—"

"If you couldn't find what you were looking for in Mother's journals then perhaps there's nothing more to them than the ramblings of a woman who allowed her obsession to spiral so far out of control it killed her and two other people."

"I know, but Grandmother—"

"Goodbye, Crimson Hunter." Sharp. Final. "Don't return until you've dealt with the situation."

Oriana left, jumping through the ether of space, Kalinda's command a cutting slash to the heart.

Crimson Hunter, she'd called her, a reminder of Oriana's duty. She would perform her duty, as she always did. As she always would.

Sitting under a tree in the Steel Rise garden, Marrok's attention was divided between reading an entry from Matriarch Helen's journal and watching his toddler play. Keira loved the outdoors as much as Marrok. So, when time permitted and the weather inviting, they would spend their afternoons among the solar cedars, kindwalnuts, and the sweet-smelling red touch-me-not and purple winterberry flowers. He read …

The residents of Bronze Ward are struggling, but it was to be expected. Few emotions, save love, are more powerful than hope. I'm hopeful. Tuncay is hopeful. The witches and werewolves of Bronze Ward are hopeful. Even

with so much hope, thick enough to choke on, fear of failure keeps me awake at night.

Tuncay wants to continue our experiments. He assures me he can handle the iron in my magic kisses. But I've seen the rashes, rubbed his back during violent vomiting spells, and called a healer when his fever wouldn't abate.

Normally I would move forward with a decision, if short-term deficits resulted in long-term gains. When it comes to my consort, however, the potential long-term benefits of our experiments do not outweigh the pain he suffers, short-term as they may be. We disagree on this point. There must be a better way.

For now, I'll concentrate on Bronze Ward—another perfectly imperfect experiment. Soon, though, I'll have to turn my attention to ensuring the line of succession. I've pretended not to notice the rumblings of discontent over how long I've waited to give Earth Rift its next matriarch. The foolish girl inside the mature woman hoped—yes, there's that word again—that I could solve the ills of the world before bringing my child into it. So very naïve of me, but I would like my daughter's reign as matriarch to be unburdened from the weight of decrees that keep us shackled to the past, our laws devoid of a vision beyond maintenance of the same mission—safeguard witches from werewolves.

"Daddy, look."

Marrok lifted his gaze from the tablet and toward the sound of his daughter's voice. Dressed in pink leggings, a white and pink polka dot shirt, and a pair of white tennis shoes scuffed from hard play, Keira wore the biggest, cutest, and the most mischievous grin he'd ever seen from his daughter.

"What do you have?" Placing his tablet on the grass, Marrok stood and walked toward Keira.

"Look. Look." She bounced on her toes. Her eyes were cheerful but not as bright as the red streaks of hair that had come loose from her ponytail. It was the only hairstyle Marrok could manage on his own. Thank the moon above, Oriana normally took care of Keira's hair. "Look."

"I see." Marrok grimaced at the ruined flowerbed behind his beaming daughter. The same white tennis shoes that looked so cute on her feet had trampled dozens of touch-me-nots. Those that remained where clutched in her chubby hands.

"Mommy."

Of course Keira had picked the flowers for Oriana. It wasn't the first time she'd done the same. Although, the last time Keira had made a similar mess he'd promised Oriana he would keep a better eye on her. *Note to self. No more reading while on dad duty.*

He scooped his daughter into his arms. "Are you trying to get me into trouble?"

"Trouble," Keira repeated.

"Yes, trouble."

Keira shook her head. "No trouble."

"Don't give me that innocent face."

In response, Keira placed a wet sloppy kiss to his cheek.

Marrok all but melted. He would do anything for his little girl.

Fight for her.

Die for her.

10: The Price of Leadership

April 15, 2243
Steelcross Realm
City of Steelburgh

Nine thousand eight hundred fifty werewolves were supposed to be residing in Steelburgh. One thousand three hundred forty-five were unaccounted for. One hundred forty-five more missing muraco than originally thought.

"Are you all right?" Oriana's hand slipped into Marrok's, but he could barely feel her comfort over the disbelief of driving through a city surrounded by a seventy-foot-high, twenty-foot-deep steel wall.

"I know it's shocking. I tried to prepare you. From the way you can't stop staring out the window and how cold your hand is, I didn't do a very good job."

Steel buildings were everywhere he looked—homes, businesses, even the roads were made of steel. No trees. No flowers. Just endless miles of metal. He'd never seen a more modern-looking city. Only Irongarde compared, except no tower of glass and iron claimed the center of that city.

Yeah, Oriana had told him about the city of metal and muracos. White werewolves were everywhere, going about their day until they caught a glimpse of Oriana's black limo driving past. They would stop, snarl, and point when they spotted the car. The Matriarch of Steelcross's flag, a steel gray spiral sun, was mounted on the center of the roof, leaving no doubt who the vehicle belonged to and who was inside. Despite the gawking and growls, no one dared attack a vehicle made of, what else, reinforced steel, and carrying the Crimson Hunter.

"I-I had no idea."

"That's because no one wants to know what the matriarchy does with muracos after they're arrested. Black werewolves don't want to support a policy that condones government-sanctioned killing of werewolves, but they also don't want muracos returned to their communities. Out of sight, out of mind works for most people."

"Who knows they're here?"

"Their families and friends. But most muracos lose one or both when they turn into a white werewolf. Although they've served their full sentence, they're too dangerous to be reintegrated into normal society. In good conscience, we can't ever permit them to rejoin the general population."

"I know but …"

The car stopped in front of a wedged-shaped building. It was thirty-five stories—the tallest in the city—and headquarters for the Steelburgh Crimson Guard.

Oriana had never lied to him. There were simply parts of being Matriarch of Steelcross she couldn't share with him until they were married. She was right. Marrok hadn't wanted to know. So, he had avoided asking questions he didn't want to know the answers to but which Oriana would've given if he had shown an interest. He relished his bubble of ignorance until over thirteen hundred muracos had disappeared.

Closing his eyes, he leaned back, letting his head fall against the leather upholstery. Oriana still held his hand, even as she told the driver, through the communication system to, "Return us to security checkpoint one, Nahara. Thank you."

The Crimson Guard, a member of Oriana's Barrage Division, and her personal driver, made a sharp U-turn. Oriana never minded the witch's questionable driving skills, probably because she drove the same way—reckless and perpetually in a hurry.

Bad witch driver aside, Marrok knew why Oriana had opted for a scenic drive around the city. It was the same reason she'd taken him to Bronze Ward before she'd begun renovations. To understand, not simply to know on an intellectual level, one had to see—not from a distance but as close as one could get and be safe while having the experience.

"By the time this is over, I'm going to have so much werewolf blood on my hands, I won't be able to wash it all off. But I needed you to see for yourself, to know I've done my best to keep them safe. And to keep everyone safe from them."

Oriana tugged her hand, but Marrok refused to let her go.

He opened his eyes, unsurprised to find Oriana staring at the palm of her free hand, as if muraco blood already stained the deceptively delicate appendage.

"By putting Steelburgh in this realm, Kalinda made you a warden."

"Someone has to rule Steelcross."

"Then it should've been her."

"It was all on her for years. Overseeing Steelburgh is part of what it means to be Matriarch of Steelcross. Irongarde is a larger realm and has all the muraco-only prisons, while Steelcross has the one muraco city. She has the more difficult job, Marrok, but I'm the one who screwed up."

Marrok wanted to hold Oriana, to comfort her the way she'd tried to soothe him earlier. He hadn't been receptive then, and he doubted she would be receptive now. So, he stopped protesting and listened without judging, interrupting, or offering solutions to a problem he didn't fully comprehend.

Oriana pointed out the window to the steel wall. "How do you feel being in here?"

Marrok didn't have to contemplate her question. His answer leapt to his mind and out his mouth. "Like a werewolf in a gilded cage. The city is beautiful in a sterile, morbid kind of way. It's depressing and, if I ever ended up here, I'd want to jump from the Crimson Guard building and kill myself."

Not hyperbole. He couldn't imagine spending the rest of his life locked away, no matter how luxurious the cage.

"That has happened. But werewolves are strong, so the fall doesn't kill them. Although, with the amount of damage their bodies suffered, they regretted the ill-planned suicide attempt. The silver snares are ineffective on muraco."

"That's not strictly true, is it? Can't you increase the dose of magic emitted from the silver snares?"

"Sure, if we want to fry their brains." Oriana shifted sideways in the seat, her long black coat parting enough for him to see her red-and-black Crimson Hunter body armor underneath. "I don't need historical documents to know Grandmother wasn't the only matriarch to perform experiments. The spells we use for rage disruptors are specific to the DNA of werewolves. It had to have taken months, if not years, to perfect. Think about it, Marrok. Imagine what had to have happened back then. Do you think werewolves volunteered to be test subjects? Or that witches got it right the first time or even the fiftieth?"

"I can't see either happening. That is so messed up."

"You do have a tendency toward understatement. The bottom line is that the slightest alteration of the spells will kill werewolves, turn their brains to mush, or invalidate the spells. I told you that witches were the true beasts, but you didn't believe me. You wondered why I didn't step down from the post of Crimson Hunter when I became matriarch, and again when I was pregnant with Keira. Do you understand now?"

Marrok thought he did. "Kalinda wanted you in both roles, didn't she?"

"She's always wanted me to become Matriarch of Steelcross. It's what I've trained to do my entire life. At the same time, Mother wants to keep me under her thumb for as long as she can. If I'm also Crimson Hunter, she can command me to do her will, and I must obey. When I'm acting in that role, we're not equals."

Marrok considered several responses, but all of them included words like "bitch," "mercenary," and "manipulative." He couldn't say anything about Kalinda that wouldn't end with Oriana defending her mother and get them into a pointless argument. But, dammit, his mother-in-law *was* a manipulative, mercenary bitch. Worse, she knew it and didn't care.

Avoiding the impulse to protect his mate against a mother she would never see through clear eyes, Marrok latched onto another thought. "You talk about me and understatements. What about you?"

Oriana frowned. "What do you mean?"

"Steelburgh is new and shiny, an old city brought back to life the same way you want to revive Bronze Ward. But this city was your first project, wasn't it?"

"Yes, I told you—"

"You told me you watched over the city because it was within the larger Steelcross Realm, not that this was your brainchild the same way a collar-free Janus Nether was your idea."

He smiled at his mate, proud of the work she'd done on behalf of werewolves, even muracos who, without this city, would still be languishing in either Moonblight Penitentiary or Dogscar Correctional Facility.

"Yes, they were all my ideas, but I didn't anticipate the backlash. Mother trusted me to be matriarch and Crimson Hunter, but I let her down."

"How? What do you mean by backlash?"

Red streaked hair fell over Oriana's face, her head dipping as if in prayer. Sighing, she breathed deeply, and pushed hair out of eyes gone wet.

"Why are you crying?"

Oriana slipped one arm out of her coat. The red of her body armor was nearly the same shade as her red streaked hair. "Do you want to know how over thirteen hundred muracos escaped Steelburgh?"

After seeing the walled-off city, he had no idea how they had.

The other arm followed the first, the garment dropping to the seat behind her. "The same way we entered."

Magic filled the car. A familiar whip encircled his waist. Marrok's stomach clenched, but the sensation didn't have him puking up his breakfast.

He braced for a hard impact, one hand on the door handle, the other clutching Oriana to him. But the teeth-rattling, spine-tingling jolt never came.

Opening eyes he hadn't known he'd closed, Marrok looked at Oriana and then to the window behind her.

When they'd stopped in front of a smooth, unified wall, no door, gate, or obvious entry point, Marrok had cast a questioning look at Oriana. She had given him a couple of minutes to prepare for the jump. This time, she'd given him none.

"Where are we?"

"Elio Desert."

Okay, yeah, he could see the barren landscape. The pink hue of the sand was breathtaking. Elio Desert was in the human territory of Aphelion Umbra. Oriana's extraction magic had taken them from the Northern Hemisphere to the Western, all in a single, only slightly nauseating, jump.

"Why are we here?"

"Because the only way the muracos could've escaped from Steelburgh and had their rage disruptors removed was with help from witches—not just any witches, but Crimson Guards."

No, that couldn't be right. "Your guards are loyal. They wouldn't betray you or the Matriarchy. Why would they?" As soon as the last sentence slipped past his lips, he regretted the naïve question.

Backlash, she'd said. Janus Nether. Steelburgh. Bronze Ward. Cyrus of Steelcross.

Snap, snap, snap, snap, all the pieces fit together. Combined, it was a canvas portrait painted with brush strokes of care and a palette of good intentions but hung in the homes of people who preferred reading to artwork. The unasked-for change jarring, like Oriana's magic jumps could be.

"I'm sorry."

"You don't owe me an apology. Even if I hadn't met and married you, I would've made the same decisions, been the same kind of matriarch, and challenged the status quo. My choices, Marrok."

She was telling him to allow her the dignity of her actions, no matter the unanticipated results. He would, not because she'd left him no option but to agree, but because she wouldn't be the witch he loved and married without her fierce heart.

Nahara's dulcet voice interrupted them. "They've arrived, Matriarch. Do you wish for me to stay in the car with Cyrus Marrok?"

"I'm not staying in the car," he yelled to Nahara, not bothering to use the communication system. Oriana's eyebrow went northward in a way that reminded him far too much of Kalinda. "We're not arguing about this," he said in a more reasonable tone. "The windows may be tinted but I sure as hell can see out. There are at least fifteen Crimson Guards out there."

"Nineteen guards, one healer, and two data technicians." Oriana grabbed his hand. "Are you sure?"

"That I want to stand by your side? Hell, yes, I'm sure."

"Not that. It's just. Well, I'm Crimson Hunter."

"I know."

Oriana rolled her eyes and shook her head. Not at all like Kalinda but very much like a mate burdened with a clueless, stubborn consort. "You really don't, but fine. Let's go."

Marrok reached across Oriana, opening the door for her like the gentleman she rarely gave him a chance to be. The woman had to do everything herself, including confronting twenty-two witches.

He followed her out of the limo. Nahara had also exited. The sun shone brightly overhead. The air was thick, the temperature uncomfortably high. The region, heat, and sun's rays sapped the strength of werewolves but bolstered the magic of witches.

Witches stood in a semicircle—some in Crimson Guard uniforms, others in civilian clothing. Remnants of extraction magic leeched away from them, a multi-looped lariat retreating to its source. Solange, captain of the Hunter Division, strolled away from the semicircle of witches to stand between Oriana and Nahara.

Marrok positioned himself to Oriana's left, his focus on the group of witches thirty feet in front of him. They neither seemed shocked nor angry at having Solange rip them away from wherever they were or whatever they'd been doing and dropping them in the middle of Elio Desert.

Removing his coat, socks, and shoes, Marrok tossed them onto the backseat of the car. He proceeded to undress, every witches' eyes on him except for the three to his right. If Oriana didn't know what Marrok meant when he'd said he would stand by her side, his shift from human to werewolf made his intention clear.

"What is this?" a tall, slim witch asked, her blonde hair cut short except for long bangs that covered a hazel eye. "Are you planning on permitting your consort to attack us?"

Oriana stepped forward.

Marrok was tempted to do the same. He didn't know what it took to push past the magic constraints of his silver snare and rage disruptor, but he'd find the strength to make it happen if those witches attacked Oriana.

A gentle hand settled on his warm arm, far enough away from his sharp claws to avoid an accidental cut.

Marrok glanced downward, taking in Solange whose gaze never left Oriana, even when she leaned in close and whispered, "As Crimson Hunter, she's duty-bound to clean her own house. As matriarch, she cannot allow a flagrant challenge to her rules to go unpunished. No one is above the law, Marrok, not even the witches sworn to uphold them."

He couldn't verbally acknowledge her words, so Marrok inclined his head. Just as there were practices and protocols unique to the werewolf culture, the same was true for witches. If Solange and Nahara could stay on the sidelines without interfering, so could Marrok.

Maybe.

Oriana didn't respond to the blonde's ridiculous question. Besides being insulting to Marrok, as if he were a trained dog Oriana commanded, the question implied the Matriarch of Steelcross was incapable of handling the situation herself.

"You should've come to me, Abelone."

Oriana dug the tip of her right booted foot into the unmarred sand. While he couldn't see his mate's face, no doubt she bit her lower lip—a telltale sign of her anxiety. Was this the price Oriana had to pay for thinking life for witches and werewolves could be different, for envisioning a future where werewolves were more valued than feared, witches more egalitarian than controlling, and families more cohesive than splintered? If so, would she view the cost a worthy payment for a dream she would still fight to achieve? Or would she succumb to self-doubt, her sun eclipsed by others' uninspired moon?

"Any of you could've come to me. Instead, you lied, violating my trust and faith."

"You wouldn't have listened."

"You say that, but you know it's not true." The foot digging into the sand stopped. Oriana's body went still. "Unless you all think me a tyrant, what Abelone said is bullshit. You didn't speak with me about your discontent, not because I'm closed-minded but because it's easier to fear and rail against change than it is to roll up your sleeves and do the hard work of rebuilding. Yes, that means making mistakes. But look at us." She swung her hand in Marrok's direction. "We make our males wear collars, and they submit because we're all convinced there's no better way to live and be safe. We've stopped trying to find a solution. Hell, maybe witches never tried because why fix a broken system that entitles us to so much, even if it condemns them to so little?"

"They don't deserve your sympathy, Matriarch."

Perhaps the blonde, Abelone, was the leader of the group because no one else spoke.

Abelone pointed to Marrok, face red more from disdain for werewolves than from the sun beating down on them.

"They are in silver snares for a reason. We can't trust them because they can't trust themselves not to hurt us. The muracos will remind everyone who and what werewolves truly are."

The way she threw her arms up at him, he thought the witch would turn her arms into deadly metal weapons. Apparently, so did Solange and Nahara because they stepped in front of him.

The physical threat never manifested. Abelone still attacked him, but with words rather than magic.

"One of these days, he'll turn on you. It's in his nature. He won't be able to help himself. He'll kill you if given a chance, no matter how much he's professed his love. No matter that you're the mother of his child. No matter that—"

"Enough!" Oriana took another step forward, shoulders squared, voice like iron. "Abelone of Copper Vale, you have been found guilty of aiding and abetting in the escape of one thousand three hundred forty-five muracos—an act of treason punishable by death. As Matriarch of Steelcross, I hereby sentence you to death by my hand."

Not as Crimson Hunter, the enforcing hand of Matriarch Kalinda, but as Matriarch of Steelcross. In what world did Kalinda think she could ever exert full control over Oriana? Certainly not this one. Yet, there was something both liberating and frightening about the depth of his mate's convictions.

Much of Earth Rift's early history was destroyed, but what remained included not only the war between witches and werewolves but the short-lived, brutal battles between witch families. When the magic smoke had cleared, the Blood of the Sun family reigned supreme, and they had ruled Earth Rift ever since.

As dissimilar as they were, Oriana and Kalinda were products of their powerful lineage. That startling truth about his mate was all too evident in her proclamation, an executioner committed to delivering the death blow because that awful responsibility fell to her alone.

Oriana's arms began to glow yellow and red. Electromagic discharges shot from her fingertips. Within seconds, the lower half of her arms were gone, replaced by Ravagers of the Lost cannons, the barrels, for the moment, pointing toward the scorching sand beneath their feet.

Abelone flicked her gaze to Marrok, her arms still raised. Hatred radiated from her toward him, more potent than the stifling heat.

He growled. Marrok could be at Abelone's throat before she had a chance to shoot Oriana or get to him. The thought of ripping her throat out in self-defense should've disturbed him. It didn't. What did unsettle him was the mouthwatering anticipation he felt at the prospect of having witch blood and magic in his mouth, coating his tongue, and sliding down his dry throat.

Disgusted at himself, he stumbled backward, at the same time Abelone lowered her arms.

"Laney of Silverwater, you have been found guilty of aiding and abetting the escape of one thousand three hundred forty-five muraco—an act of treason punishable by death. As Matriarch of Steelcross, I hereby sentence you to death by my hand."

One by one, Oriana named each of the witches, stating their crime and their sentence. No one moved or interrupted. With each recitation, Oriana's magic grew, shifting from yellow and red to bright crimson.

"You've sacrificed your honor. Will you die to restore it? Will you fight for the right to reclaim your integrity?"

Oriana's hair blew in a magic-induced wind. Pink granules levitated off the ground, joining the vortex of magic that began at Oriana's feet, spread upward, and moved outward, encircling the group of witches.

"I am Blood of the Sun, and you are my sisters. You have been judged, but you're also loved by your matriarch."

Solange and Nahara retreated behind the limo. Marrok wanted to stay close to Oriana, but her wind magic worsened, slapping against his body and pushing him backward. Claws found no traction on the sand. Oriana's tornado-like magic drove him to his knees, rattling his bones, watering his eyes, and singeing his fur.

"You will die today, but tomorrow you'll be reborn, part of the sun's chromosphere—glorious and bright red when glimpsed during a solar eclipse. That's when you'll be most remembered. Daughters of the Sun. Let's begin."

A magic whip curled around his waist, yanking him away from the ever-growing vortex. Marrok could no longer see Oriana. She'd vanished inside her magic tornado, and so had the twenty-two witches.

He could see nothing but a vicious swirl of thick crimson fog combined with hydrophobic sand. Attack spells rained down, pelting his ears with each garbled, desperate breath.

"Incineration slash."

"Frenzy blow."

"Blazing shot."

"Destruction whip."

The tornado expanded, lifting the limo and tossing it aside like an insignificant leaf in a windstorm.

"Oh hell," Nahara yelled. "Solange, we need to get out of here."

The whip on his waist tightened, and he thought Solange would jump them away from the battle.

Snarling, he yanked at the glowing whip of magic, but Solange's hold had no give.

"Calm down, Marrok. We're not leaving our matriarch."

Over the howling wind and clash of magic and metal, they jumped. Marrok roared. Solange had said they weren't leaving! Why had she lied? He had to get back to Oriana. Marrok fought against the whip tugging him further away from his mate.

Then he was falling, muzzle-first onto hot sand. They were still in Elio Desert.

Solange shoved his big, hairy leg off her two smaller ones. "I told you we weren't leaving Oriana." Once they were standing, both covered in sand, she shoved him again.

"Are you sure we're far enough away?" Nahara asked.

They hadn't gone far. Marrok could still hear the battle and see Oriana's magic fog. But Solange had put enough distance between them that his ears no longer rang, and his head no longer felt as if it would explode from the stench of heated metal.

But his mouth watered from the blood he could smell in the air.

Dropping to his knees, Marrok shifted.

"I'm glad you shifted. You're a little more reasonable when in your human form. Oriana can stop worrying about you being so close to the battle and seeing the extent of her Blood of the Sun power."

Marrok stood from his crouched position. "How in the hell can you say that so calmly? Oriana is fighting nineteen trained Crimson Guards."

Solange's scoff could've cut through Steel Rise. "If we thought those guards had any chance of beating Oriana, Nahara and I would be with her in that entanglement trap. Don't get me wrong, Oriana is going to be bloody and bruised when she gets out of there. She's atoning for her sins while also giving our sisters the respect they didn't grant her."

"What sins? Oriana didn't do anything wrong."

Rubbing her eyes free of sand, Nahara answered his question, although she coughed her way through most of it. "Sins of silence, partaking, obstinacy. Normal, everyday sins—but not when you're a matriarch, not when your reach is vast, the impact of your actions creating a ripple effect."

Unconvinced but uninterested in a topic that kept him from Oriana, Marrok ignored the witches. He listened to the battle Oriana waged, her firing cannons drowning out cries and curses. She was fighting for her beliefs, for him, for werewolves, even for witches who were victims of the same oppressive system they were afraid of altering.

Blood joined the vortex of magic and sand.

Witches raged.

Sun magic blazed.

And Oriana bellowed, "Hemorrhage Shove."

The vortex exploded, flinging blood, bones, and flesh outward, a grisly defacement of Elio Desert.

Marrok bolted toward his mate, shifting as he ran. Oriana fell.

He caught her. Blood seeped from her mouth, nose, eyes, and ears. Oriana trembled in his arms, her groans soft, breaths labored.

He nuzzled her neck and licked her face, needing her half-closed eyes to stay open and focused on him. Growling at the approaching witches for taking so long but never more relieved than when Solange's magic snaked around him, Marrok held Oriana to his chest, howling when she went limp in his arms.

11: Mother Dear

April 15, 2243
Steelcross Realm
Steel Rise

"How could this have happened? Not one of those disloyal witches should've been strong enough to hurt my daughter, not even the Crimson Guards." Kalinda whirled on Marrok and Solange. "Well, don't just stand there. One of you answer me."

Marrok looked past Kalinda to Oriana, unconscious in their bed, as she had been since passing out in his arms. "Your temper tantrum isn't helping. It didn't help when the healer came—you hovering over her shoulder and barking orders—and it's not helping now. I don't like seeing Oriana hurt any more than you do."

"Then why in the hell is she hurt, hmm? I have yet to hear an adequate response from her consort or her captain. Solange, tell me what happened."

"Umm, well, Matriarch, we—"

Marrok interrupted. "I know you have ultimate control over the Crimson Guard, which I respect. I also know Solange, and Nahara, who's waiting in the sitting area for your directive, will have to give you a report of what happened in Elio Desert. But not in here. You're loud, upset, and angry. I understand the last two. Trust me, I feel the same. But Oriana doesn't need this, not in her room while she's recuperating."

Kalinda, at five-nine, wasn't a short woman, but when she stepped into Marrok's personal space, eyes boiling over with magic, she cast the shadow of a leviathan.

Marrok refused to back up or look away. Oriana had made him Cyrus of Steelcross. Facing down her mother, he wrapped his arms around the title, clutching it to his chest and stepping into the shoes given him.

"Are you telling me to leave?" Kalinda snarled, her teeth white, threat as clear as any werewolf baring his fangs.

"I'm asking you to calm down if you want to stay. This is my home, Kalinda, and Oriana is my mate. I know you're worried about her but—"

"You pick now to grow a pair of balls. Where were they when those traitorous witches were nearly beating my daughter to death?"

The sun and moon had to be testing him. Why else would they put this egotistical, unhinged witch in his orbit? Every response he wanted to make was a statement he knew better than to let leave his mouth. So, Marrok snarled, permitting his fangs to drop from his gums. He didn't know if his eyes glowed red, but he suspected they did from the step Kalinda took backward.

"Oriana fought twenty-two witches at once."

Kalinda winced, as if she'd been struck, which someone really should do because, damn, if there was ever a witch who needed to have some sense slapped into her, it was Matriarch Kalinda.

"Oriana engaged in the drowning shatter ritual?"

"If that's a witch ritual that had her creating a magic tornado vortex and fighting a one-on-twenty-two battle, then yeah, I guess."

"I wasn't speaking to you, Marrok, and do put away those baby fangs of yours. I can barely understand what you're saying, although you've said little worth listening to. My question was for Solange, who thinks she can sneak away while I'm preoccupied with you."

Marrok couldn't fault Solange for taking advantage of what appeared to be an opportunity to get the hell away from Kalinda. He'd never seen this side of the matriarch. Fear wasn't a flattering color on her.

Hand on the doorknob, Solange stopped. For a second, her forehead fell against the closed door, and her shoulders slumped. A sigh and a curse reached his keen ears, but she'd kept it soft enough not to be heard by Kalinda. Turning, she glanced first to Marrok, dark eyes beseeching him to intervene, and then to Kalinda.

Short of tying up and gagging his mother-in-law, Marrok didn't know what in the hell Solange expected him to do. Kalinda was a force of nature who turned into a shrew when her daughter was hurt, and she felt helpless.

Oriana didn't have internal bleeding or swelling on the brain, the healer had told them. "What she does have are abrasions, bruises, and broken bones, all of which will heal. Give her magic time to knit her back together. Three days, a week, at most. She looks worse than she is. Matriarch Oriana will be fine."

The healer had closed Oriana's deeper wounds—the lacerations to her arms and legs. If not for her body armor, the damage would've been more severe. So, yeah, Marrok understood Kalinda's sense of helplessness. But she needed a serious attitude adjustment.

"Matriarch Oriana cast an entanglement trap then engaged in the drowning shatter."

"And you let her?"

"It wasn't for me to question my matriarch. She wanted to give the guilty witches an opportunity to earn their place in the sun and among the stars."

"They were traitors. They weren't worthy of her mercy."

"Perhaps not, but it was her mercy to offer. In the end, they're dead and she lives."

"Oriana is hurt."

Marrok stepped around Kalinda, planting himself next to Oriana on the side of their bed. Touching the hand closest to him, he rubbed his finger from knuckles to wrist.

In a chair on the opposite side of the bed sat Bader. When Kalinda had arrived, Oriana's father had been with her. They were dressed in evening finery—a black tuxedo for Bader and a red ballgown for Kalinda. Unless they had similar but separate plans, Kalinda and Bader had been together when Marrok had called the Matriarch about Oriana.

While Kalinda raged, Bader sat vigil, holding Oriana's hand—his fear a quiet, simmering kind of worry.

"Did she kill all of them?"

With Bader's eyes never leaving Oriana, Marrok didn't know whether his question had been for him or for Solange. Apparently, Solange didn't have the same confusion because she answered.

"All I transported to Elio Desert, yes."

"What does that mean?" For the first time since arriving, Bader's worry bled through in the harsh timber of his voice.

"Matriarch Oriana interviewed one data technician. The girl's nineteen and afraid of her shadow. As soon as Oriana called her into her office, she burst into tears and out flowed the story. She pardoned the girl and sent her back to her mother in Ironmere. The only other Steelburgh-connected witches unaccounted for are Dr. Bhavari of Copper Vale, and Misae of Cobaltpass. Dr. Bhavari is primary healer at Crimson Guard headquarters in Steelburgh and the wife of Abelone of Copper Vale, while Misae is Dr. Bhavari's assistant. My extraction spell included a mind enchantment spell."

"What is a mind enchantment spell?" Marrok asked, turning so he could see Solange.

Kalinda answered, and not, surprisingly, as if she were explaining the phases of the moon to a man-child, but with informative thoughtfulness. "The mind enchantment weaves its way inside one's brain and answers the spellcaster's single question, such as: Were you involved in helping muracos escape from Steelburgh and/or covering up the escape?"

Solange nodded. "That's close to the question I posed. I embedded that spell inside my extraction spell."

"I get it. Only those witches whose enchanted minds revealed their role in the muraco escape and cover-up were transported to Elio Desert."

"That's right. But it didn't transport Dr. Bharavi or Misae."

"Why not those two?" Bader asked.

"My magic couldn't find the healers."

"I see." Good for Bader, but Marrok didn't see. "They are likely using an obstruction spell to block your attempt to locate them, which probably means they're also using a camouflage spell to shield the muracos."

Kalinda paced, reminiscent of a caged beast of prey. "Two witches aren't strong enough to block Solange's magic. There must be other traitors out there working against us."

Now *that* Marrok understood. "How many witches would it take to prevent you from getting a read on Dr. Bhavari?"

As the center of attention, Solange had little choice but to return to the group she'd tried to flee. For better or for worse, they were in this together. With Oriana unconscious, he would speak in her stead, regardless of the objection of anyone, including Kalinda. So, he asked Solange a second question. "Do you think the unknown witches Kalinda mentioned are also hiding the muracos?"

Solange shoved the braids that had worked their way from her ponytail back into place, not that it helped much. They both looked as if they'd gone ten rounds with the desert.

"While I don't know Dr. Bhavari's magic skill level, any doctor licensed in the insertion and removal of rage disruptors has a high degree of mastery. They're precise and patient spellcasters, in a way that Crimson Guards don't have to be. Most guards are more blunt force soldiers. They're trained to efficiently take down and eliminate enemies. No finesse required. As for Misae, her magic skill level is likely less than Dr. Bhavari's."

As if by mutual agreement, they walked away from Oriana and to the other side of the bedroom. They stood in front of the window wall. In a couple of hours, the sun would set. Common sense told him Oriana wouldn't awaken by then to enjoy the sunset with him the way they did when time permitted. But common sense didn't stop Marrok from hoping all the same.

"Kalinda knows Bhavari," Bader informed them, his body angled in the direction of his mate. "If my memory serves, you handpick the healers who receive the rage disruptor certification. Is that still the case?"

"It is. I do know Bhavari, although I haven't had reason to speak with her in years. Misae is an unknown to me. To answer your question, Marrok,

Bhavari is strong enough to block Solange's locater spell, but only if she's concealing a small number of people. Perhaps one or two dozen."

Solange volunteered, "When dealing with werewolves, Oriana and I would normally track them by their rage disruptors, which you know, Marrok. With the escaped muracos, however, we were planning on using locater spells, which target a person's bio signature." Solange snatched the binding from her hair. Limp braids and pink sand fell onto her shoulders, a strange but pretty mix not matched by the witch's expression. "When the healer was in with Oriana, Nahara and I used the time to cast a locater spell. Twenty, actually."

"You're too skilled to require twenty spells to do anything. I take it you and Nahara couldn't find them."

"Not a single muraco, Marrok, and we tried damn hard."

The aku huffed. "This is bad."

Marrok smiled at Bader, hearing Oriana's voice in his head telling him he had a way with understatements.

"If we can't track the muracos, where does that leave us?" Marrok had posed the question to the one person he hated asking anything of. Kalinda would likely view it as confirmation of Marrok's inability to co-rule Steel-cross instead of a smart decision to seek help from an expert.

Kalinda's response revealed what he knew about Oriana's working rela-tionship with Kalinda—she kept nothing from her that involved the safety and rule of Earth Rift. "Oriana told me you believe the muracos are in one of the human regions, maybe Aphelion Umbra because it would've been a shorter magic jump, the region being within Steelcross Realm. But they could also be in Perilune Rille, putting them in Irongarde and closer to Janus Nether."

"If I were a betting werewolf," Bader said, "I'd wager the muraco are in Perilune Rille. I don't think the witches helped them escape just to let them run wild."

Neither did Marrok.

Bader continued, taking a quick look at Oriana first. "From everything we've heard from Marrok and Solange, the witches were upset over Oriana's push to equally include werewolves into society. What better way to undermine her efforts than to drop a large number of muraco in the middle of Janus Nether? We know what they'll do if they're loose in that area."

"Go straight for black werewolves," Marrok said, a heavy feeling of foreboding in his chest. "They'll try to turn as many as they can. Once they do, they'll head for the seat of Earth Rift's power—Kalinda and Irongarde City."

"If I didn't know better, I'd say you sound worried about my safety."

"Leave him alone, Kalinda. Your claws are bigger and deadlier than mine. Sheath them, please. It's not Marrok's fault Oriana is hurt, so stop blaming him. He didn't have a lifetime of preparation for this role any more than I did. Marrok is doing his best. Everyone can see that, except for you."

How a werewolf as self-possessed and kind as Aku Bader had married a witch like Kalinda, Marrok would never understand. But the werewolf must've been a bear tamer in a former life because Matriarch Kalinda nodded once to Bader before turning on her high heels and stalking away from them and back to Oriana. Claiming the seat vacated by her consort, Kalinda held Oriana's hand, effectively withdrawing from the conversation.

"Don't mind my mate, Marrok. Kalinda can govern a planet with ease but let someone she loves get hurt and she loses it."

"It's fine. I know Kalinda doesn't like me."

"It isn't fine, but Kalinda dislikes anyone she's forced to share her daughter with, including me." Bader tilted his head toward Solange, who appeared as if she were contemplating her odds of making it out of the bedroom before Kalinda recalled she hadn't received a full oral report from her. "Including Solange. The only exception is Keira, and that's because Kalinda views her as an extension of Oriana." As he'd done in Kalinda's library the night of Keira's birth, Bader hugged Marrok. "You'll grow on her."

"Like ringworm?"

Bader chuckled. "Yes, I'm sure Kalinda thinks of us all as fungal bacteria, as infections in need of treatment." The aku grabbed Solange and hugged her too. The witch wrapped her arms around him with a comfort that came with familiarity and trust. "Thank you and Nahara for watching over Oriana. She chose this path for herself. The physical pain she'll feel upon waking won't compare to how she'll feel on the inside after taking the lives of her sisters. Kalinda doesn't understand, but I do."

There was a hell of a lot Kalinda didn't understand about Oriana. In fairness, Marrok also took issue with Oriana permitting herself to be physically injured. The witches had earned their fate. Still, he wasn't the one responsible for following through with the death penalties. Would he view Oriana's actions differently, if it were his hands used to usher people from life into death?

Bader released Solange. "Go, and take Nahara with you."

"Are you sure?"

"You mean, will Kalinda be upset I sent you and Nahara home?" Bader shrugged. "It's nothing I can't handle. You're tired. Go. Shower. Sleep. Tell your mother I said hello, and thank her for training my daughter so well she was able to survive a fight with twenty-two witches."

Solange's grin reminded Marrok of how young they all were, despite their grown-up responsibilities.

Solange wasted no time using her magic to jump from the bedroom.

"Smart girl. Listen, Marrok, I'm here, and Kalinda's here. Go see Keira before she starts crying for her mother again."

Kalinda had selected her consort well. Bader knew how to get his way without insults, guilt, or arguments. By appealing to the father in Marrok, he circumvented any protest to the suggestion that he shower, eat, or do anything other than wait by Oriana's side.

"If Oriana's condition changes, we'll send for you right away."

Even knowing he needed to check on his daughter, the way Oriana would want him to, Marrok paused, unable to make his legs move.

Bader pushed him toward the closed bedroom door. "We'll take care of her."

He knew they would. With a final glance to Oriana, Marrok left. After spending time with Keira, Marrok would try reaching Zev again. His brother had been pissed at him since he had married Oriana and moved to Steelcross. Because Zev had refused to visit, Marrok had to drag his ass to Wild Moor whenever he wanted to spend time with his oldest brother. That had gotten old real fast, but Marrok had put in the miles anyway.

When not talking about Oriana, the brothers got along—as well as anyone could with Zev. But his brother was being an asshole and, for some reason, not answering or returning his calls. Yeah, he would call him repeatedly until the jerk got over whatever had crawled up his ass and answered his phone. If Zev didn't, he would wait until Oriana was feeling better then he would catch a Magerun transporter to Wild Moor. Either way, he would find out what was going on with his brother.

April 18, 2243
Perilune Rille
Apogean Tide Borough

Bhavari watched the werewolf on the operating table struggle against his wrist and leg shackles. The chains moored to the concrete floor and wall would do the job.

"The chains are made of steel. I've reinforced them with magic, and you're in human form. You're wasting both of our time. You can't escape."

"Fuck you. When I get out of here, I'll slit your throat and drink your blood."

Bhavari tsked from her seat in the corner of the room closest to the door. Her patience was almost gone. If this didn't work, she would throw him in with the muracos and let them turn him. She had promised the animals two things—a black werewolf who would lead them into Janus Nether and open season on the witches of Irongarde City. If the black werewolf cooperated, she would fulfill her first promise.

As for her second promise, Bhavari tsked again. Matriarch Kalinda would have every muraco's head mounted to her wall long before they stepped one white clawed foot into Irongarde City.

"Slit my throat and drink my blood? I was unaware werewolves enjoyed fantasy. Do you think yourself a supernatural creature of the night, slipping through the window and into the room of a helpless female, your vampiric scent an aphrodisiac she can't defend against? Tell you what, if you're a vampire, turn into a bat for me."

"You're a crazy soon-to-be-dead bitch."

He snapped and snarled. Muscles flexed. After jumping him from that bogus clinic, Bhavari had used the werewolf's shock as the perfect opportunity to jab a syringe in his neck, thereby incapacitating him. She had proceeded to strip him, relieved when she discovered he carried no weapon.

"I'm going to kill you. Kill you good and dead."

Vulgar curses followed more pointless struggles. The chains rattled from his efforts, her magic a strong yellow glow that kept her safe and the black werewolf where she wanted him.

"You're going to kill me?"

"Hell, yes. I'll enjoy it too. I can already taste your blood and magic in my mouth, as I rip you to shreds."

Bhavari wondered about the time, the day. This room, like the rest of the complex, had no windows. How long had she been there? When would Abelone arrive? They had known they would have until the date of the rage disruptor system's biannual audit before the data technicians' creative reporting would be discovered and the offline rage disruptors brought to Matriarch Oriana's attention.

Abelone had assured her, *"The auditor can't be bribed, bullied, or brought into the fold. I don't even want to risk going to her with our plan. She's the type to run back to the matriarch. We can't trust anyone but our small group. We're lucky to have secured the help of the data technicians. They're true believers, like us."*

Their co-conspirators had been true believers, except for the young data tech on first shift. Bhavari didn't want to know what Abelone had said or done to the girl to change her mind. For their plan to work, they had required the allegiance of the three data technicians to cover all the shifts. Matriarch Oriana would've figured that out by now. The same way she would've concluded who the likely culprits were in helping the muracos escape Steelburgh.

But figuring out the how of a plan after its execution meant little. Matriarch Oriana was still five steps behind them and wouldn't be able to prevent what came next. Bhavari and Abelone had received help from an unlikely source.

Bhavari swung her foot back and forth, the way Abelone did when she was nervous or agitated. Bhavari was both, alone with so many muracos, with only their benefactor's magic keeping them hidden. When would Abelone arrive? She was better at handling schemes and werewolves than Bhavari.

"Have you exhausted yourself?"

The black werewolf snarled something at her, likely another inventive curse. She waited, giving him another three minutes. He wasn't as bright as she had hoped. How could he have not noticed? Maybe he wasn't smart enough to get the job done. Then again, she only needed him to point the muracos in the right direction. His reign as their leader would be short-lived. But he could serve their cause well, if he calmed down and allowed her to explain.

"Notice anything?"

"Yeah, come closer so I can tell you." Sharp, deadly fangs slid against his bottom lip. "Close enough for a kiss, a taste, a," —he snapped at her— "bite."

Bhavari pushed to her feet, walked to the foot of the operating table and stopped. "Werewolves heal fast. I had to give you a little trim to get to the part of the scalp I needed, but your hair is already growing back. In another day or two, you'll never notice." She tsked again. "Not that you've noticed *anything* yet. I was in your brain, so I know you have one."

He tried reaching for his head, but the chains held him in place.

"What the fuck did you do to me, you crazy bitch?"

"I gave you what you hoped to find in Apogean Tide Borough. For the record, the underground clinic that charges exorbitant prices to remove rage disruptors is a scam that dumb werewolves like you keep falling for. They would've taken your money, shoved something in your head or neck, I have no clue what, then sent you home, thinking you were free of your rage disruptor. That is, until whatever they give werewolves that temporarily interferes with the rage disruptor wore off." Bhavari pointed to her neck. "Then you would've been right back where you started, with less money in your bank account and no legal recourse because you paid money with intent to break the law."

"What are you saying?"

"I think I was clear. You came all this way looking for a fountain of freedom. I, on the other hand, was there looking for a black werewolf from Janus Nether. Specifically, I heard you tell one of the charlatans at the clinic you were from Wild Moor, which is perfect."

"You were there? I didn't see you." He shook his head. "This is crazy. You're crazy. Do you have any idea who I am? Who my brother is?"

"I don't know, and I don't car—"

"Marrok, Cyrus of Steelcross." He laughed, a mix of snarl and mockery. "Yeah, I caught your scent change. Marrok's my baby brother and consort to Matriarch Oriana. Now let me out of these damn chains."

Bhavari's eyes roamed his body—taut and strong. She could dissect him, beginning with removing his foul, annoying tongue. She had either chosen poorly or stumbled upon something quite delicious. *Such sweet irony.*

"If you were anything like your brother, I wouldn't have found you in an underground clinic." She touched his leg, hard and smooth, like the rest of him. "I don't think you're anything like your brother. I bet he doesn't even know you came to Perilune Rille."

He flinched, from her touch or her words she didn't know.

"What does my scent tell you now?"

"That you're crazy."

"So you've said. But I have a plan. Interested?"

"Do I have any choice but to listen?"

"You don't. But I think you'll like my plan. I can only imagine what you wanted to do once you had your rage disruptor removed."

"That's none of your business."

"What if I told you, if you agreed to work with me—"

"I don't work with witches, especially ones who kidnap and operate on me. Go fuck yourself."

"—that you'll have over a thousand muracos at your disposal," Bhavari continued, unconcerned with the werewolf's hostility.

If he proved useless, there were more where he came from. She didn't relish the idea of going back out on the street and to the clinic, though. Surely, Matriarch Kalinda would've dispatched her Crimson Hunter by now, which could explain why Abelone was late.

Bhavari shoved the unpleasant thought away. Abelone was late because she was taking extra precautions to ensure her magic couldn't be traced.

"At my disposal?"

"That got your attention. Think yourself a leader, do you? Want to lead a rebellion? Kill witches? Make your brother, or yourself, Patriarch of Earth Rift?"

"Witches don't kill witches or side with werewolves. What's your angle?"

"Lead my muraco army or die on this table. Those are your options."

"Not good options, but I'm listening."

Bhavari laid out the portion of the plan he needed to know. When she finished, she realized two things about the black werewolf. One, when he smiled, it hid the vile creature he was at heart. Two, he intended to double-cross her. Bhavari would have expected nothing else from a werewolf, including his underestimation of her. His hubris would make leading him and the muracos to slaughter that much easier and more enjoyable.

"Do we have a deal?"

"Yeah." He yanked at his arm restraints. "Release me."

"I will. What's your name? I need to call you something."

"Fine. Whatever. You can call me Zev, and I'll call you Crazy Bitch. How's that?"

"Nice to meet you, Zev." Bhavari shook his hand, increasing the magic around his wrists until she heard a snap. The bone would heal in an hour or two. "Make that the last time you call me a crazy bitch. Now" —she snapped her fingers, breaking the magic and the chains that bound him— "let's go. You have clothes to put on and muracos to meet."

"Read that entry again, please."

This was the second journal entry Oriana had asked Marrok to reread. He didn't mind, though, because she was awake, talking, and "doing better," she told him every time he asked about her injuries.

Head pillowed on Marrok's chest, duvet pulled to Oriana's shoulder, he was comforted by her nearness. She would be asleep before he finished the passage. Marrok held Oriana close with one hand and the tablet with the other.

"I've tried speaking to Kalinda, as has Tuncay. She refuses to listen. I've never met a more obstinate witch. Ironically, I've heard Tuncay say the same about me. But the conversation Kalinda keeps avoiding isn't the same as my efforts with Bronze Ward or kissing experiments that still leave Tuncay sick and me feeling guilty for causing him pain. We should've never resumed that particular experiment. While I may be stubborn, Tuncay has proven that patience is the stronger character trait. Hence, my changed mind after so many years.

Yet, for all my stubbornness and Tuncay's patience, we are no closer to bridging the divide between witches and werewolves. Magic and power are at the heart of the tension. I'm afraid that will always be the case. Worse, I'm worried about Kalinda. It couldn't have been easy being raised by an "unorthodox matriarch," as witches have called me for years. I never cared what closed-minded witches thought of me, so consumed with maintaining their place in the world they've ceased caring, if they ever did, about those less fortunate than themselves.

Perhaps if Tuncay and I had given Kalinda a sibling, or spent less time focused on Bronze Ward, she wouldn't use aloofness as a form of emotional shielding while also being covetous of the few people she's let into her heart.

I need to help her understand that an egalitarian Earth Rift is our future. But first, I need to spend more time with my daughter. One day, she'll be Matriarch of Earth Rift. I question if I've prepared her well. I fear I haven't …"

12: Blinders

April 21, 2243
Perilune Rille
Apogean Tide Borough

Werewolves were everywhere, filling up every inch of the warehouse with their hostile, impatient energy and near constant whining as to when they could "leave this place" and "kill some witches."

Bhavari slammed the door, shutting out the incessant voices and locking herself in the room she used as her office. It was the same concrete space where she had kept Zev.

"I need to go home," he had told her two days ago. "My family will be worried. And what in the hell did you do with my phone? It wasn't in the stuff you gave back to me."

She had fried the device while he was unconscious. Trackers were standard on all cell phones. While she may not have known Zev's connection to Matriarch Oriana when she'd abducted him, she didn't want to risk a concerned family member finding their hideout if they came looking for Zev.

"You probably dropped it or had it snatched. The clinic you went to wasn't in the best neighborhood. A lot of unsavory people live and visit there."

"Yeah, unsavory … like you. Anyway, I'm going home."

"You can't."

"Yeah, I can. My brother, Alarick, knows I came here and why. He didn't want to know, but I told him anyway. I've already been gone too long and, without my phone, they haven't been able to contact me."

She had considered jumping him to and from Wild Moor, ensuring his return to the warehouse. In the end, Bhavari had permitted Zev to go alone, taking the Magerun back to Wild Moor as he'd planned to do before she'd taken him hostage.

"I'm in," he had said, wearing a deceptively innocent werewolf-next-door grin. "I'll be back. When I do, I'll have a list of the best areas in Janus Nether's three cities to attack. The list will include places with a lot of strong but young werewolves. Young werewolves won't put up as much resistance as older, more experienced werewolves."

Oddly enough, when she had watched Zev slip through the steel gate enclosing the complex, a middle finger his classy goodbye, Bhavari had sensed she could trust him to return when he said he would. If for no other reason than the fact that Zev of Wild Moor was the biggest asshole she'd ever met with delusions of grandeur. He thought the world owed him—and all werewolves—things like trust, faith … and power.

Bhavari slid down the wall, knees to her chest, arms wrapped around her legs. Dropping her forehead to her knees, she fought the threatening tremors but couldn't prevent her tears from falling. They were gone. She had no proof.

The warehouse was a big storage space, solar powered but without the conveniences or comforts of a home or business. Bedrolls, ready-to-eat meals, and bottled water, those were in ample supply. The benefactor Bhavari and Abelone should've known better than to trust had convinced them to use the military surplus warehouse to hide the muracos.

"Our goal is the same," she had told them.

Bhavari had no idea how the witch had learned of their plan to free the muracos, but she had, arriving at their home uninvited.

"Are your band of supporters true witches committed to the Matriarchy and maintaining our way of life? Are you, Abelone?"

Whatever apprehension Abelone had initially felt at having their plan discovered bled away with the questioning of her loyalty to the Matriarchy.

"I'm committed," Abelone had assured, placing the palm of her right hand over her heart. "We're committed. That's why we're doing this. The establishment of Steelburgh, approving a silver snare-free Janus Nether, bestowing a sun title on a werewolf … each action is a slippery slope that could once again have witches under the claws and fangs of werewolves. Those were dark times for witches."

"They were indeed. I applaud your loyalty, as will Matriarch Oriana. She'll come to see your actions as patriotism at its finest."

"What about Oriana as Crimson Hunter?" Bhavari had asked.

"As Crimson Hunter she will do what she must. That cannot be stopped. You'll be breaking planetary law, committing treason. Both will warrant action by the Crimson Hunter, and the matriarchs will be duty-bound to reestablish control of the muraco, whether that means returning them to Steelburgh or killing them."

What had gone unsaid was that there was no escaping death for the witches. The Crimson Hunter wouldn't cart them off to jail, after using a healer to inject them with a metal hardening serum, effectively preventing them from channeling magic. As a healer for the judicial system, Bhavari had performed the procedure on convicted witches. She'd never questioned that sentence. After all, adjudicators only cast down that penalty on the most reprehensible of witch criminals.

As Bhavari cried herself dry, her head aching but not as painful as her heart, she would trade a magicless existence for one with Abelone by her side.

"You go first," Abelone had told her. "We can't all disappear at the same time. The captain of the guard needs to be distracted. She won't be if we all go with you to the warehouse."

"B-but …" Bhavari had sputtered, gut churning at the prospect of leaving Abelone and dealing with the muracos on her own. "Come with me."

The smile she so loved transformed Abelone from a world-weary soldier to an idealistic revolutionary. Bhavari should've known she would never see Abelone and the others again. But she wanted to believe Abelone's lie and was desperate to ignore the very real likelihood that their plan wouldn't succeed and that they would die along with the muracos.

No matter how many times Abelone had tried to prepare Bhavari for the fate that awaited them at the end of Crimson Hunter's Ravagers of the Lost cannons, she still never quite accepted it as inevitable. She hadn't been a naïve girl in decades, but she had acted the part well, holding on to her delusions.

Eventually, Bhavari had no more tears to shed. Now that she'd stopped weeping, a warmth suffused her body as her mind no longer focused on what she had lost but on how she could make the Matriarchy pay for taking Abelone away.

With her wife gone, she had no reason to continue with the muraco plan. Zev could do whatever in the hell he wanted with the white werewolves. Whether they listened to or had him for dinner, Bhavari didn't care. The muracos wouldn't stay confined to the warehouse much longer. Eventually, they would leave the protective magic enclosure to go hunting. Once they did, humans and witches would demand action from the Matriarchy. By the time all the muracos were rounded-up or killed, the damage to Matriarch Oriana's push to elevate werewolves' standing in society would be as dead as Bhavari's wife and friends.

Shuffling to her feet, her long hair fell into her face. A sob tore through her as she pushed back the tangled wave and wished her hands were Abelone's. The muracos were raucous behind the closed door—as usual. She despised every single one of them. But not as much as she despised the Matriarchy

One gave the execution order, while the other implemented it. Both were guilty of taking Abelone away from Bhavari.

Wiping her face clean with her shirt sleeve, Bhavari composed herself. She twisted her hair in a knot and opened the door. She had a small window of opportunity to act. Zev was slated to return before the day of the white moon. She could've attempted to work around Zev, but the risk of him figuring out her plan was too great to chance.

She would proceed with her new plan while she had the muracos to herself. If she succeeded, Abelone wouldn't have died in vain. Bhavari had lost the love of her life. It was only fair that Matriarch Kalinda also lost the person she most loved.

Scanning the open room, muracos lounging everywhere, she searched for her accomplices. She would have the element of surprise, but there wouldn't be another chance if she failed.

A crowd formed around three fighting muracos. Of course, they were fighting. Her hellacious day wouldn't be complete without the animals going for each other's throats. The three ripped into each other.

Barbarians. My accomplices. Perfect.

April 24, 2243
Steelcross Realm
Steel Rise

"Did Zev say where he'd been and why he didn't return anyone's call?"

Oriana kept her voice low, speaking over their toddler who slept on the bed between them. Oriana held Keira around her waist, his daughter's back pressed to his mate's chest. The sight of mother and daughter always tugged at Marrok's heart.

He smiled.

When Keira was an infant, he could see much of Oriana in his daughter but little of himself. As Keira grew, passing her one-year milestone, she still didn't favor Marrok, but he had begun to see traces of his mother, Lita, in his daughter. To his surprise, that revelation hadn't bothered him the way it would've before Lita's declaration of love. Since he'd married, Lita had begun to reach out to him. And not only to him, but to his brothers and father, as well. Alarick and Io had been receptive—especially Io, who smiled more these days. Zev, on the other hand, had ignored Lita's overtures, claiming, "I'm a grown-ass werewolf. I don't need a mother." Thankfully, he had only said those words to Marrok and Alarick.

The new and improved family dynamics didn't alter circumstances as much as Marrok would have wished. The problems that prompted Lita to leave and stay away hadn't changed. Nothing would work for witch-werewolf families until they figured out how to get a handle on werewolves' blood-and-magic lust. He and Oriana had been circling their theory, neither knowing quite what to do with their suppositions. After what had happened at Steelburgh and Elio Desert, they needed to act sooner rather than later. Yet, there were the thirteen hundred plus muracos still unaccounted for. Capturing them took precedence.

"He didn't tell me where he'd run off to, but I think Alarick knows. Zev claims he lost his phone."

"You sound like you don't believe him."

"I'm not saying he lied but … Okay, yeah, I think he lied. If not an outright lie, he's definitely keeping something from me."

"Maybe your brother has a secret girlfriend."

"No, that's Alarick's thing. I have no idea why he and Solange are acting as if they aren't doing more than having no-strings sex." Crossing the small divide between them, Marrok kissed his daughter's forehead then his mate's lips. "Hmm, you taste good."

"So do you."

Marrok pulled back, when he felt Oriana deepening the kiss. They hadn't made love since her battle with the witches. She claimed she was "feeling better," while Marrok argued they should "take it slow." While Oriana did seem mostly back to normal, her ordeal hadn't only been physical.

"Stop looking at me like that. I told you, I'm fine."

"I know what you said. I also know what I see."

Oriana rolled off the bed. Her black, strapless tie front dress was a temptation as well as a reminder of where she had to go when she should be sleeping next to him.

Careful not to awaken Keira, Oriana picked up their daughter, carrying her through the door to the room that adjoined theirs. When she returned, Oriana sat beside him on the bed instead of joining him in it.

Marrok sat up, naked except for a pair of navy sweatpants. "It's not good for you to keep your feelings bottled inside. Talk to me." Sliding his hand over top of hers, he gentled his voice even more. "Please, talk to me."

Oriana lowered her head. He hoped she would open up to him, that she would accept his comfort. For Marrok, loving and supporting his family was what it meant to be Cyrus of Steelcross. He had no desire to rule, to have billions of people's lives impacted by his actions. He had tried, especially when Oriana had spent days in bed, to be the kind of co-ruler he thought she wanted him to be.

But on their wedding night she had told him, "Cyrus of Steelcross is a title with no ascribed meaning, Marrok. … Define it as you will."

Before and after their marriage, Marrok had watched Oriana struggle to balance the expectations of her witch sisters with the moral weight of what it would mean for her to turn a blind eye to the systematic oppression of werewolves. To fully embrace equity and equality, she risked upending a thousand-plus-year-old system that had made Earth Rift a force to be reckoned with in their solar system. That level of responsibility, of grief and guilt, wasn't an experience anyone who hadn't lived it could understand.

"I do what I must." She lifted her head, eyes shiny but tears held at bay. "They died for their beliefs while I killed to uphold the law. What makes it all so much worse is that, when it comes to our daughter and my own beliefs, I am willing to break the law I'm sworn to obey and enforce."

Yeah, this wouldn't do. Marrok grabbed Oriana's shoulders, shaking her a little to make sure he had her attention. "Don't take this the wrong way, but that's bullshit. You can't compare what they did with your wanting to spare Keira the pain of a so-called healer shoving a needle full of liquid steel into her arms. Your convictions won't hurt anyone. Those Crimson Guards and the others released over a thousand muracos, knowing innocents would die. It's one thing to fight for your beliefs, to oppose the government's unjust systems, but it's something entirely different to deliberately hurt people in your zeal, to deliberately ruin lives to make a political statement."

"But—"

"No, Oriana. I won't sit here and listen to you beat yourself up about taking steps to give werewolves a modicum of dignity and respect. You aren't the matriarch only of witches."

"But you were the one who told me to go slow to go fast."

Relaxing his hold on his mate, Marrok kept his hands where they were, thumbs stroking the points of her shoulders. "Yeah, and I still believe that to be the best strategy. But that doesn't mean you have to move at a sloth's pace. Change is hard. For some people, no matter the speed of change, it will always be too fast and too soon because they disagree with the new way of doing things."

Oriana blinked, her gaze fixed on his. He could see her processing his words. Her face was less expressive than his, but she made no attempt to conceal her feelings.

"I know killing in the name of judicial punishment is part of being Crimson Hunter. It's a necessary evil. I don't expect you to feel good about taking a life—werewolf, human, or witch." A hand lowered to her chest and over her heart. "I hate to see you upset, but it's also a good sign that what's in here is working as it should. You have the right moral compass. A conscience. You value life. Sometimes, to protect the many, you have to punish the few. Other times, to protect the few, you have to challenge the many."

With his other hand, Marrok pulled Oriana to him. She didn't cry, but she did burrow her forehead into his neck. Yeah, he would be this kind of Cyrus of Steelcross. Oriana didn't require a co-ruler of Steelcross. What she needed was a life partner, as did Marrok. Their marriage was still young. They would learn how to ask for what they wanted and needed, trusting the other person not to take advantage of their open vulnerability.

A warm wisp of breath slid across his neck. "Thank you. You always know what I need to hear." The wisps came again, followed by even warmer lips. "I love you. Need you. Want you."

"Want me?" Leaning back, Marrok quirked an eyebrow. "Want me? Like now? Yeah, I can go for that."

As he had hoped, Oriana laughed. "I tell you I love you, and all you hear is the word *want*."

"Love is great, but sex is forever."

"I'm pretty sure it's the other way around."

Up went his other eyebrow. "Sex is great, but love is forever? Nah, you got it wrong." Marrok kissed Oriana, keeping it light and shallow. No need to get himself worked up for nothing. Even if she were up for messing around, her mother was expecting her. The sooner Oriana left for Iron Spire, the sooner she could return. When she did, he would kiss and lick every delectable inch of her before letting her treat him like the stallion she enjoyed riding.

"Wait up for me?" Oriana eased off the bed, found her sandals on the other side, and slipped them on. "I promise not to be too long."

She would be longer than she intended. Kalinda would draw out the meeting if only to spend more time alone with Oriana. He had never met a more loving and devoted, yet subtly controlling, mother than Kalinda.

"I'll do my best to stay awake. But if I fall asleep, wake me when you get back."

"For sex?"

He did like the way she said that, a shy question undergirded by eyes that swept his bare upper body before settling on his lap.

Oriana crawled on the bed, a sensual witch predator on hands and knees. Across his lap she went, dress pulled up to her thighs, lips on his. "I want to have sex with you in your bleddyn form."

Marrok sputtered, but Oriana didn't retreat, neither physically nor from her statement.

"Is it so shocking?"

"Ah, n-no. It's, well, we haven't talked about it in a while."

"But you want to?"

His sudden erection, which she had to feel, if her knowing smile was a clue, answered her question, so he didn't bother playing her game.

Wrapping her arms around his neck, Oriana pressed her breasts against his chest. If she didn't stop teasing him, she would find herself naked, on her hands and knees, and him in his bleddyn form, claiming her the way he had dreamt.

"I think we should try." She kissed him, her tongue grazing the inside of his mouth, heart pounding in sync with his. "I want to know what it feels like to have you that way. Part man. Part animal. All wild for me, as I'm wild for you."

His stomach clenched. Oriana's fingernails raked his chest; the way he liked, the way she knew, made him hard. The woman was a menace.

"You want it too."

He lifted his hips, letting her know how much he wanted her like that.

They both moaned, groaning their disappointment when she slid from him, flushed and on unsteady legs.

"Do *not* fall asleep. I'll make this meeting quick."

"You better, or I'm starting without you."

Oriana's eyes traveled to his lap again, his erection tenting his sweatpants. She licked her lips, slow and tempting.

"Go before I—"

A swirl of magic whipped around Oriana and she was gone, leaving him horny, hard, and alone.

Marrok staggered to his feet, erection heavy, need unfulfilled. He would give Oriana an hour before turning in for the night. But he had to do something about his hard-on now.

April 24, 2243
Irongarde Realm
Iron Spire

"It's about time."

Oriana rolled her eyes at her mother's rigid back where she stood on the balcony of her office.

"I'm not even five minutes late for our meeting."

"That's still late." Turning, Kalinda watched as Oriana walked onto the balcony through open, sliding glass doors. "You look lovely this evening. How are you feeling?"

Between Kalinda's mothering and Marrok's smothering, Oriana could barely breathe without one of them thinking she would fall back into her sickbed. Not that Oriana had been sick, per se. Hindsight being twenty-twenty,

Oriana should've exhibited less guilt when dealing with her sisters. And she should've ended the battle sooner. She had held back, hesitant to use deadly force until she had no other choice. What her mother and consort failed to understand was that the witches had also held back. They had fought Oriana, without a doubt, but not with the same level of intensity she knew them capable of displaying, which made executing them that much more difficult.

"I'm doing well, Mother." Oriana pressed her lips to Kalinda's offered cheek, adding a heartfelt hug. "I'm healed. You don't have to continue to worry."

"I wouldn't worry if you took better care of yourself. Why didn't you bring my Keira?"

Twinkling stars that lit up the night sky drew Oriana to the edge of the balcony, her hands resting on the black cast iron railing. From this height, she could see all of Irongarde City, no building taller than Iron Spire. The buildings were made of magic and metal, growing from the ground like fantastical trees of a modern era. The past was ignored, buried under concrete and blinders of convenience. Out of sight, often out of mind, but never truly forgotten.

The scent of rain hinted at what was to come, tickling her nose and teasing her senses. Perhaps when it came, wetting the city below with big, fat droplets, it would wash away the growing tide of suspicion instead of adding to the river of pain that threatened to drown her.

For long, quiet minutes, mother and daughter stood side by side. Oriana was afraid to broach the conversation they needed to have, although not the one she'd come there to discuss. She had no idea what thoughts ran through Kalinda's mind. Oriana would like to think regret and guilt, but her mother regretted little and hadn't ever shown a propensity toward faultfinding in herself, although she found plenty in others.

Swallowing down the urge to retreat, to back away from the precipice looming before her, Oriana plunged forward, taking the scariest jump of her life.

She turned to face Kalinda, back against the railing. "Why did you give me Grandmother's journals if you didn't want me to learn the truth?" Not the most important question Oriana wanted to pose, but of her long, heartbreaking list of questions, this one was the easiest to ask. Not because the question was simple but because she thought the answer would be easier to hear … to stomach.

Kalinda didn't sigh, exhale, or prevaricate in any way. In true Matriarch Kalinda fashion, she stated her truth as if it was *the* truth … the only perspective that mattered in a world full of complementary and opposing opinions.

"You're like a dog with a bone, Oriana. Stubborn on your best day, willful on your worst. I knew you wouldn't stop hounding me for access to Mother's journals and research until I gave you something to sink your mind into."

"You didn't give me all of her journals. You gave me just enough to keep me distracted, enough to give me hope, but not enough to do anything of substance with the information. Why?"

"Must we do this now? Don't we have larger concerns?"

"More distractions, Mother? Yes, we need to do this now. I've ignored the gnawing feeling for too long." Longer than the time she'd had the journals and about more than the journals themselves. "Tell me, please."

"You know why. You've always known, but until today, you've never wanted to truly see." Kalinda waved her hand in front of her, slicing the steady appendage through the open space before her, sure in her rightness in a way Oriana had never been. "This is our realm, Oriana. We do what we must to protect the people. For me, that protection begins with you, even if that means protecting you from your own good intentions."

"You say that as if having good intentions is bad."

"Only when it's combined with naivete."

"I'm not nai—"

"You. Are. You seek answers to queries better left in the past. You offer rights and privileges to werewolves without the insight to project the long-term ramifications on a complex society."

"A society that oppresses a third of our population. There's nothing complex about that."

With slow deliberateness, Kalinda shifted her gaze from the night sky to Oriana, looking at her with a look she hadn't seen since she had entered her mother's office after being thrown from her stallion, wanting comfort but finding hard words instead.

"I suppose you want to cut into your arms and legs like Mother did? You think you can save werewolves by experimenting on yourself? Well, let me tell you something, Oriana. Your grandmother died believing she could rid her body of the metal. And, for what? Because she thought metal-free magic could curb the lust of werewolves?"

There it was, Oriana and Marrok's theory laid bare in harsh, angry tones. The missing pieces of Matriarch Helen's journals. Kalinda had known all along. In the deepest recesses of her mind, Oriana had suspected the truth. The arduous emotional journey Kalinda had taken Oriana on, her lies of commission and omission, pricked her trust and stung her heart.

"Matriarch Alba saved us." Kalinda raised her arms, covered by a lavender silk blouse with ruffles at the wrists. "If not for the metal in our arms, we would've continued to be the victims of werewolves—our magic used to feed them, to give them power, while keeping us under their clawed feet. As witches, we deserve so much more than that kind of existence."

"And werewolves deserve more than to be treated as second-class citizens. It doesn't have to be an either/or situation, Mother. Have you once considered the role witches have played in fueling the magic lust of our males?"

Oriana no longer viewed it as blood-and-magic lust, as she once had. When muracos killed witches, ripping into them like the beast they were, it was easy to assume the white werewolves, like their black counterparts, craved both magic and blood. From reading her grandmother's journals and her experiments with Tuncay, kissing him while blowing magic into his mouth, Oriana and Marrok had begun to view the relationship between werewolves and witches through new eyes.

"That's irrelevant."

Kalinda waved Oriana's bigger point away, as she had done her entire life—in ways so subtle Oriana had failed to see her actions for what they were. Some were dismissals, others indulgences. But all were executed with strategy, patience, and a bone-deep belief that Oriana would be proven wrong and Kalinda correct. The realization of Kalinda's lack of faith in her hurt more than the knowledge of the stew of lies Oriana had swallowed over the years, spoon-fed to her at regular intervals.

"Janus Nether, Steelburgh, my marriage to Marrok. You went along with those decisions, but you never believed in any of them. In me. You're the Matriarch of Patience. You were just waiting for those actions to fail—one by one by one—until there was nothing of me left but a disillusioned, closed-minded, and hard-hearted Oriana. Your perfect co-ruler because you created me in your image."

Oriana thought she would be sick. Her heart and mind battled her stomach. Her stomach won.

Spinning, she leaned over the railing, throwing up bile curdled in pain. Head whirling, throat constricting, heart raging, Oriana coughed, choked, expelling anything she could latch on to. Her body seized over and again, clenching in painful spasms.

"Oriana." A hand touched her back, rubbing the center in small circles. "Oriana. Don't. You've made yourself sick over nothing. I've always believed in you. That doesn't, however, mean I must also agree with you. I failed to protect my mother from herself. I won't make the same mistake with my daughter."

Oriana didn't know whether to curse or cry. What kind of twisted logic was that?

Wiping her mouth with the back of her hand, her tongue in need of a thorough brushing, she swallowed spit, thirsty for a glass of water.

"That's it. Get yourself under control."

She shrugged away from Kalinda's touch as much as she did her shallow words. Staring at the cityscape, glass buildings illuminated in red, pink, and blue lights, Oriana wished she could steal the serenity of the panoramic view for herself, hoarding it like a yellow pine chipmunk stockpiled food for the cold winter months.

Oriana stumbled forward, her equilibrium off. Reaching out, she caught herself on the back of a chair, the cushion soft, metal frame sturdy.

"Where are you going?"

"Away from you."

"You're being dramatic."

That pissed her off. She spun on Kalinda—angry and hurt because even now she loved her mother and wanted to wish this all way. But she couldn't. Oriana wouldn't.

"When I was recuperating, I had a lot of time to think. I no longer care that I don't know all the details because I'm done making excuses for you. That includes lying to myself."

"You're not making any sense. Why don't you sit down? I can get you a glass of water, although wine would better settle your nerves." Kalinda glanced from Oriana to the open glass doors. "Give me a minute to get you—"

"No, Mother. If either of us will leave this balcony, it'll be me. But not until I've had my say."

Inclining her head, as regal as ever, Kalinda appeared no more disconcerted by their emotional talk than she would be while taking in a fireworks display.

"I don't know how you found out or when, probably from a spy you installed in Steelburgh, but you learned of the Crimson Guards' plan to release the muracos."

Nothing in her mother's countenance changed with the accusation. Her stomach plummeted to her feet when Kalinda returned her bold statement with impassivity, and something shattered deep inside Oriana. Perhaps it was the pedestal she'd placed Kalinda on. Or maybe it was the bond they shared, not made of steel or iron but, apparently, forged from the same block of ice as Kalinda's heart.

"Unless Solange and I missed a dozen witch conspirators, the missing Dr. Bhavari and Misae aren't strong enough to conceal thirteen hundred muraco. I only know four witches powerful enough to cast an obstruction spell combined with a camouflage spell. Solange. Her mother. Me." Oriana lifted a finger and leveled it at Kalinda. "And you."

"I don't like your tone."

"You don't have to like it. Why haven't you denied anything I've said?"

"Why should I? You're clearly convinced you're right. Why waste my breath?" Crossing her arms over her chest, Kalinda had a way of looking down on Oriana, despite them being the same height. "None of what you've said alters the fact that we need to discuss how we'll handle the muracos."

"It changes everything," Oriana spat, yelling at a person unfazed by emotional outbursts. "You're using your magic to shield muracos from your own fucking Crimson Hunter."

"Watch your language."

"Really? Out of everything I've said that's what you decide to take issue with? Well, too *fucking* bad, Mother." Whatever disgust and nausea Oriana had felt vanished under the weight of her fury. "Every decision I've made since becoming Matriarch of Steelcross got nothing more than a token acceptance from you while you waited for me to fuck up and for my dreams to crumble."

"Oriana."

"But Janus Nether didn't fail. And neither did Steelburgh."

"Your own guards plotted against you. How is that not a failure?"

"They were nineteen prison guards out of thousands. I don't expect everyone on this planet to agree with me, not even my own mother. But I do … *did* expect you to trust me, to have faith in me, to not fucking lie to me and go behind my back."

"Oriana."

"I killed our sisters. I hear their screams in my nightmares, feel the spell I used to kill them surge through my body like a fucking poisonous viper."

"Oriana." Kalinda's voice rose, but Oriana was done listening to her.

"Stop saying my name. I hate the way it sounds coming from your mouth—with disapproval and sufferance. You sent me to execute them, knowing you were just as fucking culpable. At least they stood their ground, took their punishment like women, like witches. But not you. You hid behind lies and rules. Your legitimate authority is a shield you use to beat everyone into submission, including me. They died with honor, while you stayed on your iron throne. A fucking *coward*."

Smack.

Kalinda's slap came as an exclamation point at the end of Oriana's sentence. The shock, more than the power of the blow, had Oriana stumbling backward and against the chair behind her.

For all of Kalinda's sharpness, she had never raised a hand to Oriana, much less struck her.

"Oriana, I'm so sorry. I'm—"

Oriana ran from the balcony, through Kalinda's tidy office, out the door, and straight into Solange, nearly knocking the flustered witch over.

"Good. I was coming to get you. You need to return home."

"Why? What's wrong?"

"No time to explain, but Marrok and Keira need you."

With those heart-splitting words, Oriana's world turned crimson. She jumped away from Iron Spire and her mother's lies to Steel Rise where her night went from bad to worse.

13: Love Hurts

April 25, 2243
Steelcross Realm
Steel Rise

Marrok rolled over in bed, his hand instinctively going to the spot to his left—Oriana's side of the bed. She had said she wanted to have sex with him in his bleddyn form. Did that also mean she was ready for them to try having a second child—a werewolf baby?

He wanted to have more children. Marrok assumed they would. But they were new parents and a part of Marrok was like Kalinda. He shared his mate with so many people already, he wasn't ready to broaden that circle to include a second child. In another two or three years he hoped he wouldn't feel so jealous of his mate's time. Since the death of Oriana's brother, she had grown up as an only child, a lonely existence he didn't want for Keira.

Sitting up, Marrok contemplated what he could do, other than reading, to stay awake. He had taken care of his hard-on in the shower, tossing on boxers and a T-shirt afterward. He supposed he could watch a movie. Maybe even exercise, but that option would leave him sweaty and in need of another shower. Marrok could also call one of his brothers. It was after midnight Steelcross time but nearly dawn in Wild Moor.

Yeah, that idea was a no go. His brothers would curse him to the moon and back, if he called them at the break of dawn for no other reason than boredom.

Alarick would call him an asshole for waking him and Zev would … Was his oldest brother even at home?

Marrok reached for the phone on the bedside table. His last conversation with Zev had felt wrong. Off. He couldn't quite put his finger on what had unsettled him about their talk, but something had. With a guy like Zev, face-to-face conversations were better than virtual ones. When they'd last spoken, Zev had given him some bullshit reason about the video feature of his phone not working by way of explaining why he hadn't accepted Marrok's video chat request.

For all of Zev's self-professed "werewolf of the world" talk, his brother couldn't lie for shit. He hadn't even traveled beyond Irongarde Realm. How in the hell could he be a "werewolf of the world" when he didn't know what the other side of the planet looked like? Until Marrok had married Oriana, he hadn't ever set foot in the Northern Hemisphere either.

Finger poised to hit the audio/video button on the phone's display, Marrok stopped, listened, and sniffed the air. He heard nothing, except for Keira's soft breathing coming from her room. But his intuition had the hairs on his nape rising. He jumped to his feet, legs tangling in the comforter in his rush. Kicking the material out of his way, he marched to his daughter's room. Keira slept in her bed, an adorable pea atop a mattress fit for a princess. As always, Oriana had left Keira's nightlight on, a white glow that showed the way from her bedroom into theirs.

His daughter was safe, an odd thought to have, but it had come to him the moment he had seen her peacefully sleeping form. *Of course, she's safe. Why wouldn't she be?*

Marrok backed away from the adjoining door, pulling it forward but not closing it, something he and Oriana only did before having sex.

Hand on the doorknob, his werewolf instinct growled at him to close and lock the door, to keep his young safe, to defend her to the death.

Marrok spun around, heart racing, hackles rising. What in the hell was wrong with him? He was alone in the suite. Oriana wouldn't return for another thirty minutes or more, depending on how long Kalinda chose to drag out their meeting.

So, yeah, Marrok was alone. But he would have sworn he sensed *something*. Magic? Having spent so much time with witches since marrying Oriana, Marrok had become adept at catching wisps of their magic. It hung in the air like scented perfume—invisible to the eye, but there. Yet this felt different. The hairs on his arms and nape rose, triggering the elongation of his fingernails into claws and eyeteeth into fangs. Marrok readied himself.

For what, he did not know.

Io had raised three werewolves. Werewolves may not have the best track record with their witch daughters, but they were great fathers to their sons. Trusting his instincts was one of many lessons Marrok had learned from his father.

Planting himself in front of his daughter's door, Marrok waited. Eyes keen, ears sharp, he positioned himself in a fighting stance—feet staggered and placed wider than his hips, abdominal muscles tight, right arm in front of his body, the first line of defense or offense, depending on the enemy. Keeping his chin down, as if an opponent stood before him primed to strike, Marrok bared his teeth.

If Oriana found him like this, more animal than man, body shivering and blood boiling, she might reconsider the prudence of having sex with his bleddyn. More likely, though, she would take one look at Marrok, shake her head at his dramatics, and wrap herself around him until her touch and scent calmed him.

But Oriana wasn't there, and calm had abandoned him.

The scent of magic tickled his nose, the smell stronger than his sense of foreboding. Marrok shifted, not giving himself time to question what his werewolf instincts knew to be true.

Bones snapped.

Clothes ripped.

Muscles lengthened, skin expanded, hair grew and thickened, covering his body in smooth, black fur. Senses became enhanced and he went on full alert.

Marrok heard and smelled what approached. Not from the hallway or from Keira's room but from a supernatural highway created by witches that didn't adhere to the physics of space.

He knew the signs well. Only Oriana had ever magically jumped directly into their suite. The magic signature he detected in the air, however, did not belong to his mate.

A pink cloud of mist and magic formed in his bedroom near the door leading to the sitting area. One, two, three muracos emerged from the magic mist.

Io had been correct. Muraco did smell like overcooked rock doe.

Flanked by the white werewolves, a slender woman with long, black hair stared at Marrok, dark eyes wide, mouth slightly parted.

Her gaze cut to the empty, rumpled bed, and her mouth fell open even more.

Her scent betrayed the balls it had taken to jump, even with three muracos at her back, into the Crimson Hunter's bedroom.

Marrok growled.

The witch thought she could catch Oriana unawares—asleep and vulnerable to an attack by three salivating big-ass muracos. Instead, she had gotten Marrok—a pissed-off black werewolf who wouldn't tolerate the invasion of his territory nor the planned attack on his family.

Marrok closed his daughter's door, shoving a heavy armoire in front of it.

The witch disappeared.

The muracos charged.

The first muraco slammed into him, jaws snapping. Evading his teeth, Marrok countered, slashing out with a hard paw hand across the muraco's face. The blow landed, slicing snout and left eye. Marrok struck again, going for the same side. Claws dug into the muraco's face, gouging his left eye from the socket.

The muraco howled, countered with a slash to Marrok's midsection, cutting him open and drawing blood.

Marrok lunged at the half-blind muraco. If he could disable one of them, his odds of surviving the battle would increase. He had to go the distance. Marrok had to keep the werewolves' focus on himself and not the little witch in the room next door.

Keira will not become a meal for these white werewolf bastards.

He ripped into a second muraco, going straight for his throat and clamping down. His silver snare, which hummed with magic the moment Marrok had locked gazes with the black-haired witch, pulsated with the power of its magic emission.

Marrok had never enjoyed wearing his collar, but he had submitted to the requirement without much complaint. On any other day he could ignore its limitations, pretend the restrictions weren't a physical and psychological form of external control.

Blood flooded Marrok's mouth, and he fought the werewolf under him as much as he did the rage disruptor. The other two muracos crashed into him, their claws scoring his back and hindlegs.

Marrok bellowed on the inside but refused to release the muraco's throat. Burying his claws deep in the muraco's chest, Marrok used the bastard's body for leverage, yanking at his throat and ripping it out.

One of the other two muracos bit into him, and Marrok scrambled away. He bled, jagged cuts open and spilled blood. Marrok's silver snare pumped even more magic into him, working hard to dull the razor-sharp edge of his anger.

He shook his head, ears alert and muzzle wet from blood. He could hear Keira moving around in the other room, the fight having awoken her. If he could hear her, smell her, so too could the muracos.

Marrok went on the attack, driving his body into the nearest muraco. They fell over a nightstand, breaking the wood and knocking into the bed as they fought.

The muraco clamped on his shoulder, biting into bones, ligaments, and veins. Marrok grunted but countered. Arm wedged between their bodies, Marrok opened his hand wide, curled his fingers, and grabbed the muraco's muscular stomach. Twisting his wrist, he yanked with all his might.

The mouth on Marrok's shoulder loosened but didn't release him, so he stabbed the open wound, shoving his hand into the hole he'd made. That got the piece-of-shit white werewolf the hell off him.

Keira began to cry.

Marrok fought harder. His daughter was tall enough to reach the doorknob. More, she had a habit of leaving her bed and room and entering Marrok and Oriana's. That was how she had come to be in their bed before Oriana had left for Iron Spire.

Marrok felt weak, his adrenalin and strength abandoning him the longer the rage disruptor's magic assaulted his central nervous system. How in the hell did black werewolves push past the magic attack to become a white werewolf?

They must've been damned determined, must've craved the kill and the blood more than they'd valued their mind and heart.

He shoved the muraco off him, only to be slammed back to the floor by the third one. Claws raked down his back. A waterfall of blood followed.

Keira's cries grew louder, intensifying into screams and, *no, no, no*, he could hear her at the door, jiggling the doorknob.

As if controlled by a puppeteer, the muracos left Marrok, their strings pulling them away from him and toward his daughter. The armoire, a temporary stop gap, wouldn't do much to keep the muracos on this side of the door.

Seconds. That's all Marrok had.

He wouldn't make it out of this fight alive. He had been bitten too many times by the muracos, tasted their blood, swallowed it.

It's all gone. My life. My future with Oriana and Keira. No more playful banter and magic-laced kisses. No more declarations of love and conversations at midnight. No more tight hugs and gentle caresses. Gone.

Marrok struggled to his feet, woozy, muddleheaded. He felt too hot, too heavy, too …

He rushed the muracos, tackling one but missing the other. With a strength and rage he'd never known, Marrok ripped into the downed muraco, slashing over and again. Claws arced and blood spurted, splashing his fur in gooey spots of crimson and flesh.

Wood crunched behind him. Pieces of the armoire flew across the room. For blinding seconds, Marrok cared about nothing but the kill.

You came into my motherfuckin' bedroom to murder my mate. You deserve to die. You all deserve to die, and I'm going to send your asses to hell.

Marrok ravaged the muraco's throat, gnashing his teeth together and pulling until the fucker stopped mewling and twitching underneath him.

He reveled in the kill, ignoring the rage disruptor's muted chatter. The silver snare's magic ebbed, retreating like a defeated tide, the shore of Marrok's werewolf body the undisputed winner.

Raw power surged through Marrok like lightning breaking from the clouds, sharp cracks heralding its arrival and might. He roared and roared, the sound savage in its depth of intensity.

Free. I'm finally free.

Marrok roared again, smashing his hand into the dead werewolf's face. Ripping the lower jaw, he hurled it against a wall.

Freedom had never tasted so good. Tasted so—

Keira screamed. It wasn't the scream of frustration or one following a fall or scrape.

Marrok bolted to his feet. He knew all his daughter's screams. Every. Single. One. He had never heard the sounds coming from her.

Abject terror.

I must protect her.

The last muraco had removed the single barrier to Keira's room. Bits and pieces of the armoire were everywhere, as was the adjoining door—pointy shards of a father's devolution into madness.

Keep it together a little longer.

The muraco stalked forward.

Keira shrieked.

Marrok ran as fast as he could. Leaping for the muraco but knowing he was too far away to stop the inevitable, Marrok put all his power and strength behind the jump, his trajectory true but his reaction far too late.

Keira didn't so much screech as gag on her fear. She choked, trembled, eyes wide with a comprehension no toddler should ever know.

The muraco's blood-glistened claws reached for Keira, her bobbing throat his target.

Bam. Bam.

Marrok ducked, dove, and landed beside Keira. Covering her suddenly quiet body with his, he shielded her from the gunfire above him.

Bam.

"He's down. Cornered but not dead yet."

Marrok recognized the voice, the scent of magic. Not Oriana's but … Solange's.

"Nahara, finish his ass. I'm going to check the other room."

"What about Marrok?"

"Stay the hell away from him."

"But … but, he has the baby."

"Unless you want to end up like the two dead muracos I'm looking at, stay away from him. Damn, he did a number on these two in here. I didn't know Marrok had it in him to do this kind of damage."

Beneath him, Keira began to cry again. Worse, she pushed against him, her breaths coming fast.

"No, Daddy, no."

"Umm, Solange, we have an issue in here."

"I said kill the asshole."

"Not that. Wait."

Nahara's pistols rang out, four explosive sounds that had Keira screaming and Marrok scooting backward, taking his daughter with him. Holding Keira around her waist, Marrok stood, wedging himself between his daughter's bed and bookcase.

Solange returned to Keira's bedroom. "Marrok, it's over."

It wasn't. His body felt odd, different. His head ached, and why did Solange, Nahara, and Keira smell so good?

He clutched his daughter tighter, her whimpers of, "Daddy, let down," toxic vapors to his senses. Didn't she understand? He was trying to protect her. The black-haired witch could return with more muracos.

Solange should be on alert. They had only killed three of them but over thirteen hundred were still on the loose. What would they do if more arrived? No, he wouldn't let Keira down. She would stay right where she was, her delicious scent meant only for him.

He sniffed her neck, her red-and-black hair a delicious-smelling curtain of silky softness.

Solange backed away. "Watch him. I'm going to get Oriana. She's the only one who has any chance of talking him down. He hasn't changed yet."

"What if he does, while you're gone?"

Marrok growled at the witches, disliking that they talked about instead of to him.

"Do you want me to shoot him?"

He would kill her, if she tried.

"Daddy, let down. Let down."

"Don't shoot him. Shit, I don't have time for this. I need to get Oriana. Now."

Magic swirled around Solange and she was gone, leaving him with Nahara.

"Please, don't make me kill you. Do you hear me, Marrok? Stay calm and, for the love of your mate and daughter, fight the muraco clawing to take you over. You're a proud black werewolf. Stay that way. Black and proud. Don't you dare change."

Nahara's words echoed in his head. He heard her, understood her, knew she spoke the truth. But what good was the truth when every cell in his body betrayed him? He had never been so hot, a volcano ready to rupture from the crust of his black werewolf's body, spewing lava, volcanic ash, and gases in a flurry of violent rages that would consume them all.

"Daddy, let down."

No. No.

"Big teeth," Keira cried. "I want Mommy. I want Mommy."

Marrok sniffed Keira again.

Big teeth. Better to rip your throat out with.

At the sight of Marrok, Oriana nearly rushed to him in a panic. For a second, all she could see was her consort covered in blood, bites, and claw marks. Not the destroyed suite behind her or the three dead muracos, not even her sweet girl, afraid and crying, reaching for Oriana as Marrok clutched her too tightly.

For precious, agonizing seconds, Oriana only had eyes for her consort, her Marrok. "Leave us," she said, her voice so low and full of pain she wasn't sure Solange and Nahara had heard her. But Solange's equally soft curse, followed by retreating feet, had Oriana alone in her suite with her consort and daughter.

Her black werewolf.

Tears fell, blurring a vision she wished was an illusion. She had never seen the process firsthand. Oriana didn't know anyone who had. Maybe because a person unfortunate enough to be in the vicinity of the awful transformation didn't live long enough to tell the tale.

But Oriana watched in horror as Marrok's gorgeous black fur faded from a vibrant onyx to a dull, defeated gray. Not white. Not yet.

She stepped forward—but only once. His arm around Keira was too tight for Oriana's comfort. She also did not trust the nose that kept sniffing her daughter's hair.

"Marrok, love. Thank you for protecting our daughter. Thanks to you, she's safe. Keira is safe. You can let her go now."

A rumble of a growl filled the space between them.

Oriana moved closer, arms in front of her, palms up. No danger. No Ravagers of the Lost cannons.

Keira had fallen into an endless cycle of soft sobs and hiccups, her eyes red, her face a snotty, wet mess. Tiny arms reached for Oriana, fear of Marrok in every line of her body.

The sight tore at Oriana's insides. Keira had never been afraid of Marrok, in human or in werewolf form. Her daughter's body all but vibrated with tension and terror.

Not good. Werewolves, especially white ones, relished the fear they evoked in their prey. They enjoyed the hunt even more. Not that Marrok would have to run Keira to ground to claim her. All he would have to do was open his mouth and …

"I'm here now, my love. I can take care of you both. You're hurt, and Keira is afraid. Let me have her … then I can take care of you."

More black fur faded to gray, and some of the gray had turned white.

Oriana shut her eyes, revolting against the sight of her Marrok turning into a white, bloodthirsty muraco. She was losing him, and there wasn't a damn thing she could do about it.

Marrok wasn't yet lost to her, though. He was still inside the fading black werewolf. A part of him was fighting back, even as he plastered himself against the wall, refusing to relinquish their daughter to her.

Red eyes tracked Oriana, as she continued to close the distance between them.

"Please, Marrok. Give me our daughter. She's crying and is afraid. Let me have her. I know you don't want to hurt Keira."

The red of his eyes deepened as more gray gave way to white. Only a few patches of black remained on his clawed feet and left hind leg. Then at horrific metabolic speed, Marrok shifted from steel gray to pearl white.

Oriana stared at her outstretched hands. For all the magic she wielded, she was ultimately nothing more than a weapon of mass destruction, incapable of curing or saving her consort.

"Mom-my. Mom-my."

"I know, baby. Mommy's here. Don't be afraid. Daddy won't hurt you. Daddy won't—"

Marrok growled, baring his teeth.

Oriana's gaze slid over his body. The transformation was done. A muraco stood before her, eyes crimson and all traces of the black werewolf of her heart gone.

The little witch inside Keira must've sensed Marrok's complete change because she fought like a wildcat, screaming, twisting, and doing everything she could to get away from the muraco, who held her in a grip gone deadly.

Oriana lowered her hands, face awash with tears—hers silent to Keira's uncontrollable deluge. She couldn't lose them both but had no idea how to save one without killing the other. Pleading and rational talk would prove futile, as would a full-on attack. Marrok held their daughter in front of him, a flesh-and-blood shield.

She backed away, eyes on Marrok and Keira. Stepping carefully to avoid falling over broken furniture, Oriana retreated. As she hoped they would, Marrok's eyes followed her every movement. She needed him to view her as a bigger payday worth pursuing rather than settling for the easier prey he already claimed.

What would it take to have a muraco turn away from a sure meal?

Oriana released her magic, creating a vortex similar to the one she had conjured in Elio Desert. Flooding the vortex with her magic, she used the crimson fog to shield her shift.

Marrok sniffed the air. Interested.

Oriana moved farther from Keira's bedroom and deeper into their destroyed suite. The love and peace she and Marrok had found together in the suite no longer existed, marred by the ugliness that had tainted their sanctuary.

Long, sharp fangs sparkled white. Saliva dripped.

Oriana's heart thudded an erratic beat. Had she miscalculated? Would he eat Keira first before coming after her? She couldn't permit that to happen, couldn't watch her daughter die at the hands of her father.

Marrok charged Oriana, tossing Keira to the side as he dropped to all fours and rushed her. She'd fought muracos before, some larger than her consort, but none of them had meant to her what Marrok did.

Muscles rippled under white fur and thick hide. Claws scratched the floor's wood finish. Teeth bared, ready to rip Oriana to shreds.

She stood her ground. Not a cell in her body recoiled in fear, but every part of her quaked from grief.

Marrok ran into the vortex, mouth open, rows of deadly teeth aimed at Oriana.

Shutting her eyes, she lifted her arms and … fired.

14: Death Becomes Her

April 25, 2243
Irongarde Realm
Iron Spire

"I need to go." Oriana paced in the suite she'd had since she was a baby. Over the years, Kalinda had allowed Oriana to redecorate her own room instead of hiring a professional designer to do it for her. The results were never what Kalinda expected or what she would've chosen for herself, but the suite always exuded Oriana's tastes and personality—outgoing, fun, kind, and sensitive. Oriana may have moved to Steel Rise, but this would always be her suite.

Kalinda loved when Oriana visited, especially when she brought Keira with her. But this visit—Oriana holding an out-of-control Keira, an ashen-faced Solange and Nahara beside her—Kalinda would never wish to see her daughter and granddaughter under such horrific circumstances.

Kalinda placed her hand on Oriana's shoulder, a gentle persuasion her stubborn daughter looked ready to fight. To stave off a headache-inducing argument, she used her only leverage. "It took you an hour to calm Keira enough for her to fall asleep. If you leave and she awakens, she'll break down again."

"You'll be here."

"I will, but you're her mother. She'll want you, not me. Please, Oriana. Stay. Sleep."

As if someone had reached into her chest and removed her will, Oriana slumped to the bed, caving in on herself. She hadn't cried, not a single tear but, just this once, Kalinda wished her daughter would give in to her sadness. The sight of her only child, eyes depleted of their normal sunshine and replaced with gray clouds, had Kalinda sitting beside her daughter and stroking her hair.

"It'll be all right. I'll make it all right."

"It won't. You can't. I shot him. My Marrok. The father of my child."

Kalinda had forced Solange and Nahara to stay until they had given her a full report. When Oriana had stormed from her office, Kalinda had remained on the balcony, upset about her argument with her daughter but unaware of what was happening a half planet away. Despite what Oriana believed, Kalinda did not dislike Marrok. How could she when Marrok made her daughter so happy? Although she had never believed their marriage would last—none did between witches and werewolves—Kalinda had wished them many children and years of joy before the inevitable befell them.

This was not how their marriage should've ended—Oriana forced to raise a weapon against her consort, Keira witness to the violence.

"They made so much noise, we heard the fight two floors down," Solange had told her. "We rushed up there only to discover the door to their suite was blocked."

At Kalinda's raised eyebrow—a silent question—Solange had added, "There was a forcefield around the suite. We couldn't enter through the door or by jumping in. If we could've reached Marrok sooner, Matriarch, he wouldn't have had to fight three muracos on his own. He did one hell of a job defending himself and protecting Keira. But by the time we were able to counteract the forcefield it was too late."

Too late. Yes, the craven beasts had turned Marrok into a disgusting muraco, leaving Oriana no choice but to hurt him to save herself and her daughter.

"When the field finally broke, we rushed in through the nursery. Thank the sun for that choice because any other route into the suite would've ended with Keira's death. I took two shots. One to the shoulder, the other to his forearm.

Nahara finished him off. When I return home, I'll arrange for clean-up. Not every Crimson Guard is a traitor. They're loyal, Matriarch Kalinda. Once we're done here, we'll begin hunting Dr. Bhavari."

Nahara had nodded, her jaw tight, her fists balled. "We'll catch her. No one else we can think of would've had the motive and means to pull something like this off. She wanted to assassinate our matriarch. She'll regret her betrayal. The baby—" Nahara had whispered the four-letter word, anger in the two syllables she pushed through thinned lips. "Did she forget they had a baby, or was she so distraught over her wife's death she would sacrifice a child for her revenge?"

Kalinda's thoughts had run along the same lines. But that could wait. At least for a little while. First, she needed to take care of her daughter.

"You were forced to make an impossible decision. No one will blame you."

"His parents and brothers will. Dr. Bhavari came looking for me. Poor Marrok got caught in the crosshairs."

Kalinda wondered how long it would take for Oriana to blame *her* for Bhavari's actions. Once she rested, had time to grieve Marrok and the loss of her marriage, she would recall their talk on the balcony. In light of what had happened in Steel Rise and the role Oriana believed Kalinda had played in helping the Steelburgh Crimson Guards to hide the muracos, it wasn't a leap in logic to assume her daughter would come to view her as the root cause of her pain.

She couldn't allow that to happen. Kalinda refused to lose her daughter in any way.

"You were right earlier."

"About what?" Oriana kicked off her shoes then curled her tall, fit frame around a sleeping Keira, her back to Kalinda.

She stroked Oriana's hair, toying with the silky strands. "There was an employee in Steelburgh who reported directly to me."

"A spy, you mean. Who?"

"Bhavari's assistant."

Turning onto her back, Oriana leveled two accusing eyes up at her. "Did you know what they were planning?"

"I did not. I didn't find out about the plot until the night you came to me. Once you left, I called Misae. Fear kept her mouth shut longer than it should've. Misae should've come to me as soon as she suspected."

"I see. Misae was your spy."

"Do stop calling her that."

"Why? That's what she was. I tried to locate her, but she disappeared. I suppose that was *your* doing?"

"I sent her and her family on extended leave … off-planet."

"Convenient." Oriana shifted away from Kalinda again, shoulders hunched to her ears. "Go on. Tell me the rest."

The part of Kalinda that craved physical closeness considered joining her daughter and granddaughter in the bed. As out of sorts as Oriana felt, she was a loving girl who wouldn't turn away from Kalinda in her time of need, even though she was the one more in need of comforting.

"I should let you sleep. I'll go."

"No. Don't." Back still to Kalinda, Oriana reached behind her and grabbed her hand, holding it tightly. "Stay. Tell me the truth. Please."

The truth? As a child, Oriana used to grab Kalinda's hand whenever they walked the streets of Irongarde City. Not because she was small and afraid and the city vast and intimidating but because she had once told Kalinda that, "If you hold my hand and get lost, at least we'll be together. That way, you'll never be lonely." Oriana's insight at seven had frightened Kalinda. The truth of what she stood to lose now scared her even more.

"I don't want you and your Crimson Guards going after the muracos until we've confirmed their presence in Janus Nether."

The finger that had been rubbing the back of Kalinda's hand stilled. Oriana pushed herself up in bed. Kalinda was reluctant to free her hand, the separation producing a sudden beat of anxiety.

"I can capture them."

"I know you can. In Janus Nether. Not wherever in the hell they're hiding now."

"You know where they are. Just tell me, and I'll organize a team to retrieve them and Dr. Bhavari."

"Do you really think, if I knew where the escaped prisoners and Dr. Bhavari were, I would let them stay on the loose? Do you believe me as cold-hearted as everyone else does?"

"I didn't say that but … but …" Questioning, confused eyes bore into Kalinda. "If you're not the one helping Dr. Bhavari hide the muracos then I don't know who else it could be. Solange and I must've missed something during our investigation."

Oriana sounded doubtful but also relieved. Kalinda would take both emotions.

"You've been through two harrowing ordeals in a short period."

"I know, but—"

"Let Bhavari bring her muracos to us. After what she attempted in your home, it's clear she'll go to any lengths, including finishing what she and the others started. Janus Nether is likely her target. Now that Abelone is dead, she has nothing but her grief and revenge to keep her going. She'll have the muracos attack the black werewolves of Janus Nether because she wants to bring you down to her level. She may have missed her chance to kill you but Bhavari is still a threat."

"I know all of that. But I won't stand by and wait for her to jump all those muracos to Janus Nether. Mother, I … I saw what their bite does to a black werewolf." Tears formed in eyes already red. "I saw the self-control leech from Marrok, as his color bled away. I can't permit that to happen to other black werewolves. It's a brutal and sickening fate they don't deserve."

Tears fell, and Oriana let them, holding Kalinda's gaze the same way she had held her hand—tenderness overladen with determination.

"What do you suggest then?"

"I agree that Janus Nether is the target. Their silver snare-free status is the most visible and far-reaching of my matriarchal decrees. Few cared about or know of the white werewolves in Steelburgh, but a silver snare-free Janus Nether was worldwide news, creating pundits in every nook of the planet. If it's overrun by muracos, turning innocent black werewolves into faded threats to us all, we'll have more to concern ourselves with than a heartbroken healer on a murderous warpath."

"There will be chaos. Scared witches make for deadly witches, Oriana. Threatened black werewolves, even ones in silver snares, won't stand by and wait to be turned by muracos or attacked as a preemptive strike by frightened witches."

"We need to evacuate the region, as soon as possible."

"It's a large area, and you have less than two days."

Dark brows scrunched together. "Why only two days?"

Kalinda waited as Oriana contemplated her own question. Her gaze traveled to her sleeping granddaughter, calm and quiet, so unlike when she'd arrived. The sound of Keira's high-pitched screams had brought Kalinda running from the balcony.

She reached for the comforter covering Keira's petite form, hating what she would see if she pulled the blanket back, but drawn to the sight anyway. Hand on the comforter, she stopped at Oriana's firm command of, "Don't."

"I want to check on the healer's work. Her bruises should be better."

Oriana nodded and lowered her eyes but said nothing more. Kalinda took that as permission to proceed, so she pulled down the comforter. Keira slept in only a pair of panties and an undershirt. After Keira's birth, Kalinda had added a dresser to Oriana's childhood suite, stocking it with items for her grandchild. Whatever Keira may have needed when she visited Kalinda, she made sure to keep on hand, including clothing. But the healer had wanted nothing against Keira's bruised skin, so Oriana had washed and dressed her in the barest of clothing before tucking her into bed and rocking her to sleep.

"Marrok didn't mean to hurt our daughter." So she had said, a half dozen times, apologizing to Keira who cried during the non-invasive medical examination.

"I know."

"He didn't realize how tightly he was holding her. He thought he was protecting her. Marrok *did* protect her."

"I know that as well." Marrok had protected Keira to the point of nearly breaking her arms and legs in his rough grip.

Keira's body no longer bore the bright red of fresh bruises but the bluish-purple of the early stage of healing. In a few hours, they should be better still and pale green. With another treatment, maybe tomorrow, the bruises should be completely healed. But one had to be careful using strong magic on children as young as Keira. It could do more harm than good. It was a testament to Oriana's concern about Keira's health and shock over Marrok that she'd consented to Kalinda calling for her personal healer to work on Keira. It could've also been Oriana's wide-eyed worry over Keira's head wound.

Kalinda tucked the comforter back around her precious grandbaby. Bhavari would suffer for what she had done. Kalinda would see that she did.

"He didn't mean to hurt her," Oriana repeated, a mantra only necessary for herself. She raised her head. "He threw her to get to me. I heard my baby land, a hard thud. But there wasn't anything I could do to help her. I couldn't risk taking my eyes off Marrok to see where Keira had landed and if she was okay. He was right in front of me, and all I could see was him. But my mind and heart were torn between the two of them."

Pulled by their mutual love for Keira, heir to Earth Rift, Kalinda and Oriana peered down at the little girl, a bandage on her forehead. The healer had closed the wound, the bandage unnecessary except as a deterrent to keep Keira from scratching after she complained the magic was "itchy."

"The white moon is in two days. I'd forgotten. That doesn't give us much time to evacuate the citizens of Janus Nether's three cities."

"No, it doesn't, and it must be done quietly and quickly. We don't want to risk Bhavari learning of the evacuation and altering her plans. Our best chance to recapture or to kill the muracos is to have them where we know they'll be and to have our Crimson Guards waiting for them. Dividing our forces between three cities is a far better option than scouring an entire human region for them in small groups. And that's assuming you're correct about Bhavari having hidden the muracos in Perilune Rille."

Kalinda continued, her perspective firm, her tone confident. "After what she did in Steel Rise, Bhavari and the muracos could be anywhere in the world. If she's working by herself, which I doubt, Bhavari could jump the werewolves to a new location. It would take a dozen or more jumps to transport so many werewolves, but it's doable. Using an extraction spell is certainly quicker and safer than using the Magerun system. Bhavari is an intelligent woman. She would've correctly assumed you would alert the Crimson Guard Transit Authority, providing the CGTA with the name and picture of every escaped Steelburgh muraco and updating their intel to include the witch suspects."

"Everything you've said makes sense. It's all very logical and tidy, but Dr. Bhavari jumping those muracos to my home was messy and irrational. You and I know she had to have been there with them, even if only for a few seconds to ground her magic in the new location and set the forcefield."

Oriana made to leave the bed again, but Kalinda, who sat on the side of the bed beside her daughter, didn't budge, earning her a frown she couldn't care less about.

"Mother, I need to get up and get to work."

"What you need is rest."

"I don't have the time to spare. Less than two days, remember? The white moon will bolster the werewolves' strength while sapping ours, making that day the ideal time to launch an attack against us. It should've occurred to me earlier. I had wondered why Abelone and the others had waited to unleash the muracos. Now I know. The biannual white moon solar eclipse. If Dr. Bhavari doesn't move on Janus Nether during this white moon, she'll have to wait until October for the second opportunity. That couldn't have been part of Abelone's plan. I would've hunted the witches and muracos down long before then. No one as smart as Abelone would give me that kind of lead time, not if they wanted their plan to succeed."

Kalinda nodded, smiling. For all of Oriana's kindness and idealism, when it came to being Crimson Hunter, she overflowed with confidence. Kalinda had always relied on that trait in her daughter.

Right now, today, I need my daughter's idealism more than her confidence. When this series of wretched events is all said and done, Oriana's confidence will have taken a hit. Nothing she can't recover from. But her idealism will have died a painful, overdue death.

"Time is of the essence, which doesn't change the fact that you need to rest. Bader is in the other room. He'll stay and help me make evacuation plans while you get a few hours of sleep." She touched Oriana's cheek, thumb rubbing a dark circle forming under her eyes. "Nothing will happen while you rest. I promise."

"You can't keep that promise. The last time I looked away, I lost a piece of my heart."

"But the other half is right beside you. Rest, my dear girl. You'll need all your strength for the upcoming battle. Sleep for a few hours. If not for me or for yourself, then for your daughter. A girl needs her mother."

Kalinda stood, granting Oriana the space to slide down the bed. Long legs curled around Keira, right arm caging the child in and keeping her safe. The luck of the sun had been on Bhavari's side to have jumped into Oriana's suite and not to have found her there the way she was now, eyes closed, drifting into unconsciousness but deadlier for the bundle she guarded. There was no more lethal predator than a witch mother.

"Sleep well. Your father and I will be right here when you awaken. When you do, I'll need my Crimson Hunter."

"You mean your weapon of muraco destruction." Oriana huddled even closer to Keira. "Give me your order now, Mother."

"What do you—"

"The order you've wanted to give me from the beginning. The one you know I'll hate because it will make me no better than every other matriarch of Earth Rift. You know I can't say no, that this situation makes it impossible for me to do anything other than obey because not to will condemn scores of black werewolves to Marrok's fate. So, just say the words and leave me alone with my child."

Kalinda stared at Oriana's back. A black robe covered a dress splattered with Marrok's blood. She'd tried to talk Oriana into changing but her words had fallen on deaf ears. But the soiled garment would soon come off, replaced by Oriana's red-and-black Crimson Hunter body armor. Kalinda had them custom-made for Oriana, and three hung in her bedroom closet.

Placing a knee on the bed, Kalinda leaned over Oriana, kissed her head, and whispered in her ear, "Put those rabid dogs down, Crimson Hunter, that's an order from your matriarch."

April 25, 2243
Perilune Rille
Apogean Tide Borough

Bhavari needed to get off-planet. But how? She couldn't risk accessing her bank account or using her interplanetary passport. Both could be tracked.

She paced in small circles across the street from the warehouses. From this vantage point, she would see anyone converging on the complex from the outside. If Crimson Guards jumped inside the warehouses with the muracos, she would hear the battle. Either way, Bhavari would have a small window of time to get the hell away from there.

Sliding down the side of a twenty-foot, metal shipping container, Bhavari ran through her options. Before she finished her short list, she realized none of her options would include her survival. Bhavari had gone after Matriarch Oriana. Worse, the witch hadn't been in her suite.

When she had seen Matriarch Oriana's consort standing guard in front of a partially closed door, as if he'd been privy to her plan to murder his mate, Bhavari had been too frightened to do anything other than run.

It wasn't until she'd landed inside her warehouse office that the full scope of what she'd done had crashed over her. She'd sank into the chair in the corner of the room, weeping. How could she have forgotten about the matriarch's little girl? True, she had no way of knowing the matriarch's suite connected to her daughter's bedroom. But the moment she'd seen an angry, ready-to-fight Cyrus of Steelcross, a ferocious sentry, she had known who was behind the door he shielded.

Limp hair covered a face ashamed by her own cowardice. She'd escaped before the black werewolf had come for her, leaving the muracos behind to wreak havoc on Matriarch Oriana's family. Having second guessed the logic of returning to the warehouse, she'd also left those muracos behind. But she hadn't gone far, though.

Pulling knees to her chest, Bhavari wept harder. When had nationalism come to mean more to her than morality? Was revenge worth a child's life? Was she any different from the muracos?

Bhavari had once thought herself superior to every werewolf, especially white ones. She had treated them long enough and knew them well enough to know that, when it came to their blood-and-magic lust, they had little to no self-control when in the presence of a witch. She, on the other hand, had no genetic excuse she could offer to justify her actions. Bhavari had destroyed a family.

The tears came harder, faster. Had the residents of Steel Rise contacted Matriarch Oriana yet? Did she know her consort and daughter were dead? Was she looking for Bhavari? Or hell, was Matriarch Kalinda?

Bhavari rushed to her feet, tripping on her black cloak. It wasn't much of a disguise, but the hood would cover half of her face, which was enough to slow any facial recognition program she might encounter.

She flipped the hood up and prepared to jump. If Zev were lucky, he would take his brother's death as a hard lesson of what happened to werewolves who thought themselves equal to that of witches. If he were unlucky, he would return to the warehouse in time to die with the others.

The white moon would occur in less than two days. Bhavari and Abelone had planned for that day for a year. Now, as the once-anticipated date approached, Bhavari regretted letting her wife talk her into such an audacious and dangerous plot.

Bhavari called her magic to her. She envisioned where she wanted to go—her home in Copper Vale—the place where she would die surrounded by echoes of her many years of happiness with Abelone. Suicide was a coward's way out, but she had already proven herself one. Why change direction now?

Glancing around the shipping container to the warehouses, she smiled, satisfied the muracos would die along with her. With their deaths, and even her failed assassination attempt, Abelone's message had been sent. Matriarch Oriana would hate them for betraying her, despise Bhavari the most for taking away her family. But the young matriarch would've received the message loud and clear.

Equality was a fable, a fairytale parents told their children as a bedtime story. Children gobbled up those kinds of legends, fascinated by the myth of equality and the lore of equity.

In a roundabout way, Abelone's plan had succeeded in pulling Matriarch Oriana away from her fairytale thinking and into the real world.

Bhavari smiled weakly and jumped home—or rather, she intended to go home. She landed in her medical office at Steelburgh's Crimson Guard Headquarters, strapped to her chair, a glowing, red whip coiled from throat to ankles.

She wasn't surprised to see who held the other end of the whip, although the shock of having her magic overridden by a stronger extraction spell had left her teeth chattering and her heart racing.

Bhavari had wanted to die … but on her own terms. She'd intended to concoct a poison that would've had her falling asleep and never waking. Nothing bloody or violent. She'd seen too much of both and had no desire to harm herself beyond what it would take to enter into a peaceful death.

She stared into eyes crueler and deadlier than any muraco in Steelburgh.

She opened her mouth to … scream? Plead? Explain? Bhavari didn't know, and she never would because the glowing whip tightened around her throat, cutting off air and diverting her thoughts but not her gaze.

Eyes bulging, tears flowing, she watched her executioner watch her die. No satisfied smile, no contemptuous sneer, not even a baring of teeth, revealing her true nature—a wolf in matriarchal clothing.

The whip tightened.

And tightened.

Blood of the Sun Decree #1
January 1, 1300

BY MATRIARCHAL DECREE, EARTH RIFT WILL BE
FOREVER GOVERNED BY A WITCH FROM THE BLOOD
OF THE SUN FAMILY. BE IT FURTHER DECREED THAT
WITCHES ARE THE SUPREME AUTHORITY OF THE
PLANET.

Alba, Matriarch of Earth Rift

15: Crossroads

April 26, 2243
Irongarde Realm
City of Wild Moor

"That fucking bitch. I'm going to kill her." Zev rammed his fist into his living room wall. Once, twice, three times. "I'm going to rip her open from throat to stomach with my bare hands." Then he would shove his claws into her open chest, searching for the heart Marrok stupidly believed loved him. Once he found the worthless organ, he would make Oriana eat it, choking on her lies as she died.

Zev smashed the wall the way he wanted to beat Oriana to death—one brutal strike after another.

He didn't care his knuckles bled or that his brother gaped at him.

Alarick's gaze rose from Zev's bruised and bloody hands that would soon heal, thanks to werewolf's superior genetics, to his face, before falling to his neck.

Shit.

"What this side of the moon have you done?" With an impressive leap from the sofa to directly in front of him, Alarick shoved Zev in the chest. "You dumb asshole. You let one of those underground doctor freaks operate on you. I thought you were talking big shit when you said you were going to Perilune Rille. But your stupid ass actually had your rage disruptor removed. First Marrok and now you. I don't want to lose both of my brothers."

At the mention of his baby brother's name, Zev punched the wall again, splitting skin and breaking plaster. He didn't care about either. He would destroy his entire apartment if it would help ease the pain of losing Marrok.

"I went there for us."

"Bullshit. You did it for yourself." Alarick turned away from Zev, anxiety in every taut line of his back and shoulders. "You aren't the only one who wants things to change."

"Then stand with me. Fight by my side. After knowing what Oriana did to Marrok, the decision should already be made for you."

"Like I said, you're a dumb asshole." With none of the speed or grace he'd used to jump in Zev's face, Alarick slumped to the sofa. "Oriana asked you to meet us at Dad's house, but your sorry ass didn't show up." Alarick waved in the general direction of Zev's bare neck. "Now I know why. With your shitty attitude toward Oriana, it's a good thing you didn't show."

"Why? Because I would've killed her right then and there?" His scoff could've sliced through iron. "I should've gone. It would've saved me time hunting her down."

"You've always been stupid as a bag of moonrocks when it came to Oriana. Your mind is closed to seeing her in any way other than the way you think she is. I was there with Dad and Mom when Oriana arrived. I told you what she told us."

"That bitch killed our brother."

"She didn't. What happened to Marrok wasn't her fault."

"Those muracos were there because of her. You think it's a coincidence she wasn't at home?"

"What, you hate Oriana so much you think she would go to those lengths not only to have her consort murdered but to risk the life of her child and heir to Earth Rift?"

What Zev knew was that witches couldn't be trusted. The crazy doctor hadn't clued him in on that part of her plan, and he knew why. She'd waited for him to return home before she sent muracos after Oriana, knowing damn well his brother would be there. Once he finished with Oriana, the crazy bitch doctor would be next.

"All I'm saying is that shit rolls downhill."

"You have no idea what you're talking about." Alarick stood, jeans hung low, shirt wrinkled, and a day's worth of hair on his face. His brother's normal look for a Saturday except for the red, puffy eyes. Werewolves need allies in high places if we want the rights we deserve. Oriana is that ally."

"We don't need her." Zev fought hard to keep his anger in check. He needed his brother to understand. "We're begging for scraps from their table, happy with any morsel the witches toss our way. That's no way to live."

"That's not what Oriana is doing."

"Isn't it? Little scraps here and there. She gives us enough to keep us from starving, hopeful, but also dependent on her for our next meal."

"What in the hell do you expect her to do? Even as a matriarch, she's still one witch. She fought her own damn Crimson Guards because they broke one of two decrees intended to give us a modicum of liberty."

"Born of her guilt from all of her privilege. What other brainwashed bull-shit did Solange feed you after you shined her boots and kissed her ass?"

"Fuck you, you closed-minded asshole." Alarick's foot connected with Zev's sofa. The sofa skidded back, denting the wall behind it and adding to the growing damage to his living room. "Look, I don't want to fight. I came here to pass along Oriana's message. Janus Nether is under martial law. We're being evacuated. Mom has offered to let us stay with her until the Crimson Guards have secured the escaped muracos."

"Secured? Is that your word or Oriana's? They're going to kill them."

"Good. After what they did to Marrok, all of those motherfuckers deserve to die."

"Since when did you become a werewolf traitor?"

Alarick stepped into his space, so close Zev could smell the two beers he'd grabbed from the fridge and downed before telling him about Marrok.

"Nothing in this world is as black and white as you like to believe. Friends can become enemies and enemies, allies. I make zero excuses for witches, including Mom and Oriana, and I make none for werewolves. Your whole life you've been spoiling for a fight with witches."

Alarick walked past Zev, gathered the empty beer cans and crushed them before tossing them back on the table. When his brother turned back to him, smelling of sadness but looking resigned, Zev knew he'd lost another brother.

"No one else in Janus Nether knows the real reason behind the evacuations, but Oriana thought we had a right to the truth. Mom has already jumped Dad to her home in Ironmere. Like I said, we have an open invitation to join them. I came here hoping to talk you into leaving with me, even if we don't go to Mom's or Ironmere."

Again, Alarick's eyes fell to Zev's neck. "But you have no intention of leaving. You want this fight. You want to spill witch blood, even the blood of your sister-in-law, not because of a vigilante's sense of righteous revenge but because witches have the power you think belongs to werewolves. Matriarchy and patriarchy are both systems of oppression that shouldn't exist on Earth Rift, but both have. Yesterday werewolves ruled. Today witches do." Alarick shrugged, but it wasn't a movement of nonchalance but of a fatigue much older than his years. "Who knows what it'll be tomorrow."

"Stay. Fight by my side," Zev blurted, a desperate plea he couldn't resist making, even though he knew the answer he'd get.

Most of the muracos had accepted him as their leader, an intoxicating power rush he hadn't expected. But those werewolves couldn't replace the love and trust of his blood brothers. Marrok was gone, and he would have to learn to live with that hole in his life. But if there were anything he could say or do to keep the hole from gaping wider, he would do it.

"Come on. You and me. Even with your silver snare, when the white moon rises tomorrow, the effect of the silver snare will lessen. Hell, you don't have to fight, if you don't want to. Just … just don't leave. Don't turn your back on family."

Alarick swore, grabbing Zev in a hard, tight hug. "You're the biggest ass-hole ever. A selfish bastard on your best day."

A goodbye, not an acceptance.

Zev squeezed back, already missing him, the hole in his heart a deep wound not even witch blood could fill. That wouldn't prevent Zev from try-ing, however.

He released his brother, inhaling his familial scent before stepping back from him.

Alarick pressed a brass plated Magerun token into his hand. "This is from Oriana. Show it to an attendant and you'll be fast-tracked onto any transporter. With this, you can go anywhere in the world, Zev. You don't have to stay here. War is coming to Janus Nether, but you don't have to be a part of it."

"I won't die, and I won't need Oriana's guilt gift."

"If she finds you here, allied with the muraco, you'll leave her no choice but to use lethal force."

"I'm not Marrok. I won't become her prey." Zev opened his hand, permitting the token to slip through his fingers. "She'll be mine."

The stench of sadness wafting from Alarick intensified, but he accepted Zev's words as final, just as Zev accepted Alarick's decision not to stay and fight by his side.

"Take care of Dad. Let him know I did it for all of us. For werewolf freedom."

Alarick's eyes called him a lying asshole, but he refrained from saying it. But he did leave Zev with parting words that wounded even as they bolstered.

"You're a black werewolf with the delusions and bloodlust of a muraco. I didn't think that terrible combination was possible, yet here you stand." Alarick embraced Zev again. "I love you, bro. So do Dad and Mom. And so did Marrok. Remember that."

When that fateful day came—werewolves versus witches—
Zev remembered. He remembered the muracos arrival, as if birthed from the white moon. He'd joined his white brothers in claws and fangs against the Crimson Guards. He remembered when he spotted Oriana across the battlefield—tired and weak from a long day of fighting but as stubborn a warrior as he was himself.

When he went for Oriana's throat, rage overtaking him, the love he felt for Marrok was all the fuel he needed to harness the power of the white moon. Yes, Zev remembered. He slashed out, missing her throat but catching her blocking arm. Oriana blasted him with her cannon, her counterattack quick but nonlethal.

Yes, Zev remembered it all.

His love.

His hate.

April 30, 2243
Irongarde Realm
Iron Spire

Oriana sat on the couch in Kalinda' office, holding Marrok's tablet. Strange, with the amount of damage her suite had sustained from the fight, her consort's tablet had survived. Considering Marrok primarily used the device to read Helen's journal entries on muracos, its survival was more ironic than strange. Oriana had no idea why Nahara had thought it important to save the device and return it to her. Perhaps because she knew how much Marrok had loved the tablet. Or maybe Nahara could think of no other way to help ease Oriana's pain. Nahara's reasoning didn't matter, though, only her empathy, which she appreciated.

Oriana touched the tablet's screen. It lit up, and she read what was most likely the last journal entry her consort had read. The thought filled her heart with pain and her eyes with tears. Oriana blinked the tears away and forced herself to read her grandmother's journal.

It's decided. I can't say I'm happy with my decision, but I see no other way. I haven't informed Tuncay or Kalinda, and I won't. If I did, they would try to talk me out of it. In a weak moment, I would probably allow the persuasion. But that's how I've come to this crossroads, listening to Tuncay and my heart instead of following my mind and common sense.

He thinks I don't know, but very little can be kept hidden, especially from me. Metal is harmful to werewolves. We all know that, which is why witches have injected themselves with liquid steel and iron for generations.

Our metal-magic weapons can kill werewolves, and that's been our advantage since the time of Alba. After years of feeding Tuncay small doses of my magic, tainted from iron in my body, the unanticipated effect of the experiment has revealed itself as a crippling defeat.

Tuncay is fading right before my eyes. He's lost weight—his features gaunt in that way of the sick and dying. Iron poisoning, Tuncay's healer informed me when confronted. Death will eventually take him from Kalinda and me unless I discover a way to reverse the damage my magic kisses have done to his body. He thinks I don't know the real reason behind his illness. Kalinda certainly doesn't. We've become a family of liars, proficient at keeping secrets from each other and of self-delusion.

I've enlisted Farkas' assistance in what could be my final experiment. She's the best Crimson Hunter a matriarch could ever hope to have. I wish I had more time to better prepare, but I don't. Tuncay doesn't have more time either. I'll have to trust the spell Farkas and I have devised. The cuts to my arms and legs will serve as a valve through which we should be able to control the flow of blood we'll pull from me. The critical piece, the part of the plan I'm most nervous about, is the extraction of the metal from my blood.

The trial runs, with small amounts of blood, have proven successful. But are the results valid? Can I trust the reliability of the process when applied on a grander scale? I wish I knew. I wish, not for the first, or even the hundredth time since becoming matriarch, that I had the right answers.

The last time she stood on her mother's office balcony it had been too dark for her to see Wild Moor's starmount tower without the aid of her magic. But during the bright light of day, and with no fog to impair her sight, Oriana could see all the way to Wild Moor. From this very spot, Kalinda had focused her magic on the starmount towers of all of Janus Nether, turning them on and triggering the stormbringer spell.

Matriarch Alba had been the first witch to realize metal could not only be used to help witches control their magic but could also be used against werewolves. The stormbringer spell had evolved out of necessity and only been used to protect the lives of witches. Without it, the Blood of the Sun family would've perished like so many other witch families during the War of Eternal Hunger. The erection and strategic placement of starmount towers was Matriarch Alba's contingency plan. In the event of another war with werewolves, the starmount towers could be used by the matriarch to channel her stormbringer spell.

Oriana now knew the true meaning behind the title of the war between werewolves and witches. She hadn't needed the rest of her grandmother's journals to figure out the truth, not that Kalinda was willing to part with them. What she'd wanted was confirmation. Oriana wouldn't get it, at least not from Helen's journals.

Solange's magic preceded her arrival beside Oriana.

"You could've entered the office like a normal person. Mother's with Keira at the stables."

"Only Matriarch Kalinda would have a stable of horses in a big city instead of in a rural area where they belong. I've thought it strange ever since we were children."

"Mother hates the smell of trees, grass, dirt, and manure."

"Basically, she dislikes nature and everything about horses except for the prestige of owning the best thoroughbreds this side of our solar system."

Oriana peeled her gaze away from the starmount tower. During Alba's time, the stormbringer spell may have been necessary. The spell had probably even been an appropriate response to the subjugation of witches as they fought for their freedom against the physically more imposing werewolves. But that hadn't been the case when Kalinda had decided to use the spell. There were other options. Countless more. Her mother hadn't wanted to explore any of them.

"We need to be quick and decisive," Kalinda had told Oriana.

Quick and decisive had meant hand-to-hand combat when Oriana's Extraction Division could've simply transported the muracos back to Steelburgh.

Once they were in range of the guards' magic, the Extraction Unit could've saved many lives. It wouldn't have been easy to corral the muracos. Witches and werewolves would've still died, but the attempt should've been made. Kalinda, however, had overruled that as a viable strategy.

"Let's sit, and you can tell me what you've found."

Oriana ignored her mother's chaise lounge, choosing to sit beside Solange on the black leather chairs at the glass-topped table. "Did you retrieve what was left of her?"

"That's a good way of putting it." Solange, who loved gory horror movies, appeared as if she would vomit. "Half an arm, and the top half of her head. That's all that was left of Dr. Bhavari."

"Did you interview the Crimson Guard who found her?"

"I interviewed all of them. Considering what happened to the last batch who worked there, they were quick to answer my questions. Your reputation as Crimson Hunter has strengthened."

Oriana shifted in her seat. Being a killer wasn't the kind of reputation she wanted. Trust and faith inspired, while fear created unseen enemies.

"The guards have no idea how she got there or when she arrived. The guard who filed the report was the one who found Dr. Bhavari's remains. Two shifted muracos were fighting over what was left of the healer. The guard broke up the fight, and that's when she discovered the source of the were-wolves' fight. To be eaten alive … that's rough."

"You're assuming the muracos killed her. I'm not." Oriana shifted again, uncomfortable with her train of thought. Yet, it had been the same one she'd had for days. Dr. Bhavari's death, at Steelburgh of all places, solidified the terrible ideas filling her head.

"You think she was murdered then given to the muracos as evidence dis-posal? Smart." Solange's shrug could've meant anything. Most likely, though, it meant she couldn't care less how the healer died, or even who killed her, as long as Dr. Bhavari reaped her overdue punishment.

Oriana, however, very much cared who had killed the witch.

Her attention shifted to the starmount tower again. The edifice, much like a witch, was a lightning rod of immeasurable power and destruction. "Did I ever tell you my grandmother cut off her arms and legs?"

"She what?" Solange sat forward in her chair, elbows going to the table, face turned toward Oriana. "Why would she do that? Wait, I thought your grandparents died in a fire."

"They did. Wild sun-magic fire."

Like Marrok, so many of Solange's thoughts showed across her face. Oriana observed her friend work through what she thought she knew about Helen's and Tuncay's death and what Oriana had just told her. She saw the moment when her calculations bottomed out at zero.

"I have no idea what you're talking about."

"I'm fairly certain Grandmother was trying to rid herself of the liquid steel in her body. I don't think she intended to sever her limbs. Most likely, she and her Crimson Hunter used an experimental spell. They focused the spell on Grandmother's legs and arms because that's where the metal was isolated."

"Not amputation but a weird blood-cleansing spell. No offense, but your grandmother couldn't have been that naïve or st …"

"Stupid? It's fine if you say it. I've certainly thought it. Maybe I'm as crazy or as desperate as she grew to be, but I think my theory has merit. Something went wrong. That's indisputable. Her magic must've blazed out of control, damaging her arms and legs."

"You're saying Matriarch Helen blew herself up." Solange gaped at Oriana in that way of hers when she toggled between the appropriate comment to say to a friend who also happened to be her matriarch. The hand she ran over her face and the fish-like opening and closing of her mouth were enough to have Oriana taking pity on her friend.

"I'm not asking you to help me the way Grandmother's Crimson Hunter served her."

"Good, because I *won't*. Your grandmother killed herself, Oriana, and I have no idea what she hoped to achieve."

"I'll tell you, if it works."

"You mean if you don't die."

That's not what Oriana meant. If she died, the second half of her plan wouldn't matter. Although life for Keira wouldn't be the same without Oriana and Marrok in it, Oriana had made arrangements for her daughter in the event of her death. Keira would be happy with Io and Lita. There was also Solange, Alarick, and Bader, all of whom would help raise Keira the way Marrok and Oriana would've. If Kalinda knew of her updated will, she would be furious. But her mother's opinion no longer mattered. Kalinda had ruined enough lives. Keira's life wouldn't be added to the long list.

Oriana pulled up her sleeve. Zev's claw marks had closed, but they'd left a faint scar that hadn't yet disappeared. If she found her brother-in-law alive, would she repay him in kind?

An image of Zev going for her throat, not a second of hesitation in his attack, flashed through her mind.

She would repay him. For Zev, death would be preferable to what Oriana had in mind if she found the black werewolf alive and well.

Oriana stood. It was time to hunt werewolves.

16: Confrontation

April 30, 2243
Irongarde Realm
City of Wild Moor
Redwatch Suburb

Zev was being hunted. He could feel eyes on him, sense a presence other than the fifty white werewolves loping behind him. They'd traveled about twenty-five miles from downtown Wild Moor to Redwatch, a suburb of the city. The residential area, popular among single, young fathers, like Io had once been, boasted quiet neighborhoods, low crime, and good schools.

The neighborhood was still quiet, and the only crime in Redwatch was the one perpetrated by Kalinda, Oriana, and their damn starmount towers.

The suburb had been razed, magic blasts that leveled homes, memories, and each of those good schools werewolf children could never return to. Everywhere Zev's paw feet landed, he stepped in dust and ash caused by the fallout. It fell like black soot from the sky, clinging to everything it touched, including the werewolves.

Zev stopped, his keen werewolf nose sniffing. He couldn't smell anything beyond the residue left by the blasts. The dust and ash didn't affect his hearing, though, so Zev listened, ears erect. Turning in a slow circle, Zev strained to hear something other than the werewolves around him.

The muracos also halted. Phelan and Adolfus came to stand beside Zev, their snouts lifted, hairs on their backs raised.

He wasn't the only one who had sensed they weren't alone on the nameless street. Instinct told him to run. But pride kept him rooted.

Muracos growled, snapping at the air. Phelan and Adolfus joined them, jostling Zev with their anxious movements. Then the muracos darted up the street, plunging through and disappearing into a dust cloud that extended the width of the street. The sounds the werewolves made ranged from barks to howls to growls.

Zev hadn't budged, not even when Adolfus and Phelan also galloped toward the dust cloud, their muscular forms swallowed up as easily as the others.

He'd wanted to yell out to them. Warn them. He howled. Over and again, Zev howled, infusing a bark into the sounds rumbling out of him. He had to make them understand, had to draw their attention away from the futile hunt. But no one emerged from the dust cloud or returned his bark or howl.

Zev retreated, walking backward, eyes trained on the street in front of him. The sense of being hunted intensified. He barked again.

No reply.

He howled.

No answer.

A burst of sound and light filled the space between Zev and the dust cloud.

Blood pumped faster to his heart.

A swirl of yellow and red materialized from the darkness. The ravenous maw, a vortex of magic, drew dust and ash into its mouth. Muracos howled and, for a second, Zev's heart stopped pounding as relief bloomed. They hadn't abandoned him. He wasn't in this fight alone.

Their howls, however, soon turned to whines. Whatever was happening on the other side of the growing wind tunnel had Zev turning on his heels and getting the hell out of there.

The vortex followed.

He ran faster.

Zev darted around corners. Jumped over rubble. Slid on ash but didn't lose his balance.

No matter how fleet-footed he was, the vortex continued to gain on him. It nipped at his heels, as if playing a deadly game of chase.

Zev didn't know where to go. Every street he ran down looked the same—like an apocalyptic town. Charcity. Cinders. The Void. Any of those names would better suit than Redwatch. It was all in ruins.

He skidded to a stop. Where to go? Where to go? Shit, he'd run himself into what looked to be a cul-de-sac. Growling, Zev turned to face the vortex that had chased his ass all over Redwatch.

No, not chased. Hunted. He'd become prey.

The rotating column of magic, now a bright red, towered a hundred feet high and spanned two city blocks. The high winds no longer sucked in every-thing around it. It didn't have to because muracos swirled in the tornado. They had been stripped of the black dust and ash—their white fur now sparks of morbid light mixed with fatal red.

Crimson.

Crimson Hunter.

Zev waited for Oriana to appear from her death tornado. She'd blocked the only exit. He'd tried outrunning her magic. All his effort had earned him were burning lungs and cramped legs.

If Oriana wanted to fight, there the fuck he was. Standing on his hindlegs, Zev growled. Oriana may have named Marrok Cyrus of Steelcross, but once he killed her, Zev would become Alpha of Earth Rift. She'd felt his claws once. Zev could guarantee she would feel them again.

But the witch was toying with him, hiding behind her vortex which was … retreating? Not retreating but crumbling in on itself. In deafening waves, the vortex imploded, made scarier by the death whimpers of the crushed muracos. The image was like the beer cans Alarick had crushed in his strong hands then tossed onto Zev's table—trash to be discarded later.

The gruesome scene had taken less than a minute. Zev could now see the cul-de-sac clearly. It's destruction as complete as the rest of Redwatch. Gone were the dust, the ash, and the sooty curtain of air, to be replaced by a cloud-less blue sky he hadn't seen in days. For the first time, Zev found himself more grateful for the sun than for the moon.

Oriana had spared him. He didn't know why she had, nor did he trust her retreat. She'd be back, but Marrok wouldn't wait around for her return.

He took off. Moonblight Penitentiary was a half day's run from Redwatch. If he pushed himself, stopping for quick breathers and water, he would reach the prison by nightfall. When he did, he would free the muraco prisoners. Zev could still make his plan work, even without the Steelburgh white were-wolves.

Yet, when Zev reached the small town of Brassville, most buildings wrecked, Moonblight Penitentiary stood tall and strong—a pillar of iron. Zev's oasis. His army to lead. His …

Zev quirked his head to the side—listening. Creeping closer to the security gate, Zev tried to detect movement and sound within. He heard nothing, so he tried the gate. Unlocked. On high alert, he stalked inside only to find himself the only werewolf at Moonblight. The matriarchs didn't give a shit about werewolves. If they had, they wouldn't have used their starmount towers on Janus Nether. Yet, they'd evacuated a prison of convicted witch killers? Saved muracos from their attack?

This couldn't be.

Zev shifted, scampering away from Moonblight. Exhausted but fueled by an emotion he refused to name, Zev ran the length of Brassville, searching for signs of life. When he found none, he returned to Redwatch.

After a restless night's sleep, he continued his search.

Ironbark.

Mage Flame.

North Star.

Nothing. No one.

Days later, Zev found himself back in Wild Moor in the center of the same town square where he and his muracos had made their stand against Oriana and her Crimson Guards.

When he had walked through the city of his birth, the destruction from the starmount tower having made it almost unrecognizable, each unsteady step he took caused him to shift from werewolf to man. By the time he reached the square, as naked as the day he was born, Zev had drawn two conclusions.

One, he was the only person left in Wild Moor and the surrounding towns.

Two, Oriana hadn't spared him. She'd created his worst nightmare, bringing to life his greatest fear. He'd felt it after Alarick had left his apartment. The emotion doubled when he'd gone to his father's home, knowing Io had left with Lita but needing to see for himself. The feeling of aloneness had ebbed when the muracos had appeared in Wild Moor. But the discomforting sensation returned in triplicate, intensifying with each abandoned suburb he reached.

No pack. No community. Alone.

The worst fate for a werewolf.

May 7, 2243
Steelcross Realm
Steel Haven Medical Center

"I refuse."

"Yet here you are."

"Against my will."

Oriana swept her gaze over Kalinda. Hair pulled taut in a severe bun, black blouse and slacks crisp to the point of sharpness, lips painted red but set in a frown, Kalinda looked like a disgruntled teacher on her way to the funeral of a student she'd murdered.

"Against your will? Look who is being dramatic today. I'm the one in a hospital bed, not you."

Kalinda's frown deepened, and she stepped closer to Oriana's bed, arms crossing over her chest. "I'm here because your healer called me. She said I'm your next of kin, which I damn well know. Then she mentioned something about, if I wasn't available to assist with the procedure, that you had given her permission to make the request of Lita of Ironmere City."

"No need to spit Lita's name. She's my mother-in-law after all."

"You're not *her* daughter. You're *mine*. She has no place here."

Fidgeting with the white covers, more to annoy her mother than to arrange them to her liking, Oriana ignored Kalinda, an act of passive-aggressiveness that did nothing to dull Oriana's anger and hurt.

"Stop that." Yanking the covers out of Oriana's hand, Kalinda straightened them herself. "You're not sick. You shouldn't even be here."

As usual, her mother was wrong. Oriana felt sick to her soul.

"I'm going to have a blood transfusion."

"So Dr. Shams informed me. Do not do this. You know what happened to my mother."

Real pain entered Kalinda's eyes—the pain of having lost her parents and the pain of possibly losing her daughter. Until a week ago, Oriana would've never contemplated using her mother's love and grief against her—an act of insensitivity unbecoming of a daughter and of a matriarch.

"As you see, I'm taking precautions Grandmother did not." Oriana smiled as if they weren't speaking of a life-and-death procedure. "The furniture is flame retardant, although I don't think the walls are. But the sprinklers are up to code, so that's a plus."

"This isn't a joking matter."

"Dr. Shams will be here, which is more than Grandmother had. Then there's you. The second strongest witch in the realms."

If Kalinda's eyebrow arched any higher, it would be in her hairline.

"You're in rare form. Is today the day?"

Kalinda glanced around, found a chair in the corner of the room and pulled it beside Oriana's bed. Sitting with legs crossed, she observed Oriana with something akin to a snake sizing up its next meal.

Oriana sat up and swung her legs over the edge. She returned Kalinda's assessing glare. "Yes, today is the day."

"Fine."

Oriana dove off the cliff. No net. No magic. Just a free fall that could break every bone in her body, the agony of such a landing no more excruciating than the broken heart she carried.

"How about this, Mother: I'll tell you exactly how I've chosen to respond to what you've done, and you can stop the charade."

"I have no idea what you're talking ab—"

"Stop *lying* to me!" Unbidden, Oriana's Ravagers of the Lost cannons formed. She jumped from the bed. "No more lies. You know what?" Oriana rounded on Kalinda, who stared up at her with such controlled posturing, a part of her snapped.

Oriana drew her weapons upward, pointing both at her mother. She had never seen a star die but she imagined the astrological phenomenon looked very much like Kalinda's eyes—the fuel of her core running out, her star contracting, the layers expanding, ejecting critical messages sent to her brain, turning them over into a white dwarf of disbelief then finally into a black dwarf of stunned silence.

A dying star. A mother's shattered world.

Oriana had prepared for this confrontation, including what she would say and how she would react when Kalinda pretended, lied, and outright dismissed her accusations. She'd rehearsed everything, but not this. Not the soul-stealing, heart-wrenching anger that had come over her when Kalinda did exactly what Oriana knew she would.

Not only anger but a bone-deep disappointment. After all they'd been through and after all Kalinda had done, she still couldn't look Oriana in the face and speak the truth. So, there Oriana stood, weapons she'd used to kill criminals pointed at the last person she would ever want to hurt but who had brought pain to so many.

"Matriarch Kalinda of Irongarde City, you have been found guilty of aiding and abetting the escape and rebellion of one thousand three hundred forty-five muracos, of the murder of Dr. Bhavari of Cooper Vale, and of the willful destruction of Janus Nether—all acts punishable by death. As Matriarch of Steelcross, I hereby sentence you to death by my hand."

Said hands trembled slightly, but Oriana forced them to steady. No matter how much her words felt like flesh dipped in scalding oil, or how the sight of her mother's teary gaze and slumped shoulders hurt to witness —Oriana would not back down. Not this time.

"You would kill me? The woman who gave you life? Raised you? Loved and cared for you? You would sentence me to death?"

"It's the law. You forgot to add that you taught me to follow and uphold the law. As matriarch and Crimson Hunter, I'm charged with doing both."

Like Kalinda's, Oriana's cheeks glistened with tears. She cried for the little girl who thought her mother could do no wrong, for the young woman who refused to accept when she had. Who was the greater criminal then? The matriarch whose schemes ended lives or the matriarch whose gullibility made her a pawn?

With a quick movement, Oriana jerked her left cannon away from Kalinda's chest and raised it to her own head.

"Noooo, Oriana. Don't. Don't."

"We're both guilty. I didn't see, although I should've. I let you point me in your chosen direction, and I went. I followed orders, like a good little witch. I believed in you more than I trusted myself." Oriana's chest seized with pain, with guilt, with shame sharper than a werewolf's fangs. "I've killed witches and werewolves in your name, as Crimson Hunter of Earth Rift, claiming their lives with a righteous arrogance."

"They broke realm law."

"So did you!" Oriana pressed the barrel of the right cannon to Kalinda's chest. "So. Did. You," she repeated, her tone a soft contrast to her outburst. "You may continue to lie to me and to everyone else, but you know the truth. You know you're guilty of breaking realm laws, although you feel justified in your actions. You always do. But how does it feel, Mother, to have the Crimson Hunter's chosen weapon pointed at you? To know I am within my legal rights to end your life? Your judge and executioner. How does it feel?"

Oriana pushed magic into both cannons, priming them. This wasn't what she'd planned, wasn't how she wanted to die. Keira didn't deserve to grow up knowing her mother had killed her grandmother and herself. She wouldn't understand.

Kalinda wept, shoulders shaking and lips quivering. Her mother was a beautiful woman but an ugly crier. Perhaps that explained why she'd never seen her cry before. Likely, Kalinda removed her mask only when she was alone, ensconced in her suite where no one could witness the vulnerable witch who resided inside the hard-as-iron matriarch.

"I love you, Oriana."

"I know, and it's an awful, brutal love that stifles and deceives. You also love Earth Rift but to the point of violent adherence to a matriarchal system that enslaves us all. I honestly don't think you believe you did anything wrong. You wanted me to co-rule, but you had no idea what that would look like in reality, especially when my convictions diverged from yours."

Oriana powered down her cannons, letting her arms fall and shift back to normal. Despite Kalinda's crimes, Oriana couldn't kill her mother. She wasn't above scaring the shit out of her, though.

"You have a month to put your affairs in order."

"W-what do you mean?"

Snatching a tissue from a box on the nightstand, Oriana wiped her face before returning to the bed. She was exhausted, and she hadn't even had the blood transfusion yet.

"I could have you imprisoned for the rest of your life."

"You wouldn't dare. I'm matriarch of—"

"One month to get your affairs in order. That's how long you have to make the transition from Matriarch Kalinda to simply Kalinda of Irongarde City."

Kalinda shot from the chair, tumbling it backward. "You can't. You can't. I'm matriarch."

Settling under the covers, Oriana pulled them back to her waist. "No, you're a criminal I've decided to pardon, even though you don't deserve my kindness. You've never appreciated it before, perhaps you will now. Even if you don't, I won't have the former Matriarch of Irongarde carted off to prison like the common criminal she is."

"Oriana, you cannot do this to me."

"It's already done. You *will* step down from the Matriarchy. Spin whatever tale you wish. I don't care, as long as you remove yourself from the government."

Oriana waited for Kalinda's melancholic visage to morph into sharp lines of fury. But it didn't. She simply stared at Oriana, awaiting the rest of her fate.

She didn't keep her mother waiting.

"You'll also remove yourself from Iron Spire."

That had Kalinda stumbling backward, hand going to her chest and over her heart.

Oriana hated every bit of this. Practicing in front of her mirror, she hadn't felt the magnitude of what this would mean to her mother. But the full impact of her words were knife wounds to Kalinda's heart. Her mother's punishment, like Zev's, had been deliberately chosen.

Oriana had taken no more pleasure in torturing her brother-in-law than she did in ripping everything away from Kalinda that she valued and loved.

"Iron Spire is my home. You can't. Where will I go?"

"Janus Nether was the black werewolves' home, but you didn't hesitate to take it away from them." Oriana steeled herself for the most difficult part of her sentence. "Kalinda of Irongarde City, as of one month from today, you are expelled from Irongarde Realm and excluded from residing in or visiting Steelcross Realm."

Unable to watch her mother's mental disintegration, Oriana closed her eyes, crying along with Kalinda.

Kalinda had lived all her sixty years in Iron Spire and Irongarde Realm. She'd spent the last few decades as Matriarch of Irongarde. So much of her identity stemmed from being a matriarch descended from the first Matriarch of Earth Rift. If Oriana's punishment had ended there, Kalinda would've licked her wounds, settled into retirement and moved on with her life, privileged and unrepentant.

As Crimson Hunter, Oriana had blood on her hands that could never be washed away. She would have to live with each life she'd taken, even though laws of Earth Rift had supported each mortal punishment. But no law could compel Oriana to kill her mother, feeding Kalinda's doomed soul to her Ravagers of the Lost cannons.

Kalinda's crimes meant she'd forfeited her life, but there was more than one way to kill a person other than physical death.

Oriana opened her eyes at the sound of a body hitting the floor. Every instinct told her to run to her mother's side, to help her to her feet and into the chair. Her muscles ached from forcing them not to move. Oriana's mind railed against doing nothing. But she forced herself to impassively watch as a proud witch was brought low by her own machinations.

She couldn't go to her, couldn't offer her mother comfort. Her last decree, the removal of Kalinda from Irongarde Realm and her exclusion from Steelcross, had effectively taken away what mattered most to Kalinda—her family.

Kalinda's family included Bader, the two no longer as estranged as they'd once been. Her parents' relationship, no matter the status, wasn't for Oriana to weigh in on, so she'd turned a blind eye to the renewed affection between the two. Whether their marriage withstood Kalinda's duplicity depended on Bader.

The penalty hurt. Whether Kalinda understood this or not, her sentence was also Oriana's punishment. She loved her mother. Oriana always would. But she couldn't trust her. Not with Earth Rift, and certainly not with Keira.

Grandmother, mother, daughter, three generations of Blood of the Sun witches—a crimson legacy born of fear, misunderstandings, and metal. Witches and werewolves had feasted too long on all three, nearly destroying themselves. It was time to introduce something new into the equation—hope.

Oriana slid from the bed and onto the floor, cradling her weeping mother in her arms. Kalinda clung to Oriana, and she held her just as fiercely.

They stayed intertwined for long minutes, Oriana no more ready to end their bond than Kalinda.

"I love you."

"I know, and I love you, Mother."

Kalinda's hand moved to Oriana's face, wiping away her tears and kissing her cheeks. "In my final act as Matriarch of Irongarde and as Mother to Matriarch Oriana of Steelcross, I'll lend you my magic and support during your blood transfusion. I may have lost you, but I will not permit you to die."

That was good because Oriana didn't want to die. She had so much she needed to live for and even more she needed to redeem. In time, she would forgive Kalinda, but her mother would have to travel her own path of redemption.

Oriana kissed her mother's cheek, knowing by month's end they would never be like this again. She would mourn the loss of Kalinda in her life but not as much as she would grieve for the woman who'd sacrificed her morality to perpetuate a flawed system she'd been tasked with preserving long before she'd taken her first breaths of life.

It wasn't fair.

It wasn't right.

But Kalinda could've done better. Much, much better.

So could Oriana.

17: Hunger of the Hopeful

June 21, 2243
Steelcross Realm
Aphelion Umbra

Kalinda hated to cry. Yet, she'd done little else these past weeks. She thought she would miss Iron Spire, Irongarde, and serving as matriarch. Kalinda did, but not as much as she missed her beloved daughter and granddaughter. Though futile, she'd moved as close to her family as Oriana's dictate would allow. So, she'd had movers transport her belongings from Irongarde across the planet to a home she'd purchased in Aphelion Umbra.

A bottle of wine in hand, Kalinda maneuvered in her living room around boxes she hadn't bothered unpacking. Ignoring the glare from her uninvited guest, she sat on the couch, her mouth on the rim of the bottle.

"Getting drunk won't help."

Drinking deeply, Kalinda closed her eyes and tried to enjoy the rich citrus flavor of her white wine. It tasted bitter, the way every food and drink had since Oriana walked out of her life.

"I hope you're planning on sending these files to our daughter."

Bader snatched the bottle from Kalinda and threw it into the cold fireplace, shattering the bottle and causing her to jump.

"What do you want? Why are you here?"

Bader towered over a seated Kalinda. A month earlier, she wouldn't have tolerated this physical display of male dominance. She despised Bader's non-verbal reminder of how low she'd fallen.

"If you answered my phone calls, I wouldn't have had to come here." He shook her tablet in her face, as if the device was irrefutable evidence of her crimes. "After all you put Oriana through, she deserves to know the truth. All of it, Kalinda."

She reached for her tablet, but Bader was faster. He stalked away from her, kicking boxes out of his way.

Again, she should scold him for such rude behavior. The house may not be Iron Spire, but it was still her home, and Bader had no right to treat it with contempt. *Not contempt for my new home but contempt for me.*

Bader perched his tall frame on the arm of the couch identical to the one she sat on but on the other side of the room. He swiped the tablet's screen several times before stopping. "I shouldn't have left you." Dark eyes lifted to Kalinda's. "I left you both. I should've stayed. Fought harder. Been braver. So should you."

Kalinda didn't need to hear her consort's guilty ramblings. She had her own guilt from which, even in slumber, she couldn't escape.

"You've never let me read Helen's journals."

"You never asked." Kalinda removed her shoes, pulled her stockinged feet onto the couch, and waited for Bader to either finish what he'd come there to say or walk out of her life for good.

"I should've stayed," Bader repeated. "I wished I would have." His shoulders slumped and gaze drifted away before returning to Kalinda's. "We were once a team."

They had been, but those days were so long ago Kalinda could barely remember how it felt to be anything other than an island.

"What are we now?" she asked, despising the tremor that had punctuated her question.

Bader swiped her tablet twice more before stopping and reading.

"It was hiding in plain sight, as humans like to say. I've searched for decades to unearth the truth of the war between witches and werewolves. It was here all along—one of the rare bits of pre-matriarchy history Alba didn't manage to destroy. Admittedly, I understand Alba's motivations. I can't imagine what life was like for witches before Alba's time. Not just the werewolf threat—although that had to have been terrifying—but the lack of control over our witch magic.

I wonder how the witches figured it out. At what point did they realize they could not only insert liquid metal into their bodies to protect themselves and survive but that the metal could be used to manage their magic. I've heard humans say that necessity is the mother of invention. I'd say, for my witch ancestors, that adage certainly proved to be true.

The War of Eternal Hunger. If it weren't so sad, I would laugh. Instead, I've shed a fair number of tears. I once asked Mother how witches controlled their magic before the institutionalization of the rite of endometal fusion. She not only had no answer, she also had never contemplated the question. Mother was curious as to why I raised the issue but just as quickly dismissed the subject.

The question remained, though.

The War of Eternal Hunger. I have to write the words again. Armed with my new insight, I now know it wasn't a war title at all, but the name given to the witches' era of victory over their werewolf oppressors.

I can now lay my question to rest because I've discovered the answer. The way witches used to control their magic was to reduce the natural buildup in their bodies through a safe expulsion. They literally fed werewolves their excess magic, which not only helped them to control their magic but quenched werewolves' hunger for it. But when witches rebelled against werewolves, they cut off access to their magic. Thereby creating an eternal hunger within werewolves, one that witches, thereafter, refused to sate.

We were made for each other, having the ability to fulfill each other's needs. Yet, we've been locked in a battle neither side can ever win. Although I have no evidence to support my contention, I do not believe muracos existed prior to the magic starvation of werewolves. I think mura-cos were an awful yet unexpected byproduct.

I've written all my thoughts down for you, Kalinda, with the hope you'll never need to read my journals. If I don't survive tomorrow's experiment, know that I love you and your father. I ask that you not close your heart and mind to all I've done and learned. I ask that you put aside your grief and finish my life's work.

Don't allow your disappointment in me for choosing this fate over the safety of doing nothing to blind you to our world's great need for change. Please, Kalinda, do not punish our people for my mistakes. They deserve a matriarch who will work to find the balance between witches and were-wolves. It won't happen during your lifetime, perhaps not even during the next, but I have faith that, with the right leadership, the sun and the moon will align in harmony.

Like all great movements. It begins with one mind, one heart, and a sin-gle brave step into the unknown. If not you, Kalinda, then who?"

Kalinda had begun weeping halfway through Bader's flat reading of her mother's final journal entry. She kept crying minutes after he'd finished.

"We should've continued your parents' work. Solving the rift between witches and werewolves should've never fallen to our daughter and her con-sort. Now you and Oriana have lost each other, and all I can do is stand by while the two women I love mourn the loss of the other. What am I to do?"

She felt rather than heard him draw nearer. At his touch, a hand to her knee, she opened her eyes to find him kneeling in front of her.

"How can I continue our marriage after the awful crimes you've committed and the pain you've brought our daughter?"

Kalinda had no response that wouldn't have her embarrassing herself by begging Bader to forgive her and not to leave her alone with her regrets and guilt. So, she wiped her eyes dry, willed her lower lip to cease quivering, and held her consort's dark gaze with the tattered remains of her pride.

Bader sighed. "You're a stubborn witch."

"Yes."

"And ruthless."

Kalinda knew that as well. She needed more wine—preferably a case to dull her pain.

"Send the files to Oriana. The gesture won't alter her stance toward you but it's a necessary first step to rebuilding your relationship with our daughter." Bader rose, grabbed his suit jacket from off the couch where he'd been seated, and pulled it on.

Kalinda didn't watch him leave, but she did hear the firm shutting of her front door. Whether that closed door would prove a symbolic ending of their marriage, time would tell. For now, all Kalinda had was a big house, decades ahead of her, and not a soul to share either with.

July 3, 2243
Steelcross Realm
Moonvale Forest

"Are you sure you want to do this by yourself?" Alarick placed a small cooler on the ground. "I mean, what if something goes wrong?"

To Alarick's credit, he didn't look at Oriana's arms, covered by a lightweight red jacket she would exchange for a warm hoodie when the sun set and a cool front from Silentdrift Lake rolled in.

"Don't waste your breath." Solange shifted closer to Alarick, their arms grazing. "I've already asked, and she turned me down. I don't know why you bothered packing her a cooler with water and sandwiches." In a gesture unlike the Solange Oriana knew, her best friend stood on tiptoe and kissed Alarick's cheek. "It was sweet of you, though. Thank you for thinking of her."

"Ahh, umm … do I still get points if I told you Mom's the one who made the sandwiches and thought of the care package? I'm still the one who held it while you jumped us here."

Solange laughed. "Considering no one actually had to carry the cooler for me to include it in the jump, your meager physical effort counts for very little."

Alarick delivered his whispered response to Solange.

Oriana wandered away from the lovebirds.

She didn't want to think about the last time she'd been in this very spot, crying, anxious, and afraid. She hadn't known what to do, or where else to go. She'd promised she would return but had been unsure if she would be able to keep her oath. She wished she could erase that night from existence.

Oriana would rather spend her time remembering their moonless sky ceremony. He'd looked so handsome that night—her black werewolf—majestic, red eyes enchanting, full of love and hope for a happy life together.

They had been happy. But they'd also been oblivious to satellites orbiting their sun, impacted by and responding to the solar system's shifts.

"Don't go too far," Alarick warned her, sounding more amused than worried. "A little witch alone in a forest can be dangerous. What if that red jacket attracts a big, bad wolf?"

Smiling, Oriana walked away from the copse of trees and back to Solange and Alarick in the clearing. "I'm hoping to attract a big, bad wolf. Preferably a black one but a white one will do. At least for now."

They nodded, still smiling at each other, although no true humor existed in their words. Nor was Oriana's reason for being in Moonvale a laughing matter. But she'd cried enough, her ducts dry, her heart now full of hope.

Oriana missed Kalinda and Marrok. But she couldn't move on until she'd fulfilled her promise.

The destruction of Janus Nether and the deaths caused by the escaped muracos had led to an unexpected window of opportunity to address the future of Earth Rift, witches being more amenable to talk of change than in times past.

Marrok had told her his thoughts about being a prisoner. His comment had been made in reference to Steelburgh, but they had reflected the line he'd drawn between being alive and living. *"The city is beautiful in a sterile, morbid kind of way. It's depressing and, if I ever ended up here, I'd want to jump from the Crimson Guard building and kill myself."*

Alive.

Living.

Not at all the same.

Alarick approached Oriana. They'd grown closer, the last couple of months, so it didn't surprise her when he pulled her into a warm hug. Like Marrok, Alarick carried a woodsy scent, detectable even under the body oil he favored.

"Thank you for having Zev transferred to a prison in Ironmere. Having him close makes it easier for us to visit. He won't admit it, but he's grateful. I still can't believe he turned himself in." With a kiss to her cheek, Alarick stepped back. "For what he did, he's lucky he only got a fifteen-year sentence."

From behind Alarick, Solange shook her head, braids hidden under a white-and-gold head wrap that matched her dress. "Only a person who's never spent time in prison would refer to fifteen years of incarceration as *only*."

"You know what I mean."

"Of course, I do. So does Oriana. But he'll have to be moved again, once you, Lita, and Io settle in Bronze Ward. Everything is almost ready. Right, Oriana?"

She'd zoned out, her attention drawn to a spot of color across the lake.

"Hey, Oriana, what are you looking at?"

She ran away from Solange and Alarick, and to the shoreline, eyes tracking the spot of color as it moved.

"What?" Alarick caught up to her first. "What did you see?"

Oriana raised her hand to point where she'd last seen … something, but nothing was there, only rows of tall, green trees.

Alarick's sight was keener than hers, but his scan of the area was no more successful. He grunted and shook his head. "I don't see anything. Whatever you saw is gone. If you or Solange jump me over there, I could take a look. I really don't like the idea of leaving you out here by yourself."

"Neither do I. I'm giving you three hours." Solange displayed three fingers, as if Oriana needed the visual to clarify. "Three hours—then we're coming back."

"That might not be enough time."

"It probably won't, but that's all the time we're giving you."

As promised, Solange and Alarick returned in three hours. While Solange appeared unsurprised to find Oriana alone, Alarick made an admirable attempt to hide his disappointment.

And so it went for three months, Oriana jumping to and from Moonvale Forest, each trip equally uneventful and increasingly disappointing.

"We know you've done your best," Io had told her. "We don't expect more from you."

Oriana had believed Io, as well as Lita and Alarick, who'd echoed Io's sentiment. Despite their words, they were no more ready to abandon hope than Oriana.

She had used the five months since the blood transfusions, Kalinda by her side for every procedure, to learn how to use her magic without aid of a channeling device. Slow progress, for sure. It was difficult to figure out how to rewire her thinking to manipulate her magic.

Thanks to Kalinda, Oriana had finally been able to read Helen's missing journals. Her grandmother had been ahead of her time. Yet, like all of Earth Rift, also behind the times—the modern world in desperate need of catching up to the past.

Reclined on a blanket, Oriana stared up at the stars and smiled. Occurring once every twenty years, a red moon hung from the sky like a soundless wind chime. The red moon didn't sparkle or glow. It wasn't bright or even a unique shade of red. This was Oriana's first time seeing a red moon. She'd expected more, something stunning. It wasn't. It was . . . well, an uninspiring red moon.

A rustling of leaves sounded behind Oriana. Her smile grew, but she kept her focus on the sight above her and not on the sound behind her. The red moon, darker than she'd imagined, had an appeal other than visual.

There was more movement behind her.

Oriana didn't move, but she did speak. "Did you know the red moon is considered a good omen. Anyone born during a red moon will be blessed by both the sun and the moon. I'm thinking 'born' could also mean 'reborn.' What do you think?"

The sound stopped.

Oriana sat up and turned. No, the red moon wasn't particularly beautiful, but the sight before her was.

Neither a white werewolf, nor a black one, but a thin, dirty human male with untamed, bushy hair and a full beard. Gorgeous.

He opened his mouth, but only a raspy sound emerged. That was okay. She didn't need the words. All she needed was him. And he'd finally come to her. Not as the black werewolf he'd been. Nor as the muraco he'd become. But as a confused amalgam of both.

"Or-Ori-Ori-an-a."

Marrok stumbled forward, falling onto his mud-encrusted knees and into Oriana's waiting arms.

He smelled awful but felt so good. "I've got you, my love. I've got you."

As with Kalinda and Zev, Oriana hadn't been able to bring herself to kill Marrok. She'd shot to disable only. Oriana then had to decide what to do with the muraco Marrok had become. For all intents and purposes, the real Marrok was dead. Even the man she held wasn't *her* Marrok.

Marrok hadn't suddenly become a black werewolf again because he'd been left to heal and run wild in the safest place Oriana could think to leave him.

"I'm sorry it took me so long to return." By the time she had, he'd kept his distance, his white fur a spot of color she'd glimpsed on the other side of the lake. Marrok had been close enough to see, but not near enough to touch the way she held him now.

"D-don't care. H-h-ere now. Don't leave."

"I won't ever leave you again."

Marrok had said he would rather die than be imprisoned. Life as a muraco was a prison without a steel wall. One way or another, Marrok, Cyrus of Steelcross, would be set free. He would either be reborn as a black werewolf or

Oriana would grant him a true death so his soul could join mother sun and father moon.

Oriana pulled back, her neck wet from Marrok's tears and her cheeks moist from her own. "I'd like to kiss you. May I?"

Dry, cracked lips parted, and eyes lowered. "I'm d-disgusting. Stinky. Dirty." Marrok punched himself in the head with the side of his fist. "My brain isn't working right. It's telling me to do awful things to you. You shouldn't even be—"

Oriana kissed him. Yes, Marrok was all those things, but Oriana couldn't care less. He'd lived like an animal for months—hunting game and drinking from the lake. But he'd come to her as a man, in the same clearing where they'd pledged themselves to each other.

Her tongue opened his mouth for her magic. Marrok gagged. Oriana's magic was more potent than what she had fed him in the past. Marrok tried to pull away, but Oriana's firm hand to his nape kept him right where she needed him.

She wasn't completely iron free. But the transfusions had significantly reduced the amount of metal flowing through her veins and mixing with her magic. Oriana disliked having to use witches on the cusp of puberty as blood donors, but they were her only source of untainted witch blood. Perhaps it would help that Marrok's bloodlust wasn't as great as other muracos because he hadn't consumed the blood of a witch. If his bloodlust had been out of control, when in her presence his hunger would've supplanted every other desire.

"Relax and swallow my magic, Marrok. I need you to let me feed your hunger."

"But, but ..."

Oriana kissed him again, anxious to give him what his body needed, reminding herself to feed him small, digestible portions. In Marrok's fragile physical and mental state, too much magic could overload his system and kill him.

She settled them on the blanket, her hand over his heart and her mouth fused to his. Wisps of red magic swirled from their lips. In time, and with more practice, she would be able to generate a safe amount of magic from her hands, making the transfer a simple touching of skin.

Helen had many hypotheses about 'soul magic,' as she'd called the transfer. Unfortunately, her death left them unproven.

"Oriana?" Marrok's hand pushed strands of her hair from his face and behind her ears. "What is happening? I feel … I feel funny. Different."

Oriana rolled onto her back, grinning up at the red moon.

"My stomach is cramping but it doesn't hurt. It's a really weird sensation."

She laughed. "You're the king of understatements, my love." She laughed again because it felt so good. But then she sobered, afraid her celebration was premature. She learned over Marrok, scrutinizing every inch of him.

"I know I look bad. You don't have to stare at me."

"Bad? That's how you think you look?" Oriana snorted. "Not bad, Marrok. You look downright dreadful."

And yet, she wanted to kiss him again. And again. For research purposes, of course. She had to make sure the experiment worked. Helen had used the words reliable and valid.

Oriana kissed Marrok again. Bad breath had never tasted like . . . okay, bad breath was bad breath. No amount of love and relief changed that nasty fact. But Oriana kissed her consort anyway, pushing a little more soul magic into him.

It might take a generation before Earth Rift would have enough metal-free mature witches to fully integrate soul magic into their society. That would give Oriana time to work on the hearts and minds of resistant witches. She'd already begun rebuilding Janus Nether. For now, most of those residents lived in Bronze Ward. Not exactly Helen's vision of the city, but she hoped, from their place among the stars, that Helen and Tuncay could rest in peace, knowing their life's work and sacrifice hadn't been in vain.

"I want to go home." Marrok turned his face away from Oriana, weeping softly. "But I remember what I did to you and Keira. I remember … I remember I wanted to … to …"

Oriana wrapped her arms around Marrok, spooning his naked body the way she had Keira's the first few nights after the attack.

"If you recall everything, then you know you *protected* our daughter. She's only here because you were the black werewolf she needed you to be. You shielded Keira the only way you could—by pushing past your rage disruptor." Oriana turned Marrok toward her so he could see her when she said, "Thank you for saving our daughter. I thanked you that night, and I'm repeating it now. Thank you, Marrok. I love you so much."

"You must love me because I smell like shit."

"Finally." Oriana clapped. "Not an understatement. Let's go home, Marrok. You need a shower, a shave, and a real meal. In the morning, you can see our daughter. Keira has missed you as much as I have."

"Sounds like every dream I've had since being here."

Oriana stood, and Marrok followed her up, wrapping the blanket, like a toga, around himself.

"What did I miss while I was gone?"

"Nothing you want to know, but I'll tell you everything. There's a lot."

"Yeah, I assumed as much. What about sex?"

"What about it?"

"That wasn't on your list of things I need."

Oriana's gaze raked over Marrok's body. She would have to fatten him up, but a shower and shave did wonders for a man's appearance. She winked at him. "We'll see."

"What do you mean we—"

Oriana cast an extraction spell, yanking a shocked and cursing Marrok through the ether of space.

The red moon had returned her consort to her and, with more soul magic feedings, her Marrok would, once more, be his glorious black werewolf self.

They fell in a heap on their bed. Marrok glanced around the renovated suite. "Finally, you got it right."

Not yet. But Oriana would.

Go slow to go fast. Words to lead by.

Blood of the Sun Decree #190
September 1, 2243

BY MATRIARCHAL DECREE, BLOOD OF THE SUN DECREE #3 IS NULL AND VOID. WITCHES ARE NO LONGER MANDATED TO COMPLETE THE RITE OF ENDOMETAL FUSION.

Oriana, Matriarch of Earth Rift

Bonus Images

Steel Rise City

Irongarde City

City of Wild Moor

Silent Drift Lake and
Blackbridge Mountains

Moonvale Forest

About N. D. Jones

N.D. Jones, Ed.D., is an award-winning author who has achieved USA Today bestselling status for her captivating Black Fantasy and Paranormal Romance novels. She resides in the heart of Maryland with her loving family.

Driven by a passionate desire to introduce more positive, sexy, and multidimensional African American characters as soulmates, friends, and lovers, N.D. embarked on a remarkable journey of her own. Determined to address this challenge, she took it upon herself to redefine the narrative.

One of N.D.'s distinctive strengths lies in her commitment to crafting in-depth mythologies in her novels and seamlessly weaving paranormal elements into the fabric of her stories. When she creates a world of witches and shapeshifters, N.D. ensures that her readers not only witness their extraordinary existence but also gain a deep understanding of what it truly means to be part of this world.

In her novels, the paranormal is not merely a background feature; it takes center stage and is crucial to the plot, enriching the reader's experience with every turn of the page. N.D. Jones invites you to join her on an extraordinary journey where Black love intertwines seamlessly with the paranormal, creating a world where love, mystery, and enchantment reign supreme.

Books by N.D. Jones

<u>Winged Warriors Novella Series</u> (Paranormal Romance)
Fire, Fury, Faith (Book 1)
Heat, Hunt, Hope (Book 2)
Lies, Lust, Love (Book 3)

<u>Death and Destiny Trilogy</u> (Paranormal Romance)
Of Fear and Faith (Book 1)
Of Beasts and Bonds (Book 2)
Of Deception and Divinity (Book 3)

<u>Forever Yours Series</u> (Fantasy Romance)
Bound Souls (Book 1)
Fated Path (Book 2)

<u>Dragon Shifter Romance</u> (Paranormal Romance Standalone Novels)
Stones of Dracontias: The Bloodstone Dragon
Dragon Lore and Love: Isis and Osiris

<u>The Styles of Love Trilogy</u> (Contemporary Romance)
The Perks of Higher Ed (Book 1)
The Wish of Xmas Present (Book 2)
The Gift of Second Chances (Book 3)

Rhythm and Blue Skies: Malcolm and Sky's Complete Story
The Styles of Love Trilogy Complete Story Boxset

<u>Fairy Tale Fatale Series</u> (Fantasy)
Crimson Hunter (Book 1)
Bearly Gold (Book 2)

<u>Feline Nation</u> (Fantasy)
A Queen's Pride (Book 1)
Mafdet's Claws (Book 2)

<u>Resilience Series</u> (Nonfiction Self-Help)
The Color of My Resilience: A Guided Self-Care Journal for Black Men
(Book 1)
The Color of My Resilience: A Guided Self-Care Journal for Black Women
(Book 2)

<u>Seizing Freedom (Historical Fantasy Fiction)</u>
Harriet's Escape: Harriet Tubman Reimagined